winning the game AND OTHER STORIES

winning

AND OTHER

STORIES

rubem fonseca

TRANSLATED FROM THE PORTUGUESE

BY CLIFFORD E. LANDERS

the game

TAGUS PRESS | UMASS DARTMOUTH | DARTMOUTH, MASSACHUSETTS

Brazilian Literature in Translation, 1

Tagus Press at UMass Dartmouth
www.portstudies.umassd.edu

Manufactured in the United States of America

Managing Editor: Mario Pereira
Copyedited by Deborah Heimann
Designed by Mindy Basinger Hill
Typeset in Arnhem Blond

Tagus Press books are produced and distributed for Tagus Press by University Press of New England, which is a member of the Green Press Initiative. The paper used in this book meets their minimum requirement for recycled paper.

For all inquiries, please contact:
Tagus Press at UMass Dartmouth
Center for Portuguese Studies and Culture
285 Old Westport Road
North Dartmouth MA 02747-2300
Tel. 508-999-8255
Fax 508-999-9272
www.portstudies.umassd.edu

This work was published with the support of the Brazilian Ministry of Culture/National Library Foundation.

Obra publicada com o apoio do Ministério da Cultura do Brasil / Fundação Biblioteca Nacional.

Library of Congress Cataloging-in-Publication Data
Fonseca, Rubem.
[Short stories. Selections. English]
Winning the game and other stories / Rubem Fonseca ; translated from the Portuguese by Clifford E. Landers.
pages cm. — (Brazilian literature in translation ; 1)
ISBN 978-1-933227-46-7 (pbk. : alk. paper) —
ISBN 978-1-933227-47-4 (ebook)
1. Fonseca, Rubem—Translations into English. I. Landers, Clifford E., translator. II. Title.
PQ9698.16.O46A2 2013
869.3'42—dc23 2012042122

5 4 3 2 1

contents

winning the game AND OTHER STORIES

arts and trades

YOU RUIN YOUR TEETH WHEN YOU'RE A KID, but later after you make a lot of money you find a dentist who fixes your mouth. That's what happened with me; I implanted every tooth in my mouth, a marvel of odontological engineering. I'm full of teeth that don't fall out or decay, but when I laugh in front of a mirror I miss my old mouth; my lips open now in a way I don't like. In any case, I don't lack for teeth and I can champ down on women and steaks. I used to live in a lousy housing project and catch the train, squeezed in like sardines in a can. Today I live in a beautiful mansion in a gated community in the Barra, I have two cars and two drivers. I used to have one leg shorter than the other and didn't even know it. I would go out with waitresses in luncheonettes, maids, factory workers, some of them illiterate. Money got me legs of the same length, gave me a wife from a good family, ruined but with all sorts of diplomas, gave me a mistress, without a diploma but who knows how to wear elegant clothes and put on a show when she crosses a ballroom. Money, that's something I understand.

I didn't go to college either. I don't even have high school. Or elementary school, to tell the truth. That's been a concern of mine, the only thing money hasn't solved. If you're rich and don't have a diploma, people think you're stupid. If you're poor and don't have a diploma, people say you didn't go to school, don't have even a primary education, but you learned to read the best authors on your own, and you're a very smart guy. That's what they said about me when I was poor. When I became rich they began spreading it around that I was a dummy who bought books by the yard, a complete lie. I should have bought a degree as an economist as soon as I started making money. Now I can't do that anymore, people would know, the rich are always in the spotlight. Opportunity, that's something I understand.

Then I read in the newspaper:

> *Become a respected writer admired by your friends and neighbors, your family, your girlfriend. I will write for you the book you choose. Poetry, novels, short stories, essays, biographies. Absolute confidentiality. Send reply to Ghostwriter, Box 333 507. Rio de Janeiro.*

I had already seen a similar ad, by a guy offering to write masters' and doctoral theses for goof-off unscrupulous students. That day I told my wife, "I feel like writing a book, a novel. After all, if I learned how to read on my own, I can learn how to write on my own."

"You know what you want," she replied.

The next day I said the same thing to my mistress. "I think it's a good idea," she answered, "being a writer is so chic."

I went to the post office and rented a box. I didn't want to have any contact with Ghostwriter. If the book he wrote for me was good, I'd publish it and Ghostwriter would end up finding out who I was. But if it was bad, I'd toss it in the trash and the writer I was renting wouldn't need to know my identity.

> *Ghostwriter: I read your ad. I'm interested. I want a novel of at least two hundred pages, in the style of Machado de Assis. I'll pay whatever's necessary. Give me the name of your bank and your account number so I can deposit the first installment, ten percent of the total amount. I'll pay the rest in installments of thirty percent*

after delivery of seventy or more pages at a time.
Reply to Tomás Antônio, Box 432 521.

I made money in business by buying and selling things. That's the way to get rich. Buying and selling. Making money, that's something I understand. My driver is named Gaspar; my wife's is named Evanildo. My cook can make any dish, however sophisticated. By paying three times as much I was able to lure her away from one of those society types who are still brave enough to host dinners to make the social columns. When I give a dinner I also put it in the social column. I've been told that's not done anymore, that the trick is to keep a low profile here and enjoy the money abroad, away from the eyes of the envious. But then what good does it do to have the best mansion and the best cook, and the best teeth and the best clothes, and the best paintings on the wall if not to show to others? Let the envious turn green with displeasure and stew in their woe. At a dinner I gave at my house I heard a guy who was there for show whisper to the woman beside him at the table, who had also been invited just to be seen, "The money is changing hands." That's what he said: the money is changing hands. He, the old rich, was referring to me, the new rich. The old rich don't want money to change hands, but how can money not change hands if those parasites don't work? The difference between the old rich and the new rich is that the old rich, those who haven't been ruined by their hedonistic idleness, have had money longer and are misers. But it's true that both the old and the new stuff their bellies with free caviar in other people's homes. Anything that's expensive is always good, even when it's bad, that's the golden rule of consumptiveness. Ostentation, that's something I understand.

Tomás Antônio: The bank is Bradesco, agency 163,
account number 11 429 654-9. Name: M. J. Ramos.
My fee for the book, ten thousand reais. Ghostwriter.

Ten thousand, the price of a run-of-the-mill Volkswagen. My book was going to be a piece of shit. But I deposited the ten percent in Ghostwriter's account.

"Are you going to write your book on a computer?" Gisela asked. I haven't spoken of Gisela, my mistress. A rich guy has to have a mistress, for relief from bourgeois routine. A poor guy should also have a mistress, obviously, if he can; it's good for the health and makes poverty more pleasant. Wives are always a drag, both in books and real life, and a mistress makes you be more patient with her, the wife. Marriage is boring. A person's house can be something insipid, most people's houses are insipid, but they always want to transform them into showcases. People stick themselves inside the showcase, along with their knickknacks. Part of the showcase is nice teeth, good clothes and good shoes, manicured nails, a slim silhouette, domestic appliances, wedding rings, perfume, voice modulation and an imposing vocabulary, a face free of warts (did I mention I had a wart removed from my face?), and the more ornate the showcase, the greater our happiness. Exhibitionism, that's something I understand.

But I was speaking of my mistress, Gisela. First, some advice for young adventuresses: if you want to find a lover, choose a man who's new rich. They're much more generous. Don't think I suffer retrospective envy from having been poor when I was young. Nothing like it. It's because the old rich don't like money to change hands. I mean, it can change hands but only between their old-rich hands. But let's get back to Gisela.

"Yes," I answered, "I'm writing it on a computer. Isn't that what all the idiots who follow fads are doing?" Actually, just to show off, I had bought the best computer on the market, with all the peripherals, multifunctions, nets, shifts, alts, ROM, RAM, the works. I had another one, state of the art, but it was my secretary who used it. But let's get back to Gisela. A good mistress, like my Gisela, has to be pretty; has to have all her teeth; has to weigh twenty pounds less than her height in centimeters (as long as she's not a dwarf, of course); has to speak English and French; has to like cinema; has to have small feet; has to have small breasts (but her breasts, when bare under her silk blouse, must move erect when she walks without swinging, because an elegant woman doesn't swing her hips when she moves her legs); has to have large, firm thighs; has to have a small, tight ass; has to have a lot of hair on her head; has to eat with her mouth closed;

has to have long fingers; has to have large eyes; and has to like you. And all she has to give you is love. And all you have to give her is love and money. The more of both, the better. Everyone likes to receive presents, even the voodoo worshippers know that and lavish their priest with rum and flour. But don't give your mistress cheap presents. If she says she prefers a rose to a jewel, she's an impostor; women like powerful men. Money being spent profligately on a woman is the most impressive exhibition of power that a man can do for her. The prodigal male expresses for the woman benefitting from his lavishness the same venerable power that the kidnapper, the torturer, and the executioner represent to their victims. But there are cases where the guy, without being filthy rich or having life-and-death power, can exercise a certain control, insignificant to be sure, over women: they're the guys who possess a lot of charm, a lot of talent, or a lot of fame. But between a sensitive poet and a pompous landlord, women always choose the latter.

Besides a dummy, they say I'm a cynic, a misogynist, a hedonist, and a materialist. Misogynist? I don't disdain women, and I have no aversion to them. Misogynist and dummy is too much.

I received the first thirty pages from Ghostwriter.

The title of the novel was *The Forger.* Forger? What an unfortunate title. Was Ghostwriter putting me on? I took the pages Ghostwriter sent me and typed them into the computer. My character, the counterfeiter, is forging a book of memoirs, an autobiography. He's a meticulous specialist, striving for months to imitate the handwriting of the guy to whom he'll attribute authorship of the document he's forging, the capital *u* that looks like an *m,* the capital *c* similar to an *l*, etc., etc. The sheets of paper he plans to use in his scheme are already old, but he discovers a complicated process to age them even further, artificially. Here's a small excerpt: *Certain that he had succeeded in reproducing the handwriting perfectly, he sat down to begin the work. "I was born and raised in the Livramento favela, in Rio de Janeiro. My mother died when I was a child. My father remarried but died two years later. I was raised by my stepmother, a washerwoman."*

Raised by his washerwoman stepmother? Reading the first few pages wasn't enough to tell much. The story was nothing new, I think I'd already read something similar. But we readers know that a bad story well written can mean a good book, just like a good story poorly written means a bad book. The story was a bit confusing, but it wasn't badly written.

> *Ghostwriter: I received the first pages of the novel. You must remember that I asked for a novel in the style of Machado de Assis, and what you sent me has nothing of Machado de Assis. Can you change it? Tomás Antônio.*

"Are you worried about something?" Gisela asked.

"I'm not happy with the story I'm writing."

"Why don't you write about my life? Want me to tell you about my life?"

"The less we know about each other's lives, the better," I answered.

"You weren't the first, you know."

"Yes, I know, I wasn't the first."

"Or the second."

"Yeah, yeah, or the second."

"You want to know your number?"

"Yeah, yeah, I want to know my number."

"Eight, you're number eight."

"Yeah, yeah, I'm number eight."

"Stop saying yeah, yeah."

I forgot to say that mistresses are for seeing now and then. Otherwise they become as boring as wives. That was the second day in a row I'd seen Gisela. Two days in a row is too much. At most, mistresses should be seen every other day.

"My mother died when I was a child. My father remarried but died soon afterwards. I was raised by my stepmother," Gisela said.

"Incredible," I said. "In my novel the character's mother also died when he was young and the father married again and he was raised by his stepmother. Was your mother a washerwoman?"

"Are you crazy? Imagine, my stepmother a washerwoman! She came from a very good family, I'm from a very good family, my grandfather was the Baron of Laranjeiras."

"I've heard of the baron of Limeira . . ."

Gisela sulked. She removed my face from her leg, saying, "I don't like for you to bite me." But no pout can resist a jewel. I always keep a jewel in reserve for such occasions, a pair of earrings, a ring, a bracelet. I gave her a diamond ring. Actually, Gisela likes for me to bite her leg.

> *Tomás Antônio: The forger is forging an autobiography of Machado de Assis. Just as you didn't notice, the reader won't perceive it until well into the novel. The text is a lot of work. I had to research the technical processes for aging paper and am having to read all the biographies of Machado de Assis. The story of the forgery and the autobiography, apocryphal but highly accurate in its references to Machado's life, serve as a framework for each other. A framing device, understand? I'm going to have more work than I thought. Could we increase my fee to twenty thousand? Ghostwriter.*

A framing device? Was the guy trying to impress me with that theoretical claptrap? He must be a literature major. I agreed to the increase he was asking for. Intuition, that's something I understand.

Have I already spoken of my secretary? A good secretary has to have the qualities of a good dog: loyalty and gratitude. God in heaven and you on earth. The secretary can't see you naked, can't see you frightened, can't see you pick your teeth. And periodically you have to pat her on the back, the way they do with seals. No reprimands, just incentives. Some idiot told me one day that if you have the right machines you don't need a secretary. One more American stupidity. Nothing can take the place of a good secretary, nothing is better than a good secretary, not even a person's mother. Her name was Esmeralda. Nothing could be done about that. Dadá, Esmer, Meralda were all worse. I suggested, Adlaremse, a tongue twister but refined. Esmeralda didn't like it. If she doesn't like it, I don't like it either. Esmeralda is a wonder, she looks over contracts with the lawyers, I never know when she's got her period, she's never had a toothache, she takes care of my banking transactions, I only have to tell her buy, sell.

Having all this, you'll say I could only be a happy man. And I would be a truly happy man if behind my back they weren't saying I'm a dummy. I defend myself by saying it doesn't matter if others say you are a piece of shit, because you're only a piece of shit if you yourself think you're a piece of shit. But that phrase, which seems to have been inspired in one of those tenets found in so many of those brainless manuals that teach the credulous to develop their self-esteem and get ahead in life, is another of my tricks. I suffer, repeat, suffer when they call me a dummy behind my back. And they do that because I'm new rich and didn't know (in the past) how to use silverware correctly, didn't know (in the past) the difference between baroque music and twelve-tone music, didn't know (in the past) the difference between Bordeaux, Burgundy, and Beaujolais, useless knowledge that buffs the lackluster lives of the old rich. Repression, that's something I understand.

Ghostwriter took three months to finish the book. They say there are authors who take four, five, ten years to write a two-hundred-page book. Ten years have three thousand six hundred and fifty days. It would be enough for the bum to write twenty miserable words a day to have at the end of ten years the seventy-three thousand words for a book of two hundred pages. *The Forger* was made up of six hundred pages; Ghostwriter had worked hard. In summary, the story went like this: The forger, at the request of a dishonest publisher, forges a book of memoirs as if they were by Machado de Assis; the memoirs are published, everyone takes them to be real, critics go wild, the book becomes a best seller, it's all people talk about. But in the end the forger, whether from repentance or to get revenge on the publisher, the readers, and the critics, denounces the hoax, leaving everyone looking like fools.

I made six copies and sent them to six publishers. Only one answered, asking if I couldn't cut the parts of the book that spoke of the life of Machado de Assis, claiming they were unnecessary and the cuts wouldn't harm the book, that six hundred pages was a lot, that publishing houses in general were going through a difficult period because of the financial crisis, etc. The guys just didn't want to invest in a brick by some unknown author. Pretexts, that's something I understand.

I paid for a private edition. Wasn't that what all those boring prolix writers did? Nobody reads a six-hundred-page book, but its size is impressive. I didn't spare costs. I paid an expert to write the jacket flaps, my photo for the book was done by the best professional available, the cover was created by the best artist in the field. I ordered only a thousand copies printed and told the publisher to distribute five hundred. I thought, when I received the first copy with my name on the colorful cover, this piece of shit is worth as much as my tooth implants. Seeing things the way they are, that's something I understand.

For a month, nothing happened. But then the critic for a weekly magazine discovered me, said I was the greatest literary newcomer in recent years, and the five hundred copies sitting on the back shelves in bookstores sold out in a day. The publisher brought out a new printing of ten thousand copies, and another, then another. I was famous, overnight. I gave interviews to all the papers. I gave interviews on television. People asked for my autograph. My book was discussed at dinners. Who was the dummy now? Revenge, that's something I understand.

Tomás Antônio: I'm going to go on calling you that. I need to talk to you, personally. Set a time and place. Ghostwriter.

Did that surprise me? No. I was prepared for something of the kind. I had predicted that the wretched poor devil, semi-tubercular and suffering from the blunder he'd committed by selling me a book that everyone considered a masterpiece, would look me up to settle accounts.

Ghostwriter: Meet me in Nossa Senhora da Paz square, Thursday at five o'clock. You've seen my picture in the papers. I'll be sitting on one of the benches, waiting. Tomás Antônio.

That day, twenty minutes before the appointed time, I got to the square and sat on a bench near the entrance. From where I sat I had a perfect view of everyone who arrived. A guy came in carrying a newspaper, a couple came in, then a beggar, another guy in a beret, a nanny with a child, another nanny, another beggar. Time was passing and none of the people arriving came in my direction.

"Good afternoon."

The woman had appeared suddenly and stood there beside the bench, extending her hand.

"Good afternoon," I replied, shaking her hand.

"May I sit down?"

"Of course. I didn't see you come into the square."

"I was already here when you arrived. Sitting on that bench over there."

"Stupid of me not to think of it, that you might show up early. Are you Ghostwriter?"

"Yes."

"M. J. Ramos?"

"Maria José."

She spoke shyly, seemingly constrained.

"Sit down. Can you prove it?"

"That's easy. I have the whole book in my head. I'm going to tell you how I wrote it."

Cutting what she said, fifteen minutes later I said, "That's enough, I believe you. What is it you want?"

She fell silent. She must have been about thirty, delicate legs and brown eyes. She was wearing a skirt and blouse, unfashionable shoes with low heels and was carrying a small plastic purse. Her teeth were yellow from smoke.

"I feel—"

"Nonsense. You can speak."

"I need an operation."

"You or your mother?"

"Me."

"How much?"

"Well, there's the doctor, the hospitalization . . . I don't have any health insurance . . ."

"What type of operation?"

"I'd rather not say. But I've already scheduled the operation. I knew I could count on you."

A con job, that's something I understand.

"Okay, I have a proposal for you. I'll give you some dough today for your urgent expenses. I'll deposit in a bank account of your choosing all the money the book has brought in so far and will bring in later, for the rest of my life. Give me the number of your account."

"You know it; you've already made deposits to it. I shouldn't ask for anything else. A deal's a deal."

"Don't worry about it. You deserve much more."

I signed a check and gave it to her. "This is just the first payment."

"I don't need this much," she said, putting the check in her purse. "And I don't want anything more."

"With what's left, buy yourself some clothes. Would you like a lift? Where do you live?"

"It's out of your way. Jacarepaguá."

"I'll take you."

It was getting dark when we got the car. We took Avenida Niemeyer. When I was a nobody, I used to dream about having a car to drive around the Barra. Now that I lived in the Barra, driving on that avenue was a nuisance. She sat mutely beside me. What could be going through her head? That I was street smart and had tumbled to her story about an operation, but that the scam she had pulled on me wasn't enough to repair the error she had committed by selling me the book? Or maybe that I was a generous guy who had put an end to her difficulties? Or—?

"How many commissioned books have you written?"

"This was the first. I mean, I've always written since I was a girl, but I tore them up."

"The first? We could write another. What do you think?"

"I don't know. I don't want to do it anymore."

"Regrets?"

"Something like that."

The houses were becoming less frequent, and we drove along a dark deserted highway. I pondered about a way to solve my perplexity once and for all. In case of doubt, don't hesitate. That's how you make money. I could grab her by the neck, strangle her and dump her body by the beach. But that wasn't how I did business. Buying and selling, that's something I understand.

"Look," I said, "I can't let you go without settling our matter."

"I thought we'd already done that."

In the dark Maria José wasn't so plain. For some moments I imagined what she would look like in Gisela's clothes. There are those who say that to be elegant a woman has to have slim legs.

"We won't settle the matter just yet. I'm going to tell you how the story can have a happy ending."

I spoke for half an hour. She listened in silence.

"Well?" I asked.

"I never could have expected that you—that someone would propose that to me . . . I never—When I was a girl, boys didn't look at me, later, men didn't look at me . . . You just met me today, how is it that—"

"Symbiosis," I said.

She lit a cigarette, and examined my eyes by the light from the match.

"I know you'll be patient and delicate with me. Symbiosis," she said.

"Then we agree. One question: were you really going to have an operation? A man and a woman have to trust one another."

I heard her answer, and the answer wasn't very important.

It's complicated having two mistresses. Logistical problems. Not forgetting the woman you married, she has to enter into the things you do with the others, and those things are many: there's the distribution of endearments and laughter, you can't do without that, and then there's the buying of jewels, which is easy, it's enough for a jewel to be very expensive for it to be appreciated, and there's the buying of clothes, which is very complicated—some like to show their legs, others like to show their breasts—and there are visits to friends, which is even more convoluted; certain friends can't meet certain other friends, and then there are trips, it always happens that all three like the same city that you hate, and the premiere on Friday of the musical all of them want to go to, and there's the confidential and embarrassing visit to the gynecologist that you can't get out of, and there's the painter and the carpenter and the electrician, women love remodeling, and there's the decorator and the relatives, I shudder just thinking of the relatives, and even if you manage to set up all these things in perfect order, like a tile roof or the scales of a fish, so as to let the water flow without making puddles or getting swept into the whirlpool, you're going to have to program your life the way a general plans a war.

I came to an agreement with Gisela; I don't like to see anyone suffer.

Maria José stopped smoking and her teeth are no longer so yellow.

The new book is almost completely written. It's going to be even better than the first.

Success, that's something I understand.

the hunchback and botticelli's venus

FLUTTERING LOCKS OF REDDISH HAIR whipped by the wind and rain, smooth and radiant skin, she is Botticelli's Venus walking down the street. (The one in the Uffizi, born from a seashell, not the one in the Staatliche Museen, with a black background, which is similar but has dry hair arranged around the head, descending evenly down the body.)

Don't think that I boast any extraordinary perspicacity, but the fact is that if the woman I observe is as motionless as a statue, I can still tell the rhythm of her steps when she moves. I understand not only muscles, but also skeletons and, according to the symmetry of the bone structure, can predict the articulation of the ankles, knees, and ilium, which determine the rhythm of the body's movement.

Venus walks unbothered by the rain, sometimes turning her head toward the sky to wet her face even more, and I can say without the slightest poetic stuffiness that it's the walk of a goddess.

I have to create an elaborate strategy to get close to her and achieve what I need, a difficult task, as women, at first contact, feel repulsion towards me.

I follow her to where she lives. I watch the building for several days.

Venus likes to walk in the streets and to sit in the square near her home, reading. But she stops all the time, looks at people, especially children, or else feeds the pigeons, which in a way disappoints me; pigeons, like rats, roaches, ants and termites, don't need any help. They'll be around after bacteria finally put an end to us.

Looking at her from a distance, I am more and more impressed by the harmony of her body, the perfect balance among the parts that make up her wholeness—the extension of the members in relation to the vertical dimension of the thorax; the length of her neck in relation to the face and head; the narrowness of her waist in combination with the firmness of the buttocks and chest. I need to approach this woman as soon as possible. I'm racing against time.

On a day with heavy rain, I sit beside her under the downpour, on a bench in the square. I have to find out right away if she likes to talk.

"Too bad the rain doesn't allow reading today," I say.

She doesn't answer.

"That's why you didn't bring a book."

She pretends not to hear.

I insist: "He makes the sun shine on the good and the bad, and sends the rain on the just and the unjust."

The woman then stares at me quickly, but I keep my gaze on her forehead.

"Are you talking to me?"

"God makes it rain on the just and the—" (My eyes on her forehead.)

"Ah, you were speaking of God."

She gets up. Standing, she knows she's in a favorable position to thwart the advances of an intruder.

"Don't take it wrong. I saw that you must be one of those evangelicals looking to save souls for Jesus, but don't waste your time; I'm a lost cause."

I follow her as she walks slowly away.

"I'm not a Protestant pastor. In fact, I doubt you can guess what I do."

"I'm very good at that. But I don't have time today; I have to get to an art exhibit."

Her voice displays less displeasure. She possesses the virtue of curiosity, which is very good for me. And another essential quality as well: she likes to talk. That's even better.

I offer to accompany her and, after a slight hesitation, she agrees. We walk, with her a short distance away from me as if we weren't together. I try to be as inconspicuous as possible.

At the exhibit there is a single attendant, sitting at a table, filing her nails. Negrinha, my current lover, says that women who file their nails in public have trouble thinking, and filing their nails helps them reflect better, like those women who reason more clearly while removing blackheads from their nose in front of the mirror.

While I look at the paintings with studied indifference, I say to her, "Avant-garde from the last century, spontaneous abstract vestiges, subconscious, sub-Kadinski; I prefer a Shakespearean sonnet."

She doesn't reply.

"I'm trying to impress you."

"It wasn't enough, but mentioning poetry helped a little. I'd like to understand poetry."

Poetry isn't to be understood; poetry is no pharmaceutical instruction sheet. I'm not going to tell her that, not for the time being.

"How about getting an espresso?" she asks.

I look for a place where we can sit. Being taller than I, Venus makes my hump look larger when we're standing side by side.

"Now I'm going to find out what you do," she says, appearing to be amused by the situation. "You do something, don't you? Don't tell me, let me guess. Well, we already know you're not a Protestant pastor, and you're not a teacher; teachers have dirty fingernails. Lawyers wear ties. Not a stock broker, obviously not. Maybe a systems analyst, that hunched-over position in front of the computer . . . Uh . . . Sorry."

If I had looked in her eyes, what would I have seen when she referred to the spinal column of a guy bent over in front of the computer? Horror, pity, scorn? Now do you understand why I avoid, in the initial contacts, reading their eyes? True, I might have seen only curiosity, but I prefer not to risk glimpsing something that could undermine my audacity.

"And you, do you know what I do?"

"Clean nails without polish. You like to read on a park bench. You like getting wet in the rain. You have one foot larger than the other. You want to understand about poetry. You're lazy. Disturbing signs."

"Does it show?"

"You could be a photographer's model."

"Does it show?"

"Or an idle, frustrated housewife who goes to a fitness center where she does dance, stretching, bodybuilding, specific exercises to strengthen the gluteus. The, the—"

"The ass. Is that the word you're looking for? What about the ass?"

"After the breasts, it's the part of the body most exposed to danger," I add.

I'm a bit surprised at her naturalness in using that vulgar word in a conversation with someone she doesn't know, despite the fact that I know from long experience that no one employs euphemisms with hunchbacks. Or other niceties: it's common for people to belch and fart absentmindedly in my presence.

"Does it show?" she repeats.

"Or else it's none of that, and you have a bookbinding workshop in your house."

"You didn't answer. Does it show?"

"What?"

"That I have one foot larger than the other?"

"Show me the palm of your hand. I see you're planning a trip. There's a person that has you concerned."

"Right again. What's the trick?"

"Everyone has one foot larger than the other, is planning a trip, has somebody who makes life difficult for them."

"It's my right foot."

She extends her leg, shows her foot. She's wearing a flat leather shoe styled like a sneaker.

"But, anyway, what's my profession?"

"Bookbinding. A woman who works with books has special charm."

"There you're wrong. I don't do anything. But you got one part right. I'm lazy. Is that one of my disturbing signs?"

"It's the main one," I reply. "A famous poet felt laziness to be a delicious state, a sensation that relegated poetry, ambition, and love to a secondary plane. The other unique sign is enjoying reading on a park bench. And finally, liking to get wet in the rain."

I don't tell her that lazy people suffer from the instinctive impulse to achieve something but don't know what. The fact of Venus being lazy was, to me, great luck. All the women I've seduced were lazy, dreaming of doing or learning something. But, especially, they enjoyed talking—speaking and listening—which in reality was what was most important. I'll get back to that.

"You're a professor of some kind; your clean fingernails threw me off."

"You can call me professor."

"All right, professor. And what about you? What're you going to call me? Lazy girl?"

"I already have a name for you. Venus."

"Venus? Horrible."

"Your Venus is the one by Botticelli."

"The painting? I can't remember what it's like anymore."

"Just take a look in the mirror."

"Silly flattery. Why is liking to get wet in the rain a disturbing sign?"

"That's something I'm not going to tell you today."

"Here's the book. I couldn't read it in the rain," she says, taking a book from the pocket of her raincoat. "Ciao."

It was only then that I saw her blue eyes: neutral. She had already become accustomed to my appearance and, perhaps, managed to see that my face wasn't as ugly as my body.

That was our first meeting. Venus's liking poetry was going to help me, but if she appreciated music, or theater, or cinema, or the plastic arts it wouldn't change my strategy at all. Negrinha only liked music and wasn't a lot of trouble, as she liked to talk, especially to complain about the man who lived with her before me, who only spoke of practical things—short-, medium- and long-range plans, schedules, notes in appointment books, errands, cost-benefit analysis of expenses, whether for a trip or buying a garlic press, and when she wanted to talk about some other topic, he simply didn't hear.

Besides being a good listener, I can say interesting things, trivia from almanacs as well as more profound things that I've learned from books. I've spent my life reading and becoming informed. While others were kicking balls around, dancing, dating, strolling, driving cars or motorcycles, I was at home convalescing from failed operations and reading. I've learned a lot; I've deduced, thought, verified, discovered. I've become a bit prolix, it's true. But I grew, during my martyrdom of shadows, by studying and planning how to reach my objectives.

A guy who's had twenty operations on his spine, one failure after the other, has to have, among his major virtues, that of persistence. I discover, through the doorman of the building where she lives, that Agnes is the name by which Venus is known in the world of mortals. I leave an envelope with a note for her at the reception desk in her building.

The note: *I suspect that you've read little poetry. You read the books in the park and skip pages. They must be short stories; no one reads poems that way. Lazy people like to read short stories; they finish one story on page twenty, then skip to the one on page forty, and in the end they read only part of the book. You need to read the poets, even if it's only in the manner of that crazy writer for whom books of poetry deserve to be read only a single time and then destroyed so that dead poets can yield way to the living ones and not leave them petrified. I can make you understand poetry, but you'll have to read the books I indicate. You need me, more than you need your mother or your Pomeranian. Here's my telephone number. P.S.: You're right; it's better to be named Agnes than Venus. Signed: The Professor.*

To make a simpleton understand poetry! But she liked that literary genre, so the topic of our conversations would therefore be poetry. The things a hunchback is capable of doing to make a woman fall in love with him.

When I'm looking for a new girlfriend, the old one is discarded; I need to concentrate on the main objective. It was time to say good-bye to Negrinha.

Astutely, I write some obvious love poems to Agnes and leave them, on purpose, in the printer tray on the computer table, a place that Negrinha always pries into. She's all the time going through my things; she's very jealous.

Negrinha becomes furious when she discovers the poems. She curses me, utters hard words, which I answer gently. She beats against my chest and my hump, says that she loves me, that she hates me, while I respond with soft words. I read somewhere or other that in a separation it's the one who doesn't love that says affectionate things.

Truthfully, I was very interested in Negrinha until she fell in love with me. But I am not and never was in love with her, or with any other woman I've been involved with. I'm a hunchback: I don't need to fall in love with a woman, I need for some woman to fall in love with me—and then another woman, then another. I remember the pleasant moments I spent with Negrinha, in bed, talking, listening to music, and mixing our saliva. They say that this transparent liquid secreted by the salivary glands is tasteless and serves merely to fluidify food and facilitate ingestion and digestion, which only proves that people lack the sensitivity to perceive the taste of even their own saliva, and, worse yet, the necessary gustative subtlety to take delight in the taste of another person's saliva. When they mix, the two salivas acquire an ineffable flavor, comparable only to the nectar of mythology—an enzymatic mystery, like others in our body.

I'm sad at having made Negrinha suffer. But I'm a hunchback. Goodbye, Negrinha, your saliva was delectable and your green eyes possessed a luminous beauty.

It takes Agnes a week to reply to my letter.

Her note: *I do need my Pomeranian, but I don't need my mother, maybe her checkbook. I'm going to stop by there.*

When Agnes arrives, I'm already prepared to receive her. How does a hunchback prepare to receive a beautiful woman who must be arduously induced to give herself to him? By making plans beforehand—all the contingencies, as is the essence of planning; remaining calm, as we must when we receive the surgeon or the plumber come to fix the toilet in the bathroom; wearing loose clothing and sticking out the chest; remaining alert so that our face always appears benign and our gaze permanently gentle. A distracted hunchback, even if not Quasimodesque but having a good-looking face, as in my case, always exhibits a sinister mien.

Agnes comes in and observes the living room with a keen feminine eye. I've been living here for only a year; I move constantly, and my living room, despite being elegantly furnished, has something vaguely incomplete about it, as if it lacked light fixtures, furniture with no function, and other useless ornaments that result from the prolonged occupation of domestic spaces. The fine wooden bookcases—which hold my books, CDs, and DVDs of film, music, opera, and the plastic arts and always go with me when I change residences—are modular and easily disassembled.

Agnes stops in front of the bookcases that cover the walls of the living room and asks, without turning toward me, "Do you own this apartment?"

"It's rented."

"What are the books mentioned in your note?"

"You'll find out in due time. It's a schedule without preset period of duration. You'll read a poem daily. The poets will never be repeated. You'll have the entire day to read the poem. At night you'll come here, we'll have dinner, and you'll talk to me about the chosen poem. Or about anything you wish, if you don't feel like talking about the poem. I have the best cook in the city. Would you like something to drink?"

Agnes, who has kept her back to me till then, suddenly turns, exclaiming, "I don't know what I'm doing here. I must be mad. Am I going to become a student? Is that it?"

"You're a pretty woman, but you feel an emptiness inside, don't you?"

"Ciao."

Over twenty operations to correct a hump that never went away. Constant awareness of furtive expressions of contempt, blatant mockery—*Hey, little man, can I rub my hand on your hump for luck?*—daily and immutable reflections of repugnant nakedness in the mirror in which I contemplate myself, not to mention what I read in the gaze of women, before I learned to wait for the right moment to read women's gazes—if all of that didn't break me, what effect can an oblique ciao followed by a disdainful withdrawal have? None.

To select what Agnes should read, I decide, for the sake of convenience, to use the works I have in my bookcase. I think about beginning with a classical licentious poet, but it's too early to introduce poems that say *questo è pure un bel cazzo lungo e grosso* or *fottimi e fà de me ciò che tu vuoi, o in potta o in cul, ch'io me ne curo poco;* she might get scared. This obscene poet is to be used in the phase when the woman has already been conquered. I forgot to say that I choose poets who are already dead, despite the existence of living poets much better than certain renowned poets who've kicked the bucket, but my decision is dictated by convenience; the best of the dead had the opportunity to find their way to my shelves, and I can't say the same about the living ones.

I send Agnes a poem that says that the art of losing is not hard to learn. I know it will provoke a reaction. Lazy people are constantly losing things, not to mention missing flights.

It's raining on the first day of the program. As soon as she enters, Agnes asks, "How did you know that for me losing things is always a disaster, despite all the rationalizations I make?"

"The same way I knew that you have one foot larger than the other. Shall we talk more about the poem? We can have dinner afterward."

"Tomorrow. Another thing, the foot of Botticelli's Venus is very ugly. Mine's prettier. Ciao."

A hunchback knows how he sleeps. He goes to sleep on his side, but he wakes up in the middle of the night lying face up, with pains in the back. Sleeping face down demands that one leg be bent and the opposite arm stuck under the pillow. We hunchbacks wake up several times during the night, looking for a comfortable position, or at least a less uncomfortable one, tormented by nocturnal thoughts that haunt our sleep. A hunchback never forgets, he is always thinking about his misfortune. People are what they are because they once made a choice; if they had chosen otherwise, their fate would be different, but a born hunchback makes no choice; he didn't intervene in his lot, didn't roll the dice. This intermittent affirmation robs him of sleep, forces him to get out of bed. Besides which, we hunchbacks like being on our feet.

When Agnes arrives the next day, the cook is already preparing dinner. A guy with his vertebrae in place can take the woman he wants to seduce to get a hot dog on the street. I can't allow myself that luxury.

"The poet—Is it poet or poetess?"

"The dictionary says poetess. But you can call all of them poet, man or woman."

"The poet says that when talking to the man she loved, she realized that he was hiding a tremor, the tremor of his mortal suffering. I sensed that when I spoke with you."

"Interesting," I said.

"Do you find it . . . bothersome to be a hunchback?"

"I've gotten used to it. Besides that, I've seen without anguish all the movie hunchbacks of Notre Dame, and I'm familiar with all the Richard IIIs—did you know that the real Richard III wasn't a hunchback, as can be deduced from his armor, which has been preserved to the present day? I also know by heart Dylan Thomas's poem about a hunchback in the park."

Agnes imitates me.

"Interesting."

I ask her to read me the new poem she's chosen. She leafs through the pages, reading poorly, her face buried in the book. You can't read decently with your face stuck in the book. And reading a poem is even more difficult; poets themselves don't know how to do it.

"Talk about the poem."

"The woman laments the death of the man she loved . . . Her fate was to celebrate that man, his strength, the brilliance of his imagination, but the woman says she's lost everything, forgotten everything."

"Did you feel anything?"

"A certain sadness. The poem bothered me a lot."

"Talk some more," I request.

Agnes speaks, I listen; she speaks, I listen. I intervene only to provoke her to speak more. As I know how to listen, it's very easy. Making them speak and listening to them is my tactic.

"I think that in Russian it must be even more tormenting," she says.

"That's the problem of poetic translation," I reply.

"The reader either knows all the languages in the world," says Agnes, "or has to get used to it: poems being less sad or less happy or less pretty or less meaningful, or less et cetera when translated. Always less."

"An American poet said that poetry is what's lost in translation."

"Who was it?"

"You're going to have to discover that. How about our having dinner?"

I'm not going to describe the delicacies of the dinner, the wines of noble provenance that we drank, the specifications of the crystal glasses we used, but I can say that the table of the greatest gourmet in the city is no better than my own. My father was skilled in matters of business, and when he died—my mother died first, I think she couldn't bear my misfortune, *her* misfortune—he left me in a comfortable situation. I'm not rich, but I can move, when necessary, from one beautiful residence to another even better, and I have a good cook and free time to accomplish my plans.

I call a cab. I accompany her to her home, despite her protests that she could go by herself. I return very tired.

I get out of bed quite early, in doubt as to the next poet to recommend. Choosing the books makes me feel even more shameless, like one of those know-it-all scholars who make their living by creating canons, or rather, catalogs of important authors. Actually, as I've already said, I only want to use the authors I have on my shelves, and even the bookcases of a hunchback don't necessarily have the best authors.

I ask Agnes to read the poem in which the author describes allegorically an act of cunnilingus.

"Please read this poem to me."

She reads. Her French is perfect.

"Talk about the poem."

"The poet, after saying that his loved one is nude like a Moorish slave, contemplates the thighs, the woman's hips, her breasts, and her belly, *ces grappes de ma vigne,* observes, enthralled, the narrow waist that accentuates the feminine pelvis, but what leaves him in ecstasy and sighing is the haughty red of the woman's face."

"Was that what you understood? The poet sees her pelvis and becomes ecstatic over the rouge on her face? Remember, he's staring at the lower part of the woman's trunk; the haughty red part that catches his attention can only be the vagina. Except he's not lecherous enough to dispense with metaphors."

"It could be. What's on today's menu?"

"You're the one who said she wanted to *understand.*"

"What's on today's menu?"

"Grenouille."

"Love it."

Several days have passed since our first encounter. I maintain control; patience is one of the greatest virtues, and that's true also for those who aren't hunchbacks. Today, for example, when Agnes, upon sitting down in front of me, shows her knees, I feel like kissing them, but I don't even look at them for long.

Agnes picks up the book.

"This here: 'the lover becomes transformed into the thing loved, by virtue of so much imagining . . . what more does the body desire to achieve?' What the devil does the poet mean by that?"

"Agnes, you read the poem unwillingly. It was you who chose this poem. There were other easier ones."

"Can we say it's a solipsistic sonnet?"

"Just for the pleasure of alliteration?"

"That too. Or should we call it an ascetic sonnet? Or a Neo-Platonic sonnet? See, I'm starting to sound like my own professor."

"Can one have a philosophy without knowing the philosopher who conceived it?" I ask.

Her face remains immobile; she has the habit of being like that, without moving her eyes, much less her lips—those gestures of someone wanting to demonstrate that they're meditating. It's as if she has gone deaf. But she quickly resumes speaking, with enthusiasm. And I listen. Knowing how to listen is an art, and enjoying listening is part of it. Anyone who feigns liking to listen is soon unmasked.

I don't touch her, either that day or in the days that follow.

There are women with dull white skin, others with an almost verdigris whiteness, others faded like plaster or bread-crumb flour, but Agnes's white skin has a splendid radiance that makes me want to bite it, sink my teeth into her arms, her legs, her face; she has a face meant to be bitten, but I restrain myself.

I give her another erotic poem to read. I confess that I'm taking a calculated risk. How will she react when she reads *the tongue licks the red petals of the pluriopen rose, the tongue tills a certain hidden bud, and weaves swift variations of subtle rhythms, and licks, languorously, lingeringly, the liquory hirsute grotto?* Agnes had changed the subject when I tried to make an erotic exegesis (isn't that what she wants—to *understand?*) of the cunnilingus poem, read by her two days earlier. How would she act now, after reading another poem on the same topic and even more daring?

"I thought that poetry didn't show such things, that fellatio and cunnilingus were only clichés used in films," Agnes says, after reading the poem. "I don't know if I liked it. 'Licks, languorously, lingeringly' is an amusing alliteration. But 'liquory hirsute grotto' is horrible. Is the next one going to be like that?"

I don't fathom the true implications of what she's telling me. Displeasure, disappointment? Mere curiosity? An opening? Better not to go into it too deeply.

We have been at the game for several days.

We read a poem about a guy who asks if he dares to eat a peach.

"Eating peaches?"

I play her game: "Let's say it's about old age."

"And old men don't have the courage to eat peaches?"

"I think it's because old people wear dentures."

"I thought that poems always spoke of beautiful or transcendental things."

"Poetry creates transcendence."

"I hate it when you show off."

"I'm not showing off. Prostheses are not merely the thing they represent. But some are more meaningful than others. Penis implants more than false teeth."

"Mechanical legs more than false fingernails?"

"Pacemakers more than hearing aids."

"Silicone breasts more than wigs?"

"Right. But always transcending the thing and the subject, something outside it."

"Is that implant much used? The one—"

"For the penis? Put yourself in the place of a man who has that implant. See the poetic simplicity of the metaphysical gesture of rebellion against the poison of time, against loneliness, anhedonia, sadness."

"May I ask an indiscreet question?"

"Go ahead."

"Do you use, or rather, would you use that prosthesis?"

"I'm a true hunchback. A hunchback doesn't need it."

I could have told her that a hunchback from birth, like me, either sublimates his desires forever—in which case, why the implant?—or else, as an adult, like me who until twenty-eight never had a sexual relationship, comes to be dominated by a paroxysmic lubricity that makes his dick get hard at the slightest of stimuli. A hunchback either becomes impotent or burns in a fire of lasciviousness that never cools for a single instant, like the heat of hell. But she'll find that out for herself in due time.

"There are no dentures in the poem," says Agnes, "or any kind of implant."

"Poets never show everything clearly. But the dentures are there, for one who knows what to look for."

"Old age is there, and the fear of death."

"And what is old age in a man?" I ask.

"I agree: it's false teeth, baldness, the certainty that the sirens no longer sing to him. Yes, and also the fear of acting. 'Do I dare?' the poet asks the whole time. He hates the horrendous symptoms of old age but doesn't dare commit suicide. 'Do I dare to eat a peach?' means will I have the courage to put an end to this shit that is my life? The peach is a metaphor for death. But I accept that there's also a denture involved. Am I learning to understand poetry?"

"Yes. The poem can be understood any way you like, which in itself is a step forward, and other people may, or may not, understand it in the same fashion as you. But that's not important in the least. What matters is that the reader must feel the poem, and what one feels upon reading the poem is exclusive, it's unlike the feeling of any other reader. What needs to be understood is the short story, the novel, those lesser literary genres, full of obvious symbolism."

"I think you talk too much," she says, good-naturedly.

Caveat: if a woman doesn't have a minimum of humor and intelligence, I am not able to fuck her. How could I carry on a conversation with her?

That's awful for a lascivious hunchback who must confront a real uphill battle to seduce women, whose first impression on seeing him could be the same one they'd have upon seeing a basilisk, if that cross-eyed reptile with lethal breath existed. Can you imagine me investing, blind with desire, days and days on a seduction only to discover later, in the middle of the undertaking, that I'm dealing with a dummy who'll make me go limp at the moment of truth? Once a hunchback goes limp, he's limp for the rest of his life, as if infected by a polyresistant bacteria. You'll say that if Agnes were intelligent she'd find me prolix and an exhibitionist. But in actuality I merely provoked her so she would talk. She was impressed with herself, believed she was learning not just to see but to understand that though the person may be nearsighted, he can't keep his eyes closed.

Another thing: just as for the poet writing is choosing—creating options and choosing—I too had to create options and choose.

My member is rigid. The hardness and the size of my penis give me confidence, very great courage, greater even than my cerebral astuteness. I feel like placing her hand on my dick, but the moment for that hasn't arrived yet. The alternative hasn't been created yet.

I don't know if I've mentioned already that the name of my cook is Maria do Céu, or Mary from Heaven. She deserves that name, and tonight she graces us with a magnificent meal.

After dinner we talk until the early hours. Several times I ask: Isn't it late for you? And she replies that she's not sleepy and doesn't feel like going home. We have wine, but I'm careful to avoid getting her drunk. Lucidity, both hers and mine, is essential to my plan.

I tell pointless jokes that make her laugh, precisely because they're pointless. For the first time she speaks of personal matters, the least complex ones, like her mother's grouchiness. There are women who even after they're no longer adolescents continue to feel resentment towards their mother. I listen to everything, attentively. Agnes also speaks of her former boyfriend, who was a good person but didn't talk to her. On one occasion, they went out for dinner and she decided that she'd keep quiet the entire evening. At the restaurant, her boyfriend consulted the menu, suggested the dishes, placed the order, and, once served, asked Agnes if her dish was tasty. He didn't say anything else, and didn't even note the silence. He might have noticed if she had refused to eat, but she was hungry. When they returned home, they went to bed and made love in silence. Then the boyfriend said "Good night, dear," rolled over, and went to sleep.

I listened to it all, attentively, making neutral but appropriate comments, which she interpreted as obvious interest on my part in what she was saying and feeling.

I choose another English-language poet. I have no predilection for the English language but cultivate English for the same reason that Descartes knew Latin. Agnes arrives with a basket of tangerines.

"You never have tangerines in the house."

"They're out of season," I said.

"But I found some. I chose this poem."

"Oh?"

"The poet says he knows the night, he has walked and still walks in the rain, beyond the lights of the city, without looking at the people, without the desire to give explanations, imagining the sounds of distant houses; the time that the clock shows is neither wrong nor right. You know I'm enjoying this?"

"Why?"

"I wanted to understand what poets say, and I learned with you that it's secondary," says Agnes. "Every literary text is capable of generating different readings, but besides that wealth of meanings, poetry has the advantage of being mysterious even when it says two and two is four."

"You're right. And, especially, poetry is never totally consumed. However much you devour a poem, the feeling it evokes is never exhausted."

"How complex life is," says Agnes, pretending to sigh.

"You'll see that's how it is," I say, lightly touching her arm. She moves away from the contact unaffectedly, without drama.

"How what is?"

"Life is complex."

"Is that what poets say?"

"I don't know. Let's have dinner."

Did I blunder by touching her? I think, as we eat the gastronomic delicacies prepared by Maria do Céu.

I've been at this undertaking for many days. I sense that Agnes is starting to become more vulnerable. But as the Bible says, for everything there is a season, and it's not yet time to harvest.

"Is there such a thing as feminine poetry?" Agnes asks. "If someone didn't know the author's name, would he discover that this verse—'the deepest feeling always shows itself in silence; not in silence, but restraint'—was written by a woman? Is that a masculine or a feminine sentence?"

"It was a woman who wrote it, but it could have been written by a man."

We've finished dinner and are in the middle of our conversation when the doorbell rings. Maria do Céu goes to open the door and returns immediately, with an apologetic expression, followed by Negrinha.

"I didn't know you had company," says Negrinha.

"I told her you were with someone," protests Maria do Céu, who knows that this unexpected appearance by Negrinha can only mean trouble: she witnessed Negrinha hit my hump when I gave her the pink slip.

"I didn't hear her," says Negrinha, noticing the book on the table. "Ah, poetry. Am I interrupting chitchat about poetry? This devil is full of tricks."

Agnes gets up from her chair.

"It's time for me to go."

"You haven't introduced me to your friend," says Negrinha.

"Some other time," says Agnes. "Ciao."

Agnes's ciao is always a bad sign. I go to the door with her.

"Wait a moment, I'm going to get the book."

She takes the book and leaves in a rush; I barely have time to give her a kiss on the cheek.

"It's always the same magic," says Negrinha sarcastically. "The man who can talk about the beauty of music, painting, poetry. And that fools the idiots, doesn't it? It worked with me. Music here, poetry there, and when the imbecile opens her eyes you're already sticking your dick in her."

"Negrinha, stop it."

"You're a prick. That hussy left before I could tell her what a 24-carat son of a bitch you are."

"Negrinha—"

"I came here because I was feeling sorry for you, thinking you were by yourself, but no, I find another idiot being seduced, the next victim. Does she know that after you screw her you'll kick her out on her ass?"

"Do you want something to drink? Sit here. Some wine?"

"Water."

I bring her a glass of water. Negrinha takes a swallow. She's calmer now.

"I think I'm going to accept that wine."

I place the glass and the bottle of Bordeaux, the wine she likes, beside her.

"Who is that woman? Is she that Venus, the one you wrote love poems for?"

"I already told you: that Venus was a fictitious figure."

"You said you were in love with another woman. With that hussy, the classical dumb blonde?"

"She's a redhead."

"The same shit."

Negrinha empties and refills the wine glass.

"And how could you fall in love with another woman when you were screwing me all the time? Why did you leave me? You liked me; you still like me, don't you?

She reaches out her hand, but I move away.

"You're afraid, aren't you? Just wait till you let me grab your dick."

She downs another glass of wine, in a single gulp.

"Negrinha, remember Heraclites—"

"Fuck Heraclites. You've never read a book on philosophy; you read those *For Dummies* books."

"I have to go out, Negrinha."

"Don't call me Negrinha. My name is Barbara."

"I have to go."

"You're afraid to go to bed with me."

"I have an important appointment."

"Coward."

I go to my bedroom and start changing clothes, rapidly. Negrinha invades the room. She seems a little drunk. As I quickly dress, she undresses with the same haste. We finish at practically the same time. Negrinha lies down, nude, on the bed, showing me the tip of her moistened tongue.

"I came here to talk with you," she says.

I run out of the room and descend the stairs. In the street I take the first taxi I see.

Agnes disappears for a couple of days. When we meet again, she seems calm, and different.

"I liked that poem," Agnes says.

"Why?"

"I don't know. Maybe because it's only three lines."

"And what does the author say in those three lines?"

"Does it matter?" Agnes asks. "Or is what's important what I felt?"

"Yes, what you felt."

"The poet says that she doesn't like poetry, but when she reads it, with total disdain, she discovers after all in poetry a place for the truth. I understood something, but I think she means something different. I was overcome by a feeling that I can't explain. That's how it should be, isn't it?"

"Yes."

"Who was that woman who came here? She's very pretty."

I kiss Agnes, lightly, on the cheek.

"Do you think I could be your girlfriend?" she asks.

"I think so."

"You have a handsome face, but you're a hunchback. How can I be your girlfriend?"

"After a time you won't even notice this physical characteristic of mine."

"What will other people say?"

"Others won't know, or suspect, or imagine. We'll go live somewhere else. We'll tell the neighbors we're brother and sister."

"And who was that woman? I have to admit that she's beautiful."

"Must be some crazy."

"I'm speaking seriously."

"She's a woman who has a thing for me."

"I'm not lazy."

I kiss her again, this time on the lips.

"This is very good," she says.

I take her by the arm and lead her gently to the bedroom. We remove our clothes in silence.

After the surrender, she sighs in exhaustion. Lying beside her, I feel in my mouth the delectable taste of her saliva.

"Promise you'll always talk to me," says Agnes, embracing me.

I'm going to live with Agnes in a different house, in a different area.

The deafening street howls around me when a woman dressed completely in black, with long black hair, passes by, tall and slim, enhancing by her movements her beautiful alabaster legs. (Life imitates poetry.) I follow her to where she lives. I have to create an elaborate strategy to get close to her and achieve what I need, a difficult task, as women, at first contact, feel repulsion towards me.

the game of dead men

THEY WOULD MEET EVERY NIGHT in Anísio's bar. Marinho, who owned the largest pharmacy in town, Fernando and Gonçalves, partners in a grocery store, and Anísio. None of them was a native of the city or even of the Baixada. Anísio and Fernando were from Minas Gerais and Marinho from Ceará. Gonçalves had come from Portugal. They were small-businessmen, prosperous and ambitious. They owned modest summer homes in the same development in the lake region, belonged to the Lions, went to church, lived a quiet life. They also had in common a strong interest in all forms of gambling. They would bet, among themselves, on card games, soccer, horse races, car races, beauty contests, anything with an element of chance. They bet big, but they usually wouldn't lose much money, since a losing streak was normally followed by a string of wins. In the last few months, however, Anísio, the owner of the bar, had been losing steadily.

They were playing cards and drinking beer the night the game of Dead Men was invented. Anísio invented the game.

"I bet the squad kills over 20 this month," he said.

Fernando observed that "over 20" was very vague.

"I bet the squad kills 21 this month," Anísio said.

"Just here in the city or in the whole Baixada?" Gonçalves asked. Despite being in Brazil for many years he still had a strong accent.

"A thousand that the squad kills 21 this month, here in Meriti," Anísio insisted.

"I bet they kill 69," Gonçalves said, laughing.

"I think that's a lot," Marinho said.

"I'm joking," Gonçalves said.

"Joking my ass," said Anísio, forcefully throwing a card on the table. "What's said is said, and it's just too bad for anybody who talks nonsense. I'm sick of losing out that way."

It was true.

"Did you hear the one about the Portuguese guy and sixty-nining?" Anísio asked. "They had to explain to him what sixty-nining was; he was horrified and said, 'God that's sickening. I wouldn't do that even with my dear mother.'"

Everyone laughed but Gonçalves.

"You know, this is a good game," Fernando said. "A thousand says the squad kills a dozen. Hey, Anísio, how about some cheese to go with the beer. And some of that salami."

"Write it down there,'' Anísio told Marinho, who noted the bets in a book with a green cover, "plus a thousand more that out of my 21, 10 are mulattos, 8 are black, and 2 are white."

"Who decides who's white, black, or mulatto? Here everything's a mixture. And how will we know who does the killing?" Gonçalves asked.

"Whatever it says in the newspaper is what counts. If it says he's black, he's black; if it says it was the squad, it was the squad. Agreed?" asked Marinho.

"Another grand that the youngest of mine is 18 and the oldest 26," Anísio said.

At that moment the False Perpétuo came into the bar and the four immediately stopped talking. The False Perpétuo had straight dark hair, bony facial features, and an impassive gaze, and like the True Perpétuo, a famous detective who had been assassinated some years earlier, he never smiled. None of the players knew what the False Perpétuo did; perhaps he merely worked in a bank or as a civil servant, but his presence, when he showed up now and then in Anísio's Bar, always frightened the four friends. No one knew his real name; the False Perpétuo was a nickname given him by Anísio, who claimed to have known the True Perpétuo.

He had carried two .45s, one on each hip, and a wide cartridge belt could be seen above his pants. He'd had the habit of lightly running the edge of his jacket through his fingers, as babies do with their diapers, a sign of alertness, always ready to pull out his weapons and shoot with both hands. When he was killed, they'd had to do it from behind.

The False Perpétuo sat down and ordered a beer, not looking at the players but turning his head slightly, his neck taut; he could be listening to what the group was saying.

"I think it's just our impression," murmured Fernando, "and anyway, whoever he is, why should we care? No debts, no worries."

"I don't know, I just don't know," Anísio said pensively. They went back to playing cards, in silence, waiting for the False Perpétuo to leave.

At the end of the month, according to the newspaper, the squad had executed 26 people—16 mulattos, 9 blacks, and 1 white, the youngest, an ex-reformatory inmate, being 15, and the oldest, 38.

"Let's celebrate the victory," Gonçalves said to Marinho, who between them had won the majority of the bets. They drank beer, ate cheese, ham, and meat turnovers.

"Three months of bad luck," Anísio said somberly. He had also lost at poker, on the horses, and on soccer; the lunch counter he had bought in Caxias was losing money, his credit with the bank was getting worse, and the young wife he had married a little over six months before was spending a lot.

"And now August is coming," he said, "the month Getúlio shot himself in the heart. I was a kid, working in a bar on the same street as the palace, and saw it all, the crying and the screams, the people filing past the coffin, the body being taken to the airport, the soldiers firing machine guns into the crowd. If I was unlucky in July, just think of August."

"Then don't bet this month," said Gonçalves, who had just lent Anísio 200,000 *cruzeiros*.

"No, this month I plan to win back part of what I lost," said Anísio with animosity.

The four friends, for the month of August, expanded the rules of the game. Besides the quantity, age, and color of the dead, they added national origin, marital status, and occupation. The game was becoming complicated.

"I think we've invented a game that's going to be more popular than the numbers game," Marinho said. Already half drunk, they laughed so hard that Fernando wet his pants.

The end of the month was approaching, and Anísio, more and more irritated, argued frequently with his companions. That day he was more exasperated and nervous than ever, and his friends, ill at ease, were looking forward to when the card game would end.

"Who's for an even-money bet with me?" Anísio asked.

"What kind of even-money bet?" asked Marinho, who had won more frequently than any of them.

"I'll bet that this month the squad kills a young girl and a businessman. Two hundred thousand bills."

"That's crazy," said Gonçalves, thinking of his money and of the fact that the squad never killed girls and businessmen.

"Two hundred thousand," Anísio repeated in a bitter tone, "and you, Gonçalves, don't call other people crazy, you're the one who's crazy for leaving your homeland to come to this shithole of a country."

"You're on," said Marinho. "You don't have a prayer of winning; it's almost the end of the month."

Around eleven o'clock the players ended the game and quickly said goodnight.

The waiters left and Anísio was alone in the bar. On other nights he would rush home to be with his young wife. But that night he sat drinking beer until shortly after one a.m., when there was a knock at the rear door.

The False Perpétuo came in and sat down at Anísio's table.

"Want a beer?" Anísio asked, avoiding either the polite or familiar form of address with the False Perpétuo, uncertain of the degree of respect he should show.

"No. What's this about?" The False Perpétuo spoke quietly, in a soft voice, apathetic, indifferent.

Anísio told him about the bets he and his friends made every month in the game of Dead Men. The visitor listened in silence, erect in his chair, his hands resting on his legs; at times it seemed to Anísio that the False Perpétuo ran the edge of his jacket through his fingers the way the true one did, but he must have been mistaken.

Anísio began to regret the man's gentleness; maybe he was nothing more than a bureaucratic functionary. God, Anísio thought, 200,000 down the drain; he'd have to sell the lunch counter in Caxias. Unexpectedly he thought about his young wife, her round, tepid body.

"The squad has to kill a young girl and a businessman this month for me to get out of the hole," Anísio said.

"And what does that have to do with me?" Smoothly.

Anísio summoned up his courage. He had drunk a lot of beer; he was on the verge of ruin and felt awful, as if he couldn't breathe properly. "I think you belong to the death squad."

The False Perpétuo remained inscrutable.

"What's the deal?"

"Ten thousand if you kill a young girl and a businessman. You or your colleagues, it's all the same to me."

Anísio sighed unhappily. Now that he saw his plan close to realization, his body was overcome by a feeling of weakness.

"You got the money here? I can do the job right now."

"It's at home."

"Where do I start?"

"Both at once."

"Anybody special?"

"Gonçalves, the owner of the grocery, and his daughter."

"That Portuguese friend of yours?"

"He's not my friend." Another sigh.

"How old's his daughter?"

"Twelve." The image of the girl having a soft drink in his bar flashed through his head, like a twinge of pain.

"All right," said the False Perpétuo, "show me his house." That was when Anísio noticed that above his waist he also wore a wide cartridge belt.

They got into the False Perpétuo's car and headed for Gonçalves's house. At that hour the city was deserted. They stopped fifty yards from the house. The False Perpétuo took two pieces of paper from the glove compartment and drew two crude death's-heads with the initials D.S. below.

"It'll be quick," the False Perpétuo said, getting out of the car.

Anísio put his hands over his ears, closed his eyes, and curled up on the seat until his face touched the plastic seat cover, which gave off an unpleasant odor that reminded him of his childhood. There was a buzzing in his ears. A long time went by, until he heard three shots.

The False Perpétuo returned and got into the car.

"Let's get my money. I took care of them both. I threw in the old woman for free."

They stopped at the door to Anísio's house. He went in. His wife was in bed, her naked back facing the bedroom door. She usually slept on her side, and the view of her body seen from behind was prettier. Anísio got the money and left.

"You know, I don't know your name," Anísio said in the car, while the False Perpétuo counted the money.

"It's better that way."

"I gave you a nickname."

"What?"

"The False Perpétuo." Anísio tried to laugh, but his heart was heavy and sad.

Could it have been an illusion? The other man's expression had suddenly become alert and he was delicately fingering the edge of his jacket. The two looked at each other in the half shadow of the car. As he realized what was about to happen, Anísio felt a kind of relief.

The False Perpétuo took an enormous weapon from his waist, pointed it at Anísio's chest, and fired. Anísio heard the roar and then an immense silence. Forgive me, he tried to say, tasting the blood in his mouth and attempting to remember a prayer, while at his side the bony face of Christ, illuminated by the streetlight, faded rapidly.

the blotter

1.

Detective Miro brought the woman to see me.

"It was her husband," Miro said, uninterested. In that precinct in the outskirts, husband-and-wife squabbles were common.

Two of her front teeth were broken, her lips injured, her face swollen. Marks on the arms and neck.

"Did your husband do this?" I asked.

"He didn't mean to, sir, I don't want to file a complaint."

"Then why are you here?"

"At the time I was angry, but not now. Can I go?"

"No."

Miro sighed. "Let the woman leave," he said between his teeth.

"You've suffered bodily harm; that's a prosecutable crime independent of your lodging a complaint. I'm going to send you for questioning to see if a crime has been committed," I said.

"Ubiratan is high-strung but he's not a bad person," she said. "Please, don't do anything to him."

They lived nearby. I decided to go have a talk with Ubiratan. Once, in Madureira, I had convinced a guy to stop beating his wife; two others, when I worked in the Jacarepaguá precinct, had also been persuaded to treat their wives decently.

A tall, muscular man opened the door. He was in shorts, shirtless. In one corner of the room was a steel bar with heavy iron rings and two weights painted red. He must have been doing exercises when I arrived. His muscles were swollen and covered with a thick layer of sweat. He exuded the spiritual strength and pride that good health and a muscle-packed body give certain men.

"I'm from the precinct," I said.

"Ah, so she did file a complaint, the stupid bitch," Ubiratan grumbled. He went to the refrigerator, took out a can of beer, opened it, and started drinking.

"Go tell her to come home right now or there's gonna be trouble."

"I don't think you understand why I'm here. I came to ask you to make a statement at the precinct."

Ubiratan threw the empty can out the window, grabbed the barbell and hoisted it overhead ten times, breathing noisily through his mouth as if he were a locomotive.

"You think I'm afraid of the police?" he asked, looking admiringly and affectionately at the muscles in his chest and arms.

"There's no need to be afraid. You're just going there to make a statement."

Ubiratan grabbed my arm and shook me.

"Get the hell outta here, you lousy cop, you're starting to get on my nerves."

I took my revolver from its holster. "I could arrest you for insulting an officer of the law, but I'm not going to do that. Don't make things worse; come down to the precinct with me, you'll be out of there in half an hour," I said, calmly and politely.

Ubiratan laughed. "How tall are you, midget?"

"Five-eight. Let's go."

"I'm going to take that piece of shit outta your hand and piss down the barrel, midget." Ubiratan contracted every muscle in his body, like an animal making itself bigger to frighten the other, and extended his arm, his hand open to grab my gun. I shot him in the thigh. He looked at me, astonished.

"Look what you did to my sartorius!" Ubiratan screamed, pointing to his own thigh, "you're crazy, my sartorius!"

"I'm very sorry," I said, "now let's go or I'll shoot the other leg."

"Where you taking me, midget?"

"First to the hospital, then to the precinct."

"This isn't the last of it, midget, I got influential friends."

Blood was running down his leg, dripping onto the floor of the car.

"You bastard, my sartorius!" His voice was more piercing than the siren that opened a path for us through the streets.

2.

A warm summer morning on São Clemente Street. A bus struck down a ten-year-old boy. The vehicle's wheels ran over his head, leaving a trail of brain matter several yards long. Beside the body was a new bicycle, without a scratch on it.

A traffic cop caught the driver at the scene. Two witnesses stated that the bus was moving at high speed. The site of the accident was carefully roped off.

An old woman, poorly dressed, with a lit candle in her hand, wanted to cross the police line, "to save the little angel's soul." She was stopped. Along with the other bystanders, she contemplated the body from a distance. Separated, in the middle of the street, the corpse appeared even smaller.

"Good thing it's a holiday," a cop said, diverting traffic, "can you imagine if it was a weekday?"

Screaming, a woman broke through the barrier and picked the body up from the ground. I ordered her to put it down. I twisted her arm, but she seemed to feel no pain, moaning loudly, not yielding. The two cops and I struggled with her until we managed to pull the dead boy from her arms and place him on the ground where he should be, waiting for the coroner. Two cops dragged the woman away.

"All these bus drivers are killers," said the coroner, "good thing the scene is perfect, it means I can do a report that no shyster can shake."

I went to the squad car and sat in front for a few moments. My jacket was dirty with small remnants of the victim. I tried to clean myself with my hands. I called one of the uniforms and told him to get the prisoner.

On the way to the station I looked at him. He was a thin man who appeared to be about sixty, and he looked weary, sick, and afraid. An old fear, sickness, and weariness, which didn't come from just that day.

3.

I arrived at the two-story house on Cancela Street and the cop at the door said, "Top floor. He's in the bathroom."

I climbed the stairs. In the living room a woman with reddened eyes looked at me in silence. Beside her was a thin boy, cringing a little, his mouth open, breathing labored.

"The bathroom?" She pointed me toward a dark hallway. The house smelled of mold, as if the pipes were leaking inside the walls. From somewhere came the odor of fried onion and garlic.

The door to the bathroom was ajar. The man was there.

I returned to the living room. I had already asked the woman all the questions when Azevedo, the medical examiner, arrived.

"In the bathroom," I said.

It was getting dark. I turned on the living room light. Azevedo asked for my help. We went into the bathroom.

"Lift the body," the M.E. said, "so I can undo the rope."

I held onto the dead man by the waist. A moan came from his mouth.

"Trapped air," said Azevedo, "funny isn't it?" We laughed without pleasure. We placed the body on the wet floor. A frail man, unshaven, his face gray, he looked like a wax dummy.

"Didn't leave a note, nothing," I said.

"I know the type," said Azevedo. "When they can't take it any longer, they kill themselves fast; it has to be fast before they can change their minds."

Azevedo urinated into the toilet. Then he washed his hands in the basin and dried them on his shirttails.

lonelyhearts

I WAS WORKING FOR A POPULAR NEWSPAPER as a police reporter. It had been a long time since the city had seen an interesting crime involving a rich, young, and beautiful society woman, along with deaths, disappearances, corruption, lies, sex, ambition, money, violence, scandal.

"You don't get crimes like that even in Rome, Paris, New York," the editor said. "We're in a slump. But things'll change soon. It's all cyclical. When you least expect it, one of those scandals breaks out that provides material for a year. Everything's rotten, just right, all we have to do is wait."

Before it broke out, they fired me.

"All you have is small-businessmen killing their partners, petty thieves killing small-businessmen, police killing petty thieves. Small potatoes," I told Oswaldo Peçanha, editor-in-chief and owner of the newspaper *Woman.*

"There's also meningitis, schistosomiasis, Chagas's disease," Peçanha said.

"Out of my area," I said.

"Have you read *Woman?*" Peçanha asked.

I admitted I hadn't. I prefer reading books.

Peçanha took a box of cigars from his desk and offered me one. We lit the cigars, and soon the atmosphere was unbreathable. The cigars were cheap, it was summer, the windows were closed, and the air conditioning wasn't working well.

"*Woman* isn't one of those colorful publications for bourgeois women on a diet. It's made for the Class C woman, who eats rice and beans and if she gets fat, tough luck. Take a look."

Peçanha tossed me a copy of the newspaper. Tabloid format, headlines in blue, some out-of-focus photographs. Illustrated love story, horoscope, interviews with TV actors, dressmaking.

"Think you could do the 'Woman to Woman' section, our advice column? The guy who was doing it left."

"Woman to Woman" carried the byline of one Elisa Gabriela. *Dear Elisa Gabriela, my husband comes home drunk every night and—*

"I think I can," I said.

"Great. You start today. What name do you want to use?"

I thought a bit.

"Nathanael Lessa."

"Nathanael Lessa?" Peçanha said, surprised and offended, as if I'd said a dirty word or insulted his mother.

"What's wrong with it? It's a name like any other. And I'm paying homage to two people."

Peçanha puffed his cigar, irritated.

"First, it's not a name like any other. Second, it's not a Class C name. Here we only use names pleasing to Class C, pretty names.

"Third, the paper only pays homage to who I want it to, and I don't know any Nathanael Lessa. And finally"—Peçanha's irritation had gradually increased, as if he were taking a certain enjoyment in it—"here no one, not even me, uses a masculine pseudonym. My name is Maria de Lourdes!"

I took another look at the newspaper, including the staff. Nothing but women's names.

"Don't you think a masculine name gives the answers more respectability? Father, husband, priest, boss—they have nothing but men telling them what to do. Nathanael Lessa will catch on better than Elisa Gabriela."

"That's exactly what I don't want. Here they feel like their own bosses, they trust us, as if we were all friends. I've been in this business twenty-five years. Don't come to me with untested theories. *Woman* is revolutionizing the Brazilian press; it's a different kind of newspaper that doesn't run yesterday's warmed-over television news."

He was so irritated that I didn't ask exactly what *Woman* was out to accomplish. He'd tell me sooner or later. I just wanted the job.

"My cousin, Machado Figueiredo, who also has twenty-five years' experience, at the Bank of Brazil, likes to say that he's always open to untested theories." I knew that *Woman* owed money to the bank. And a letter of recommendation from my cousin was on Peçanha's desk.

When he heard my cousin's name, Peçanha paled. He bit his cigar to control himself, then closed his mouth, as if he were about to whistle, and his fat lips trembled as if he had a grain of pepper on his tongue. He opened his mouth wide and tapped his nicotine-stained teeth with his thumbnail while he looked at me in a way that he must have considered fraught with significance.

"I could add 'Dr.' to my name. Dr. Nathanael Lessa."

"Damn! All right, all right," Peçanha snarled between his teeth, "you start today."

That was how I came to be part of the team at *Woman.*

My desk was near Sandra Marina's, who wrote the horoscope. Sandra was also known as Marlene Katia, for interviews. A pale fellow with a long, sparse mustache, he was also known as João Albergaria Duval. He wasn't long out of communications school and constantly complained, "Why didn't I study dentistry, why?"

I asked him if someone brought the readers' letters to my desk. He told me to talk to Jacqueline in the office. Jacqueline was a large black man with very white teeth.

"It won't go over well being the only one here who doesn't have a woman's name; they're going to think you're a fairy. Letters? There aren't any. You think Class C women write letters? Elisa made them all up."

> DEAR DR. NATHANAEL LESSA. *I got a scholarship for my ten-year-old daughter in a fancy school in a good neighborhood. All her*

classmates go to the hairdresser at least once a week. We don't have the money for that, my husband drives a bus on the Jacaré–Caju line, but he says he's going to work overtime to send Tania Sandra, our little girl, to the hairdresser. Don't you think that our children deserve every sacrifice? DEDICATED MOTHER. VILLA KENNEDY.

ANSWER: *Wash your little girl's head with coconut soap and wrap it in curling paper. It's the same as the hairdresser. In any case, your daughter wasn't born to be a doll-baby. Nor anyone else's daughter, for that matter. Take the overtime pay and buy something more useful. Food, for example.*

DEAR DR. NATHANAEL LESSA. *I am short, plump, and shy. Whenever I go to the outdoor market, the store, the vegetable market, they trick me. They cheat me on the weight, the change, the beans have bugs in them, the cornmeal is stale, that kind of thing. It used to bother me a lot, but now I'm resigned to it. God is watching them and at the day of judgment they will pay.* RESIGNED DOMESTIC. PENHA.

ANSWER: *God doesn't have his eye on anybody. You have to look out for yourself. I suggest you scream, holler, raise a scandal. Don't you have a relative who works for the police? A crook will do also. Get moving, chubby.*

DEAR DR. NATHANAEL LESSA. *I am twenty-five, a typist, and a virgin. I met this boy who says he really loves me. He works in the Ministry of Transportation and says he wants to marry me, but first he wants to try it out. What do you think?* FRENZIED VIRGIN. PARADA DE LUCAS.

ANSWER: *Look, Frenzied Virgin, ask the guy what he plans to do if he doesn't like the experience. If he says he'll dump you, give him what he wants, because he's a sincere man. You're not some Kool-Aid or stew to be sampled. But there aren't many sincere men around, so it's worth a try. Keep the faith and full speed ahead.*

I went to lunch.

When I got back Peçanha called me in. He had my copy in his hand.

"There's something or other here I don't like," he said.

"What?" I asked.

"Ah, good God, the idea people have of Class C," Peçanha exclaimed, shaking his head pensively while he looked at the ceiling and puckered his lips. "It's Class A women who like being treated with curses and kicks. Remember that English lord who said his success with women came from treating ladies like whores and whores like ladies."

"All right. So how should I handle our readers?"

"Don't come to me with dialectics. I don't want you to treat them like whores. Forget the English lord. Put some happiness, some hope, tranquility, and reassurance in the letters, that's what I want."

> DEAR DR. NATHANAEL LESSA. *My husband died and left me a very small pension, but what worries me is being alone and fifty years old. Poor, ugly, old, and living a long way out, I'm afraid of what's in store for me.* LONELY IN SANTA CRUZ.
>
> ANSWER: *Engrave this in your heart, Lonely in Santa Cruz: neither money, nor beauty, nor youth, nor a good address brings happiness. How many rich and beautiful people kill themselves or lose themselves in the horrors of vice? Happiness is inside us, in our hearts. If we are just and good, we will find happiness. Be good, be just, love your neighbor as yourself, smile at the clerk when you go to pick up your pension.*

The next day Peçanha called me in and asked if I could also write the illustrated love story. "We turn out our own stories, not some translated Italian *fumetti*. Pick a name."

I chose Clarice Simone, two more homages, though I didn't tell Peçanha that.

The photographer of the love stories came to talk to me.

"My name is Monica Tutsi," he said, "but you can call me Agnaldo. You got the pap ready?"

Pap was the love story. I explained that I had just gotten the assignment from Peçanha and would need at least two days to write it.

"Days, ha ha," he guffawed, making the sound of a large, hoarse domesticated dog barking for its master.

"What's so funny?" I asked.

"Norma Virginia used to write the story in fifteen minutes. He had a formula."

"I have a formula too. Take a walk and come back in fifteen minutes; your story'll be ready."

What did that idiot of a photographer think I was? Just because I'd been a police reporter didn't mean I was stupid. If Norma Virginia, or whatever his name was, wrote a story in fifteen minutes, so could I. After all, I read all the Greek tragedies, the Ibsens, the O'Neills, the Becketts, the Chekhovs, the Shakespeares, the *Four Hundred Best Television Plays*. All I had to do was appropriate an idea here, another one there, and that's it.

> A rich young lad is stolen by gypsies and given up for dead. The boy grows up thinking he's a real gypsy. One day he meets a very rich young girl, and they fall in love. She lives in a fine mansion and has many automobiles. The gypsy boy lives in a wagon. The two families don't want them to marry. Conflicts arise. The millionaires order the police to arrest the gypsies. One of the gypsies is killed by the police. A rich cousin of the girl is assassinated by the gypsies. But the love of the two young people is greater than all these vicissitudes. They decide to run away, to break with their families. On their flight they encounter a pious and wise monk who seals their union in an ancient, picturesque and romantic convent amidst a flowering wood. The two young people retire to the nuptial chamber. They are beautiful, slim, blond with blue eyes. They remove their clothes. "Oh," says the girl, "what is that gold chain with a diamond-studded medallion you wear on your neck?" She has one just like it! They are brother and sister! "You are my brother who disappeared!" the girl cries. The two embrace. (Attention Monica Tutsi: how about

> an ambiguous ending? Making a non-fraternal ecstasy appear on their faces, huh? I can also change the ending and make it more Sophoclean: they discover they're brother and sister after the consummated fact; the desperate girl leaps from the convent window and creams herself down below.)

"I liked your story," Monica Tutsi said.

"A pinch of Romeo and Juliet, a teaspoon of Oedipus Rex," I said modestly.

"But I can't photograph it, man. I have to do everything in two hours. Where do I find the mansion? The cars? The picturesque convent? The flowered wood?"

"That's your problem."

"Where do I find," Monica Tutsi continued as if he hadn't heard me, "the two slim, blond young people with blue eyes? All our models tend toward the mulatto. Where do I get the wagon? Try again, man. I'll be back in fifteen minutes. And what does Sophoclean mean?"

> Roberto and Betty are engaged to be married. Roberto, who is very hard working, has saved his money to buy an apartment and furnish it, with a color television set, stereo, refrigerator, washing machine, floor polisher, dishwasher, toaster, electric iron, and hair dryer. Betty works too. Both are chaste. The date is set. A friend of Roberto's, Tiago, asks him, "Are you going to get married still a virgin? You need to be initiated into the mysteries of sex." Tiago then takes Roberto to the house of the Superwhore Betatron. (Attention Monica Tutsi: the name is a pinch of science fiction.) When Roberto arrives he finds out that the Superwhore is Betty, his dear fiancée. Oh heavens! What a horrible surprise! Someone, perhaps a doorman, will say, "To grow up is to suffer." End of story.

"One word is worth a thousand photographs," Monica Tutsi said. "I always get the short end of things. I'll be back soon."

> DR. NATHANAEL. *I like to cook. I also like to embroider and crochet. And most of all I like to wear a long evening gown and put on crimson lipstick, with lots of rouge and eye shadow. Ah, what a sensation! What a pity that I must stay locked in my room. No one knows that I like to do these things. Am I wrong?* PEDRO REDGRAVE. TIJUCA.
>
> ANSWER: *Why should it be wrong? Are you doing anyone harm? I had another reader who, like you, enjoyed dressing as a woman. He carried on a normal, useful, and socially productive life, to the point that he was chosen a model worker. Put on your long gowns, paint your lips scarlet, put some color in your life.*

"All the letters should be from women," Peçanha reminded.

"But this one is real," I said.

"I don't believe it."

I handed the letter to Peçanha. He looked at it with the expression of a cop examining a badly counterfeited bill.

"You think it's a joke?" Peçanha asked.

"It might be," I said. "And it might not be."

Peçanha put on his reflective look. Then: "Add some phrase of encouragement to your letter, like for example, 'write again'."

I sat down at the typewriter: *Write again, Pedro, I know that's not your real name, but it doesn't matter; write again, count on me. Nathanael Lessa.*

"Shit," said Monica Tutsi, "I went to do your great piece of drama and they told me it was stolen from some Italian film."

"Wretches, band of idiots—just because I was a police reporter they're calling me a plagiarist."

"Take it easy, Virginia."

"Virginia? My name is Clarice Simone," I said. "What idiocy is this of thinking only Italian fiancées are whores? Look here, I once knew an engaged woman, a really serious one, who was even a sister of charity, and they found out she was a whore too."

"It's okay, man, I'm going to shoot the story. Can Betatron be mulatto? What's a Betatron?"

"She has to be a redhead, with freckles. Betatron is an apparatus for the production of electrons, possessing great energy potential and high velocity, impelled by the action of a rapidly changing magnetic field," I said.

"Shit! That's really a name for a whore," said Monica Tutsi admiringly, on his way out.

> UNDERSTANDING NATHANAEL LESSA. *I have worn my long gowns gloriously. And my mouth has been as red as tiger's blood and the break of dawn. I am thinking of putting on a satin gown and going to the Municipal Theater. What do you think? And now I'm going to tell you a great and marvelous confidence, but you must keep my confession the greatest secret. Do you swear? Ah, I don't know if I should say it or not. All my life I've suffered the greatest disillusionment from believing in others. I am basically a person who never lost his innocence. Betrayal, coarseness, shamelessness, and baseness leave me quite shocked. Oh, how I would like to live isolated in a utopian world of love and kindness. My sensitive Nathanael, let me think. Give me time. In the next letter I shall tell more, perhaps everything.* PEDRO REDGRAVE.
>
> ANSWER: *Pedro. I await your letter, with your secrets, which I promise to store in the inviolable reaches of my recondite consciousness. Continue this way, confronting aloofly the envy and insidious perfidy of the poor in spirit. Adorn your body, which thirsts for sensuality, by exercising the challenges of your courageous mind.*

Peçanha asked: "Are these letters real too?"

"Pedro Redgrave's are."

"Strange, very strange," Peçanha said, tapping his nails on his teeth. "What do you make of it?"

"I don't make anything of it," I said.

He seemed preoccupied about something. He asked about the illustrated love story but took no interest in the answers.

"What about the blind girl's letter?" I asked.

Peçanha got the blind girl's letter and my reply and read aloud: "Dear Nathanael. I cannot read what you write. My beloved granny reads it to me. But do not think I am illiterate. I am blind. My dear granny is writing this letter for me, but the words are my own. I want to send a word of comfort to your readers so that they, who suffer so much from small misfortunes, may look at themselves in the mirror. I am blind but I am happy. I am at peace, with God and my fellow man. Happiness to all. Long live Brazil and its people. Blind but Happy. Unicorn Road. Nova Iguaçu. P.S. I forgot to say that I am also paralyzed." Peçanha lit a cigar. "Moving, but Unicorn Road doesn't ring true. You'd better make it Windmill Road or something like that. Now let's see your answer. 'Blind but Happy, congratulations on your moral strength, your unwavering faith in happiness, in goodness, in the people, and in Brazil. The souls of those who despair in their adversity should take nourishment from your edifying example, a flambeau of light in the darkness of torment.'"

Peçanha gave me the papers. "You have a future in literature. This is a great school we have here. Learn, learn, dedicate yourself, don't lose heart, work hard."

I sat at the typewriter:

> Tesio, a bank employee, resident of Boca do Mato, in Lins de Vasconcelos, married to Frederica in his second marriage, has a son, Hipolito, from his first marriage. Frederica falls in love with Hipolito. Tesio discovers their sinful love. Frederica hangs herself from the mango tree in the back yard. Hipolito asks his father for forgiveness, leaves home and wanders desperately through the streets of the cruel city until he is run over and killed on the Avenida Brasil.

"What's the seasoning here?" Monica Tutsi asked.

"Euripides, sin, and death. Let me tell you something: I know the human soul and don't need any ancient Greek to inspire me. For a man of my intelligence and sensitivity it's enough to look around me. Look closely at my eyes. Have you ever seen anyone more alert, more wide awake?"

Monica Tutsi looked closely at my eyes and said, "I think you're crazy."

I continued: "I cite the classics only to demonstrate my knowledge. Since I was a police reporter, if I don't do that the cretins don't respect me. I've read thousands of books. How many books do you think Peçanha has read?"

"None. Can Frederica be black?"

"Good idea. But Tesio and Hipolito have to be white."

> NATHANAEL. *I love, a forbidden love, an interdicted love, a secret love, a hidden love. I love another man. And he also loves me. But we cannot walk in the street holding hands, like others, exchange kisses in the gardens and movie theaters, like others, lie in each other's arms on the sandy beaches, like others, dance in night clubs, like others. We cannot get married, like others, and together face old age, disease, and death, like others. I do not have the strength to resist and struggle. It's better to die. Good-bye. This is my last letter. Have a mass said for me.* PEDRO REDGRAVE.

> ANSWER*: What are you saying, Pedro? Are you going to give up now that you've found your love? Oscar Wilde suffered like the devil, he was ridiculed, tried, sentenced, but he stood up to it. If you can't get married, shack up. Make a will in each other's favor. Defend yourselves. Use the law and the system to your benefit. Be selfish, like the others, be sly, implacable, intolerant, and hypocritical. Exploit. Plunder. It's self-defense. But, please, don't carry out any deranged gesture.*

I sent the letter and reply to Peçanha. Letters were published only with his approval.

Monica Tutsi came by with a girl.

"This is Monica," Monica Tutsi said.

"Quite a coincidence," I said.

"What's a coincidence?" asked the girl Monica.

"The two of you having the same name," I said.

"His name is Monica?" Monica asked, pointing to the photographer.

"Monica Tutsi. Are you Tutsi too?"

"No. Monica Amelia."

Monica Amelia stood chewing a fingernail and looking at Monica Tutsi.

"You told me your name was Agnaldo," she said.

"On the outside I'm Agnaldo. Here inside I'm Monica Tutsi."

"My name is Clarice Simone," I said.

Monica Amelia observed us attentively, without understanding a thing. She saw two circumspect people, too tired for jokes, uninterested in their own names.

"When I get married my son, or daughter, is going to be named Hei Yoo," I said.

"Is that a Chinese name? " Monica asked.

"Or else Wheet Wheeo," I whistled.

"You're becoming a nihilist," Monica Tutsi said, withdrawing with the other Monica.

NATHANAEL. *Do you know what it is for two people to like one another? That was the two of us, Maria and I. Do you know what it is for two people to be perfectly attuned? That was us, Maria and I. My favorite dish is rice, beans, kale, manioc meal, and fried sausage. Guess what Maria's was? Rice, beans, kale, manioc meal, and fried sausage. My favorite precious stone is the ruby. Maria's, you guessed it, was also the ruby. Lucky number 7, color Blue, day Monday, film Westerns, book The Little Prince, drink Beer on Tap, mattress Anatom, soccer team Vasco da Gama, music Samba, pastime Love, everything the same between her and me, wonderful. What we would do in bed, man—I don't mean to brag, but if it were in the circus and we charged admission, we'd be rich. In bed no couple was ever so taken by such resplendent madness, was capable of such a dexterous, imaginative, original, pertinacious, splendiferous, and fulfilling performance as ours. And we would repeat it several times a day. But it was not just that which linked us. If you were missing a leg I would continue to love you, she would say. If you were a hunchback I would not stop loving you, I would reply. If you were a deaf-mute I would continue to love you, she would say. If you were cross-eyed I would not stop loving you, I would respond. If you had a paunch and were ugly I would go on loving you, she would say. If you were all scarred with smallpox I would not stop loving you, I would respond. If you were old and impotent I would continue to love you, she would say. And we were exchanging these vows when a desire to be truthful struck me, as deep as a knife-thrust, and I asked her, what if I had no teeth, would you love me? And she replied, if you had no teeth I would still love you. Then I took out my dentures and threw them on the bed with a grave, religious, and metaphysical gesture. We both lay there looking at the dentures on top of the sheet, until Maria got up, put on a dress, and said, I'm going out for cigarettes. To this day she hasn't come back. Nathanael, explain to me what happened. Does love end suddenly? Do a few teeth, miserable pieces of ivory, mean that much?* ODONTOS SILVA.

As I was about to reply, Jacqueline came by and said that Peçanha was calling me.

In Peçanha's office was a man wearing glasses and a goatee.

"This is Dr. Pontecorvo, who's a—just what are you?" asked Peçanha.

"A motivational researcher," Pontecorvo said. "As I was saying, first we do a survey of the characteristics of the universe we're researching, for example: who is the reader of *Woman?* Let's suppose it's the Class C female. In our previous research we've surveyed everything about the Class C female—where she buys her food, how many pairs of panties she owns, what time she makes love, what time she watches television, which television programs she watches, in short, a complete profile."

"How many pairs of panties does she own?" Peçanha asked.

"Three," Pontecorvo replied without hesitation.

"What time does she make love?"

"At 9:30 p.m.," Pontecorvo replied promptly.

"And how did you find all this out? Do you knock at Dona Aurora's door in the housing project, she opens the door and you say, good morning, Dona Aurora, what time do you get it on? Look here, my friend, I've been in this business for twenty-five years, and I don't need anybody to tell me what the Class C woman's profile is. I know from personal experience. They buy my newspaper, understand? Three pairs of panties . . . Ha!"

"We use scientific research methods. We have sociologists, psychologists, anthropologists, statisticians, and mathematicians on our staff," said Pontecorvo, imperturbable.

"All to get money from the patsies," said Peçanha with undisguised scorn.

"As a matter of fact, before coming here I put together some information about your newspaper which I believe may be of interest to you," Pontecorvo said.

"And what does it cost?" said Peçanha sarcastically.

"This I'll give you for free," Pontecorvo said. The man seemed to be made of ice. "We did a miniresearch on your readers, and despite the small sample size I can assure you, beyond the shadow of a doubt, that the great majority, almost the entirety, of your readers is made up of Class B men."

"What?" screamed Peçanha.

"That's right, Class B men."

First Peçanha turned pale. Then he began to turn red, then purple, as if he were being strangled. His mouth open, his eyes bulging, he rose from his chair and, arms spread, staggered like a crazed gorilla in Pontecorvo's direction. A shocking sight, even for a man of steel like Pontecorvo, even for an ex-police reporter. Pontecorvo retreated before Peçanha's advance until, his back against the wall, he said, trying to maintain his calm and composure, "Maybe our technicians made a mistake."

Peçanha, who was within a centimeter of Pontecorvo, underwent a violent tremor and, contrary to what I expected, did not pounce upon the other like a rabid dog. He seized his own hair forcefully and began tearing it out, as he screamed, "Con men, swindlers, thieves, exploiters, liars, scum of the earth." Pontecorvo nimbly made his way toward the door, as Peçanha ran after him throwing the tufts of hair yanked from his own head, "Men! Men! Class B!" Peçanha snarled madly.

Later, after calming down—I think Pontecorvo escaped by the stairs—Peçanha, seated behind his desk again, told me, "That's the kind of people Brazil's fallen into the hands of—manipulators of statistics, falsifiers of information, con men with computers, all of them creating the Big Lie. But they won't pull it off with me. I really put that wretch in his place, didn't I?"

I said something or other in agreement. Peçanha took the box of El Ropos from the drawer and offered me one. We smoked and talked about the Big Lie. Afterwards he gave me Pedro Redgrave's letter and my reply, with his okay, for me to take to the composing room.

On the way I saw that Pedro Redgrave's letter wasn't the one I had sent him. The text was different:

"Dear Nathanael, your letter was a balm for my afflicted heart. It has given me the strength to resist. I will not make any deranged gesture. I promise to—"

The letter ended there. It had been interrupted in the middle. Strange. I didn't understand. Something was wrong.

I went to my desk, sat down, and began writing the answer to Odontos Silva:

> *He who has no teeth also has no toothache. And as the hero of the well-known play put it, "There's never been a philosopher who could bear a toothache with patience." Besides, teeth are also instruments of revenge, as Deuteronomy says: an eye for an eye, a tooth for a tooth, a hand for a hand, a foot for a foot. Dictators despise teeth. Remember what Hitler told Mussolini about another meeting with Franco?—I prefer having four teeth pulled. You're in the situation of the hero of that play All's Well If Nobody Gets Shafted—no teeth, no taste, nothing.* ADVICE*: put your teeth back in and bite. If biting doesn't do the trick, try punching and kicking.*

I was in the middle of Odontos Silva's letter when I suddenly understood everything. Peçanha was Pedro Redgrave. Instead of returning the letter in which Pedro asked me to have a mass said for him and which I had given him together with my answer about Oscar Wilde, Peçanha had handed me a new letter, unfinished, surely by accident, and which was supposed to come into my hands by mail.

I got Pedro Redgrave's letter and went to Peçanha's office.

"May I come in?" I asked.

"What is it? Come in," Peçanha said.

I handed him Pedro Redgrave's letter. Peçanha read the letter and, seeing the mistake he had committed, turned pale, as was his wont. Nervously, he shuffled the papers on his desk.

"It was all a joke," he said, trying to light a cigar. "Are you angry?"

"For real or a joke, it's all the same to me," I said.

"My life would make a novel . . ." Peçanha said. "Let's keep this between the two of us, okay?"

I wasn't sure what he wanted to keep between the two of us, his life making a novel or his being Pedro Redgrave. But I replied: "Of course, just between the two of us."

"Thanks," said Peçanha. And he breathed a sigh that would have broken the heart of anyone who wasn't an ex-police reporter.

mandrake

I WAS WHITE AND HAD FIANCHETTOED MY BISHOP. Berta was mounting a strong center pawn position.

"This is the office of Paulo Mendes," my voice said on the answering machine, giving whoever had called thirty seconds to leave a message. The guy said his name was Cavalcante-Meier, as if there were a hyphen between the two names, and that they were trying to frame him for a crime but—click—his time ran out before he could say what he planned to do.

"Every time we're in a close game some client calls," Berta said. We were drinking Faísca wine.

The guy called back and asked me to call him at home. A number in the South Zone. An aged voice answered, its vocal cords reverential. It was the butler. He went to get the master.

"There's a butler in the story. I already know whodunit." Berta didn't think it was funny. Besides being hooked on chess, she took everything seriously.

I recognized the voice from the answering machine: "What I have to say has to be in person. Can I come by your office?"

"I'm at home," I explained, and gave the address.

"So much for the game, B.B. (Berta Bronstein)," I said, dialing.

"Hello, Dr. Medeiros, what's the situation?"

Medeiros said the situation wasn't serious but was no laughing matter either. Medeiros thought about nothing but politics. He'd held some position or other at the start of the revolution and, despite having the biggest office in town, had never shaken off the nostalgia of power. I asked if he knew a Cavalcante Meier.

"Everybody knows him."

"I don't. I even thought the name might be a phony."

Medeiros said the man owned plantations in São Paulo and the North, exported coffee, sugar, and soybeans, and was an alternate senator for the state of Alagoas. A rich man.

"What else? Does he have any weaknesses, is he involved in any shady financial transactions, is he a sexual pervert as well as a landowner?"

"You think the whole world's no good, don't you? The senator is a very highly respected public figure, a business leader, a model citizen, unimpeachable."

I reminded him that J. J. Santos, the banker, had also been unimpeachable and that I'd had to rescue him from the clutches of a crazed transvestite in a motel in the Barra.

"You got a Mercedes out of it. Is this how you show your gratitude?"

I hadn't "got" the Mercedes, I had extorted it, the way bankers do with their interest rates and management fees.

Medeiros in a mellifluous voice: "What's the problem with Cavalcante Meier?"

I said I didn't know.

"Let's finish the game," Berta said.

"I can't meet the guy naked, can I?" I said.

I was getting dressed when the bell rang, three times in ten seconds. An impatient man, accustomed to doors that opened quickly.

Cavalcante Meier was thin, elegant, fiftyish. His nose was slightly crooked. His eyes were deep-set, brownish green, and intense.

"I'm Rodolfo Cavalcante Meier. I don't know if you know me."

"I know you. I have your file."

"My file?"

"Yes." I saw him looking at the glass in my hand. "Care for some Faísca?"

"No thanks," he said, evasively. "Wine gives me a headache. May I sit down?"

"Planter, exporter, alternate senator for Alagoas, services rendered to the revolution," I said.

"Irrelevant," he cut me off, sharply.

"Member of the Rotary Club," I said, to rattle his cage.

"Just the Country Club."

"A leader, a man of integrity, a patriot."

He looked at me and said firmly, "Don't joke with me."

"I'm not joking. I'm a patriot too. In a different way. For example, I don't want to declare war on Argentina."

"I have your file too," he said, imitating me. "Cynical, unscrupulous, competent. A specialist in extortion and fraud cases."

He spoke like a recording; he reminded me of a laugh-box that you wind up and it makes a sound that's neither animal nor human. Cavalcante Meier had wound himself up, his voice that of a plantation owner talking to a sharecropper.

"Competent yes, unscrupulous and cynical no. Just a man who lost his innocence," I said.

He rewound the laugh-box. "Have you seen the papers?"

I answered that I never read newspapers, and he told me that a young woman had been found dead in the Barra, in her car. It had been in all the papers.

"That girl was, uh, my, er, connected to me, do you know what I mean?"

"Your lover?"

Cavalcante Meier said nothing.

"It was already over. I thought Marly should find someone her own age, get married, have children."

We lapsed into silence. The telephone rang. "Hello, Mandrake?" I turned off the sound.

"Yes, and then?"

"Our relationship was very discreet, I'd even say secret. No one knew anything. She was found dead on Friday. Saturday I got a phone call, a man, threatening me, saying I had killed her and that he had proof we were lovers. Letters. I don't know what letters they could be."

Cavalcante Meier said he hadn't gone to the police because he had political enemies who would take advantage of the scandal. Besides, he knew nothing that could help clear up the crime. And his only daughter was getting married that month.

"My going to the police would be a socially and ethically useless gesture. I'd like you to find that person for me, see what he wants, defend my interests in the best way possible. I'm willing to pay to avoid scandal."

"What's the guy's name?"

"Márcio was the name he gave. He wants me to meet him tonight at ten at a place called Gordon's, in Ipanema. He'll be on a motorcycle, wearing a black shirt with 'Jesus' on the back."

We agreed I'd keep the appointment with Márcio and negotiate the price of his silence. It could be worth a lot or worth nothing.

I asked where he'd heard about me.

"Dr. Medeiros," he said, getting up. He left without shaking hands, with just a nod of his head.

I went to look for the laugh-box. I rummaged through the closet, the bookshelf, the drawers, until I found it in the kitchen. The maid loved to listen to the laughter.

I took it to the bedroom, lay down, and turned it on. A convulsive and disturbing guffaw, stuck in the glottis, purple, as of someone with a funnel stuck up his anus whose deadly laughter had gone through his body to come out his mouth, clogging lungs and brain. This called for a bit more Faísca. When I was a boy, a man sitting in front of me in the movie theater had a laughing fit so severe that he died. From time to time I remember that guy.

"Why're you listening to that awful noise? You look like you're crazy," Berta said. "Shall we continue the game?"

"I'm going to read the papers now," I said.

"Shit," Berta said, knocking the chessboard and pieces to the floor. An impulsive woman.

All the newspapers were on the night table. Young secretary killed in her car in the Barra. A bullet in the head. The victim still had her jewelry and documents. The police ruled out robbery. The victim was in the habit of going straight to work from her house and returning early. She didn't go out much at night. No boyfriend. The neighbors said she was friendly and shy. Her parents said she would go to her room to read after coming home from work. She read a lot, her mother said, she liked poetry and novels, she was gentle and obedient, without her our life is empty, meaningless. The papers ran several photos of Marly, tall and thin, with long hair. Her expression seemed sad, or was that my imagination? I'm an incurable romantic.

Finally I went back to play with Berta. Playing Black, I opened with king's pawn. Berta copied my move. I moved my knights, Berta following me, creating symmetrical positions that would bring victory to the more patient player, the one who made fewer mistakes, in other words Berta. I'm very nervous. I play chess to irritate myself, to blow up *in camera;* on the outside it's too dangerous, I have to stay calm.

I tried to recall Capablanca's game with Tarrash, St. Petersburg, 1914, which featured a four-knight opening and the springing of a terrible trap, but what trap was it? I couldn't remember; my head was full of the biker at Gordon's.

"It's no use giving me that victorious gloating look," I said, "I'm going to have to leave now."

"Now? In the middle of the game? Again? You're a coward, you know you're going to lose so you run away."

"That's true. But besides that I have to see a client."

Berta raised her arms and began to pin back her hair. A woman's armpit is a masterpiece, especially when she's thin and muscular like Berta. Her armpit also smells very nice, when she doesn't use deodorant, that is. A sweet-and-sour odor that turns me on. She knows it.

"I'm meeting a motorcyclist at Gordon's."

"Ah, a motorcyclist."

"There's a Hitchcock at eleven on TV."

"I don't like television; I detest dubbed films," Berta said in ill humor.

"Then study the Nimzovitch opening; it offers some good positional traps. I'll be back soon."

Berta said she'd wait for me, adding that I had no consideration for her, no respect.

When I stopped in front of Gordon's, still in the car, I saw the biker. He was a short, husky young man with dark brown hair. He was arguing, insolently, with a girl. Her hair was so dark it looked dyed. Her face was very pale, unlike the suntanned girls who hung out at Gordon's. Perhaps her pallor made her hair look darker and her hair in turn made her face look paler, which in turn—

While I amused myself with this proposition, thinking about the Quaker Oats I used to eat when I was a child—a Quaker holding a box of oatmeal that showed another Quaker holding a box of oatmeal, etc., ad infinitum—the girl got on the back of the motorcycle and they left quickly down Visconde de Pirajá. I couldn't follow them; my car was blocked. I got out, went to the counter in Gordon's, and ordered a coke and sandwich. I ate—slowly. I waited an hour. They didn't return.

Berta was in bed asleep, the television on.

I called Cavalcante Meier.

"The apostle didn't show up," I said. There was no point telling what had happened.

"What are you going to do?" He spoke in a low voice, his mouth close to the phone. My clients always talk that way. It bothers me.

"Nothing. I'm going to bed. We'll talk tomorrow." I hung up.

I kissed Berta lightly on the lips. She woke up.

"Tell me you love me," Berta said.

I woke up in the morning with an urge to have some Faísca. Berta didn't like me to drink so early, but Portuguese wine does no harm at any time of day or night. I turned on the answering machine and found a message from Cavalcante Meier.

I called.

"Have you seen the papers?" Cavalcante Meier asked.

"I just got up," I lied. "What time is it?"

"Noon. Have you read the papers? No, of course you haven't yet. The police say they have a suspect."

"They always have a suspect, who's usually innocent."

"Since I'm innocent, I may be the suspect, following your logic. Another thing. That guy Márcio called. He says he's coming to my house this afternoon."

"I'll be there. Introduce me as your personal secretary."

"What time did you start in on the wine?" Berta asked, coming into the living room.

I explained to her that Churchill used to get out of bed, have some champagne, smoke a few cigars, and win the war.

I read the papers, smoking a dark Suerdieck panatela. Marly's death got a lot of space, but there was nothing new. No mention of a suspect.

I called Raul.

"That crime with the girl in the Barra. What's the word on it?"

"Which girl? The one who was strangled, the one who got run over, the one shot in the head, the one—"

"Shot in the head."

"Marly Moreira, the secretary at Cordovil Meier. My boys are on the case."

"They say there's a suspect. Know anything about it?"

"I'll check it out."

Cavalcante Meier lived in Gávea Pequena. I stopped the car at the gate and blew the horn. A private guard came out of the gatehouse. He wore a pistol in his belt and the look of someone who didn't know how to use it. He opened the gate.

"Are you Dr. Paulo Mendes?" he asked.

"Yes."

"Go on in."

"You ought to ask for some identification."

Disconcerted, he fingered his kepi, then asked for my ID. These false professionals are everywhere these days.

I went up a tree-lined drive with bushes on both sides, over a well-kept lawn. English grass, without a doubt. The butler opened the door. He was as old as I had expected, with hate in his expression and a back bent from long years of licking boots. In his reverential voice he inquired my name and asked me to wait.

I paced back and forth in the marble vestibule. A large staircase led to the second floor. A young woman came down the stairs, a Dalmatian at her side. She had blond hair and was wearing jeans and a tight-fitting knit blouse. I couldn't take my eyes off her. As she came up to me, she asked impersonally, "Are you waiting for someone?" Blue eyes.

"Mr. Cavalcante Meier."

"Does Daddy know you're here?" She looked through me as if I were made of glass.

"The butler went to tell him."

Without another word, she turned her back, opened the door, and left, with the dog.

Once when I was a teenager I saw a beautiful woman walking down the street and fell instantly and overpoweringly in love. She came past me and we continued in opposite directions, me with my head turned, watching her walk away *agile et noble, avec sa jambe de statue,* until she was lost in the crowd. Then, on a despondent impulse, I turned around, away from that passerby, and banged my head against a lamppost.

I stood there looking at the door the girl had gone through, fingering the scar on my forehead, which time had not erased.

"Please come with me," the butler said.

We went through an enormous room with a large round table in its center, surrounded by velvet chairs. Then another, with armchairs and large paintings on the walls.

Cavalcante Meier was waiting for me in his book-lined office.

"Who's the girl with the dog?" I asked. "The pretty blonde."

"My daughter, Eve. She's getting married on the twenty-third, as I told you."

Cavalcante Meier was smartly dressed, like the first time. His hair was neatly combed, parted on the side, not a single hair out of place. He looked like Rudolph Valentino in *Camille,* with Alia Nazimova.

I asked if he'd seen the film. No, he wasn't even born when the film was shown. Nor was I, but I liked to go to art theaters.

"Do you have any connection to Cordovil & Meier?"

"It's my export firm."

"Then the dead girl was your employee?"

"She was the secretary of my international marketing director."

A shadow passed over Cavalcante Meier's face. Few actors can make a shadow pass over their face. Everett Sloane could; Bogart couldn't. Grimaces are something else.

The telephone rang. Cavalcante Meier answered.

"Leave it to me," he said.

I heard the noise of a motorcycle. It stopped for a time, and then I heard it again. Cavalcante Meier appeared to attach no importance to the sound and instructed the butler to show in immediately the person who had just arrived.

Márcio, the biker, came into the room, wearing the same arrogant expression I'd seen at Gordon's. Up close, it looked like a badly fitting mask.

"You said we'd be by ourselves. Who's this guy?"

"My secretary."

"The talk's just between the two of us. Lose him."

"He stays," Cavalcante Meier said, controlling his anger.

"Then I'm outta here," Márcio said.

"Wait, take it easy. I don't want any trouble. I can wait outside," I said.

I quickly left for the large hall. From the window I saw Eve sitting on the lawn, the Dalmatian at her side. The sunlight filtering through the branches made her hair even more golden.

The office door opened and Márcio went hurriedly past without looking at me. I heard the noise of the motorcycle. At the same instant the girl rose quickly to her feet.

"Everything's taken care of," Cavalcante Meier said, at the door to his office.

"How so?" I asked, without leaving the window. Eve ran across the lawn, followed by the dog, and vanished from my field of vision.

"I came to an understanding with that fellow. I won't have any further need of your services. How much do I owe you?"

"Who was it said that language exists to conceal thought?" I said, coming away from the window.

"I don't know and don't care. How much do I owe you?"

"Nothing."

I turned my back on him. The butler was in the vestibule. He gave the impression of skulking behind doors eavesdropping on all the conversations.

I got my car. There was no sign of Eve. The guard opened the gate for me. I asked him if the biker had stopped along the drive before going into the house.

"He stopped near the pond, to talk to Miss Eve."

The guard looked at something past the hood of the car. I looked also and saw a pale girl with dark hair standing about twenty yards away. It was the girl I had seen on the back of the motorcycle at Gordon's. When she saw I was looking at her, she began walking slowly away.

"Who's that girl?" I asked.

"The boss's niece," the guard said. Her name was Lilly, and she lived at her uncle's house.

The telephone in the gatehouse rang. The guard went to answer it. When he returned, he opened the gate. I approached with the car.

"Has that guy on the motorcycle ever been here before?"

"I don't know anything," the guard said, turning away. He must have received orders not to talk to me.

I got home, opened the refrigerator, took out a bottle of Faísca. There was a note on the table: *You could have used Wurtzberg's gambit. All you had to do was sacrifice the queen, but you never do that. I love you. Berta.*

I called Wexler, my partner.

"I'm not coming in to the office today."

"I know," Wexler said. "You're going to play chess with a woman and drink wine. I work my butt off while you lay women."

"I'm working on a case Medeiros put me onto." I told him the whole story.

"Nothing will come of it," Wexler said.

I called Raul. He had set up dinner at the Albamar with the detective handing the Marly case.

"Downtown?" I complained.

"That's where Homicide is. His name is Guedes."

Guedes was a young man, prematurely balding, thin, with brown eyes so light they looked yellow. He ordered a coke. Raul drank whiskey. They didn't have Faísca, so I ordered Casa da Calçada. I prefer something with more age to it, but there are times when a well chilled young wine is just the ticket.

"Marly was wearing a gold Rolex, a diamond ring, and had a hundred dollars in her purse," Guedes said.

"That helps," Raul said.

"It helps, but we're still in the dark," Guedes said.

"The newspapers say you have a suspect."

"That's to throw them off the scent."

"Have you come across the name of her boss at Cordovil & Meier, the head of marketing?" I asked.

"Arthur Rocha." Guedes's suspicious yellow eyes scrutinized my face.

"I saw his name in the papers," I said.

"His name wasn't in the papers." Guedes's eyes burned into mine. There was no way I was going to bullshit this guy. He seemed like a decent enough cop.

"I did a little job for the president of the firm, Senator Cavalcante Meier."

"I took down Arthur Rocha's statement myself. He swore he didn't know anything about the secretary's private life," Guedes said.

"You think he's telling the truth?"

"We turned his life inside out. The girl was killed on a Friday, between eight and nine p.m. At eleven Rocha was in Petrópolis, at the home of friends. He's not interested in women; his thing seems to be flaunting his wealth. He had a riding area built at his place in Petrópolis, and I hear he can barely mount a horse. Get the idea? The lesser big shots have their tennis courts and pools. Besides all that, he has a riding area and horses for his friends to use."

"If a director earns that much, just imagine the president," Raul said.

"He's probably not on salary; he must be a partner. We're on a salary—Raul and me I mean, not you, Mr. Mendes."

"Hey, no need for formalities. Call me Mandrake," I said.

"They say you're a rich lawyer."

"Don't I wish."

"Mandrake's a genius," Raul said, already halfway through the bottle of whiskey. "A real sonofabitch. He had my wife. You remember that, Mandrake?"

"I'm still suffering because of it," I said.

"I forgave you, Mandrake," Raul said. "And that bitch too."

"His wife went down for the troops. They weren't married any longer. That's the story."

"The crime, in principle, conforms to the pattern of a crime of passion," Guedes said, uninterested in my conversation with Raul. "Arthur Rocha is incapable of falling in love or killing for passion, or money, or anything. But I still think he's lying. What do you think?"

"When I investigate a crime, even my own mother is a suspect," Raul said.

Guedes was still looking at me, waiting for an answer.

"People kill when they're afraid," I equivocated, "when they hate, when they envy."

"Right out of the Farmer's Almanac," Raul said.

"I know he's lying," Guedes said.

Alone in my car, I told the rearview mirror, "Everybody's lying."

The next day Marly's death had dropped off the front pages. Everything wearies, my angel, as the English poet said. The dead must be renewed, the press is an insatiable necrophile. An item in the society pages caught my attention: the marriage of Eve Cavalcante Meier and Luis Vieira Souto would not be held next week. Some of the columnists lamented the calling off of the nuptials. One exclaimed, "What will be done with the mountain of presents the once-future couple has already received from every corner of the country?" Truly a grave problem.

I got the car and went to Cavalcante Meier's house. I stopped a hundred yards from the gate. I put a Jorge Ben cassette in the tape deck and kept time with him on the dashboard.

The first to show was the Mercedes. Cavalcante Meier in the back seat. The chauffeur in navy blue, white shirt, dark tie, black cap. I waited another half hour until the gates opened, and a Fiat sports car came roaring through like a shot.

I followed it. The car took the curves at high speed, tires squealing. It wasn't easy to keep up with it. This is the day I die, I thought. Which one of my women would suffer the most? Maybe Berta would stop biting her nails.

The Fiat stopped in Leblon, in front of a small building. The girl got out of the car, went in a door marked *Bernard—Aerobics for Women.* I waited two minutes.

A carpeted waiting room, walls covered with reproductions of Degas ballerinas and dance posters. A bleached, heavily made-up receptionist in a pink uniform said hello from behind a metal-and-glass table and asked if I wanted something.

"I'd like to enroll my wife in the aerobics class."

"Certainly," she said, getting a card.

I scratched my head and said I didn't want my wife going to just any class, maybe I'm old fashioned but that's my way.

The receptionist smiled with her whole mouth, the way only people with all their teeth can, and said I'd come to the right place, an academy frequented by ladies and young women from society. She emphasized the word "society." Her nails were long and painted dark red.

"What is your wife's name?"

"Pérola . . . Uh, er, is the teacher a man or a woman?

A man, but there was nothing to worry about, Bernard was very respectful.

I asked if I could see a little of the class.

"Just a tiny bit," the blonde said, getting up. She was my height, with a willowy body, small breasts, really solid.

"Do you work out too?"

"Not me, this is the body God gave me. But it could be Bernard's work; he can perform miracles."

She glided in front of me till she came to a door with a mirror on it, which she opened slightly.

The women were following the pounding rhythm of music from speakers spread around the floor. In quick succession they bent their trunks forward, their heads down, stuck their hands backwards between their knees, then straightened their bodies, raised their arms again, and began to repeat the entire process.

There were about fifteen women, in leotards. Most were blue but there was also red, pink, and green. In the middle of the room stood Bernard, also in a leotard, holding a swagger stick. He must have been a ballet dancer; he was certainly proud enough of his firm buttocks.

"Don't bend your knees, Pia Azambuja! Pull in your buttocks, Ana Maria Melo!"

Smack! The swagger stick rapped Ana Maria Melo's fanny.

"Follow the rhythm, Eve Cavalcante Meier! Don't stop, Renata Albuquerque Lins!" Bernard used the students' full names; they were the names of important fathers and husbands.

The receptionist closed the door.

"You've seen everything, haven't you?"

"Does he always hit the students?" I asked.

"It's just a tap, it doesn't hurt a bit. They don't mind. They even like it. Bernard is marvelous. When they come here the students are full of cellulite, flabby, have bad posture, awful skin, and Bernard gives them the body of a beauty queen."

We filled out my wife's card.

"Pearl White?"

"My wife's an American. Pearl means Pérola."

I don't know what I see in making jokes nobody gets, but I do it all the time.

I paced back and forth in front of the Fiat, playing White, controlling the center: K3, Q3, KB4, K4, Q4, QB4, KB5, K5, Q5, QB5, K6, and Q6. Power and focus of action. Gioco Piano. Sicilian. Nimzo-Indian.

Eve came out with her hair wet, wearing long cotton pants and a knit blouse, her arms bare. She carried a large handbag.

"Hello." I planted myself in her path.

"Do I know you?" she asked coldly.

"From your father's house. He hired me as his lawyer."

"Oh . . . ?"

"But he already fired me."

"Oh . . . ?" She spoke brusquely but made no move to leave. She wanted to hear what I had to say. Women are curious as cats. (Men are like cats too. Whatever.)

"Someone was trying to involve him in the death of Marly Moreira, the girl they found in the Barra with a bullet in her head."

"Is that it?"

"A blackmailer named Márcio claims he has papers that incriminate your father."

"Anything else?"

"The police suspect him. I have more to say, but not here in the street."

When the waiter came she ordered mineral water. God, Bernard, and Strict Dieting had created that marvel. I ordered Faísca. We sat there in silence.

"If my father is in danger, you should speak to him. I don't see what good it does to talk to me."

"Your father released me from his service."

"He must have had some reason."

I told her of the interviews I'd had with Cavalcante Meier, my trip to Gordon's, the meeting between her cousin Lilly and Márcio the biker. Her expression remained unreadable.

"Do you think my father killed that girl?" A scornful smile.

"I don't know."

"My father has a lot of shortcomings. He's vain and weak, and worse, but he's not a murderer. Anybody can take one look at him and see I'm right."

I mentally ran through the faces of all the murderers I'd known. None of them looked guilty.

"Somebody killed the girl, and it wasn't a robbery."

"It wasn't my father either."

"Márcio the biker stopped to talk to you in the garden when he went to see your father."

"You're mistaken. I don't know who that person is."

I looked into her innocent face. I knew that she knew that I knew she was lying. Eve had a face by Botticelli, un-Brazilian on that sunny day, which perhaps made her more attractive to me. I don't like suntanned women. It's a device. The skin knows its color, like the hair, the eyes. It's stupid to use the sun as a cosmetic.

"You're very pretty," I said.

"You're an unpleasant, ugly, ridiculous person," she said.

Eve got up and left, walking the way Bernard had taught her.

I went home, turned off the answering machine. Berta had gone to her place. All my life I've either not dreamed or forgotten most of what I dreamed. But there were two dreams I always remembered, always those two and no others. In one I dreamed I was sleeping and dreamed a dream I forgot upon waking, leaving the feeling of having lost an important revelation. In the other I was in bed with a woman and she touched my body and I experienced her sensations as she touched my body, as if my body weren't of flesh and blood. I woke up (in reality, outside the dream) and ran my hand over my skin and felt as if it were covered with cold metal.

I woke up to the sound of the doorbell. Wexler.

"What've you been getting into? Do you know who's after you? Detective Pacheco. Are you involved with the commies now?"

Wexler told me that Pacheco had come by the office early that morning, looking for me. Pacheco was famous throughout the country.

"He wants you to go down to the station and have a talk with him." I didn't want to, but Wexler convinced me. "Nobody gets away from Pacheco," he said.

Wexler went with me. Pacheco didn't keep us waiting long. He was a fat man with a pleasant face that belied his unsavory reputation.

"Your activities are under investigation," Pacheco said with a sleepy air.

"I don't know why I'm here; I'm corrupt, not subversive." Another joke.

"You're neither one nor the other," Pacheco said in a tired voice, "but it wouldn't be hard to prove you're both." He looked at me like someone looking at his naughty kid brother.

"A friend told me you've been bothering him. Stop doing it."

"May I ask your friend's name? I bother a lot of people."

"You know who he is. Leave him alone, joker."

"Let's go then," Wexler said. His father had been killed before his eyes in the Warsaw ghetto pogrom in 1943, when he was eight. He could read people's faces.

"Be careful with that Nazi," Wexler said in the street. "Look, just what kind of mess are you involved in?"

I told him about the Cavalcante Meier case. Wexler spat vigorously on the ground—when he's angry he doesn't swear, he spits on the ground—and grasped my arm firmly.

"You have nothing to do with the case. Drop it. Those Nazis!" He spat again.

I called Berta.

"B.B., you open with the Ruy Lopez and I'll beat you in fifteen moves."

It was a lie. Black has real problems with that opening when the players are equal, as was our case. I just wanted someone near who loved me.

"You look awful," Berta said when she arrived.

My face is a collage of several faces, something that began when I was eighteen; until then my face had unity and symmetry, I was only one. Later I became many.

I set the bottle of Faísca beside the chessboard.

We began to play. As agreed, she opened with the Ruy Lopez. By the fifteenth move I was in a tight spot.

"What's going on? Why didn't you use the Steinitz defense to leave the king file open for the rook? Or the Tchigorin defense, developing the queen side? You can't be that passive against a Ruy Lopez."

"Look, Berta, Bertie, Bertola, Bertette, Bertier, Bertiest, Bertissima, Bertina, B.B."

"You're drunk," Berta said.

"Right."

"We're not going to play any more."

"I want to hug you, rest my head on your breasts, feel the warmth between your legs. I'm tired, B.B. And I'm in love with another woman."

"What? Are you pulling a Le Bonheur on me?"

"A mediocre film," I said.

Berta threw the chessmen on the floor. An impulsive woman.

"Who's the woman? I had an abortion because of you; I have a right to know."

"The daughter of a client."

"How old is she? My age? Or are you already looking for younger ones? Sixteen? Twelve?"

"Your age."

"Is she prettier than me?"

"I don't know. Maybe not. But she's a woman I'm attracted to."

"You men are such childish, weak braggarts! A fool, you're a fool!"

"I love you, Berta," I said, thinking of Eve.

When we went to bed, I thought of Eve the entire time. After we made love, Berta fell asleep, belly upwards. She snored lightly, her mouth open, torpid. Whenever I drink a lot, I only sleep for half an hour, and I wake up feeling guilty. There was Berta, her mouth open, sleeping like the dead. Sleeping is such a weakness! Children know that. That's why I don't sleep much, the fear of being unarmed. Berta was snoring. Strange, in such a gentle person. The sun was coming up, with a fantastic light somewhere between red and white. That called for a bottle of Faísca. I drank it, showered, got dressed, and went to the office. The watchman asked, "The bed catch on fire last night, sir?"

I sat down and did the final brief for a client. Wexler arrived, and we started talking about inconsequential matters, things that wouldn't get us excited.

"It must be hell being the son of Portuguese immigrants," Wexler said.

"What about the son of a Jew killed in a pogrom?" I asked.

"My father was a Latin professor, my mother played Bach, Beethoven, and Brahms on the piano. Your father fished for cod, your mother was a seamstress!"

Wexler went to the window and spat.

"Bach, Beethoven, Brahms, Belsen, and Buchenwald. The five B's of the piano," I said.

He gave a painful look, an expression only Jews can achieve.

"Forgive me," I said. His mother had died at Buchenwald, a young and pretty woman in her photo, with a sweet, dark-complexioned face. "Forgive me."

The day ended and I decided not to go home. I didn't want to face Berta, the answering machine, anyone, or anything. All I could think of was Eve. My passions are brief but overwhelming.

A cheap hotel on Correa Dutra Street, in Flamengo. I got the key, went up to the room, lay down, and stared at the ceiling.

There was one bulb, a dirty globe of light, which I turned on and off. The street sounds blended with the silence into an opaque, neutral mucus. Eve. Eve. Cain killed Abel. Someone's always killing someone else. I spent the night tossing in bed.

In the morning I paid the hotel and went for a shave and haircut.

"The Steinitz defense," I told the barber, "isn't really that effective. The rook's mobility is limited; it's a powerful piece, although predictable."

"You're right," the barber said cautiously.

"The Tchigorin defense jeopardizes the queen, something I never do," I continued. "Everything's wrong, the idiotic lyrics of the national anthem, our positivist flag without the color red—what good is the green of our forests and the yellow of our gold without the blood of our veins?"

"It's scandalous," the barber said.

While the barber talked about the cost of living, I read the paper. Márcio Amaral, also known as Márcio the Suzuki, had been found dead in his apartment in the Fátima section. One bullet in the head. In his right hand was a .38 Taurus revolver with one spent cartridge in the cylinder. The police suspected homicide. Márcio the Suzuki was said to be involved in the drug trade in the city's South Zone.

"I don't care any more. Screw them all, that bastard of a senator and his ice queen daughter, the pale shadow, the dead secretary and her gabby parents, the biker, Guedes—they can all go to hell. I've had it."

The barber looked at me uneasily.

There was a note for me in my apartment: *Where have you been hiding? Are you crazy? Wexler wants to talk to you, urgently. I'm at the store. Call me. I love you. I miss you like mad. Berta.*

I still liked Berta, but my heart no longer beat faster when I heard her voice or read her messages. Berta had become the perfect person to marry, when I was old and decrepit.

I called Berta, set up a meeting for that night. What else could I do? I dialed Wexler.

"I thought Pacheco had you," Wexler said. "Raul is looking for you. Says it's important."

Raul's telephone rang and rang and rang. He answered just as I was about to hang up.

"I was in the bathroom. Guedes really wanted to talk to you. Stop by Homicide," he said.

I told Raul about Pacheco's threats. Raul said to be careful.

At Homicide, Guedes saw me right away.

"I'll play straight with you," he said. "Read this."

The handwriting was rounded, the dots over the *i*'s little circles. *Rodolfo, don't think you can treat me like this, like an object you use and then throw away. I feel like doing crazy things, having a talk with your wife, raising a scandal in the company, going public in the newspapers. You have no idea what I'm capable of. I don't want an apartment anymore, you can't buy me the way you do everybody else. You're the man of my life, I never had another, I didn't want to and I still don't. You've been avoiding me, and that's no way to end a relationship like ours. I want to see you. Call me, right away. I'm really out of my head and nervous. I might do anything. Marly.*

"Well?" Guedes said.

"Well what?"

"You have any ideas?"

"What idea could I have?"

"What do you make of the letter?"

"Has the handwriting been analyzed?"

"No, but I'm sure it's Marly Moreira's. Know where the letter was found? On one Márcio Amaral, commonly known as Márcio the Suzuki. The person who killed Márcio searched the room, possibly looking for the letter, but forgot to look in the victim's pockets. That's where the letter was."

"An amateur," I said.

"A real amateur. They tried to fake a suicide without knowing the tricks. No sign of gunpowder on Márcio's fingers, the bullet's path was downward; lots of mistakes. The killer was standing, and the victim was seated. I think I know who the murderer is. An important man."

"Be careful. Important men can buy everybody."

"Not everybody's for sale," Guedes said. He could have said he was incorruptible, but the ones who really aren't for sale, like him, don't brag about it.

"Senator Rodolfo Cavalcante Meier killed Marly," Guedes went on. "Márcio, we don't know how, got hold of the letter and started blackmailing the senator. To cover up the first crime, the senator committed a second one, killing Márcio."

I was looking at a decent man doing his job with dedication and intelligence. I felt like telling everything I knew, but I couldn't. Cavalcante Meier wasn't even my client, he was a disgusting millionaire and maybe a vile murderer as well, but even so I couldn't turn him in. My job is to get people out of the grasp of the police; I just can't bring myself to do the opposite.

"Well?" Guedes asked.

"The senator wouldn't have to kill anyone himself. He'd find somebody to do the job for him," I said.

"We're not in his home state," Guedes said.

"We also have hit men here who'll kill for next to nothing."

"But they can't be trusted. The police get hold of them, rough them up a bit, and they spill their guts. They're not mafiosi working under some code of silence," Guedes said. "Besides, you agreed that both crimes were the work of an amateur."

I repeated that I knew nothing about the crimes and that my opinion was off the top of my head.

"Raul said you could help," Guedes said, disappointed, as I left.

I set up the chessboard and put a bottle of Faísca in the ice bucket.

"I don't feel like playing chess or drinking wine," Berta said.

"What is it, honey?" I asked, knowing only too well.

"The only way I'll stay with you is if you give up that girl."

“There’s nothing between us. How can I give up what doesn’t exist?”

“You care about her, that exists. I want you to stop caring about her. You once told me you only care about those who care about you, that you only care about those you love. I want you to care only about me. Otherwise, good-bye, no more chess games, no balling any time you feel the urge, no wine binges. I hate wine, you idiot—I drink it because of you. I hate it, I hate it, I hate it.”

“What about chess?”

“Chess I like,” Berta said, wiping her tears. Berta was a protagonist in my life, instead of her own.

I promised to make an effort to forget Eve. I let her beat me using the Blemenfeld countergambit. To tell the truth, she’d have won anyway, since the whole time I was asking myself how Marly Moreira’s letter had fallen into the hands of Márcio the Suzuki. P-Q4, N-KB3. Cavalcante Meier would surely have kept it in a safe place. N-KB3, BP-Q3. Why didn’t he destroy it? Maybe he never received it, maybe someone intercepted it. P-B4, P-B4. In that case it had to be someone in his house, assuming the letter was sent to his house; it might have gone to his office. I had a hunch it was the house. The butler? I laughed. P-Q5, P-QN4. “You’re laughing, are you?” Berta said, “In a few minutes you’ll see.” PXKP, BPXP. It was Berta’s turn to laugh. Someone in security, or the wife, whom I’d never seen, or the daughter, or the niece. As Raul said, you have to suspect even your own mother. PXP, P-Q4. “Mate!” Berta said.

“B.B.,” I said, “not even Alekhine could have played so brilliantly.”

“You just played badly,” Berta said.

I was willing to forget Eve, as I had promised Berta, but when I got to Cavalcante Meier’s house it was Eve who opened the door, and my enthusiasm returned. I had first gone to his office, where they told me the senator was at home, sick. I had a newspaper in my hand with a story about the death of Marly Moreira. The case was back on page one. Ballistics had proved that Márcio the Suzuki was shot with the same gun that killed Marly. Detective Guedes had said in an interview that a big name was involved and that the police were close to arresting him, whatever the consequences. There was also talk of drug dealing.

“I want to speak with your father.”

“He can’t see anyone.”

“It’s in his interest. Tell him the police have the letter. Just that.”

She looked at me with her impassive doll’s face. Her healthy skin had the appearance of porcelain, rosy cheeks, red lips, bright blue eyes, a luxuriant growing thing in the prime of life. She was like a color slide projected in the air.

“He can’t see anyone,” Eve repeated.

“Look, girl, your father’s in a bind, and I want to help him. Tell him the police have the letter.”

Cavalcante Meier received me wearing a short red velvet robe. His hair had been carefully combed and oiled, recently.

“The police have the letter,” I said. “They know it was sent to a certain Rodolfo and think you’re that Rodolfo. Fortunately the envelope hasn’t been found, so they can’t prove anything.”

“I tore up the envelope,” he said. “I don’t know why I didn’t destroy the letter too. I kept it in a drawer in the table by my bed.”

“A banker’s failing, keeping documents,” I said.

“I didn’t kill Marly. I haven’t the faintest idea who did.”

“I’m not sure I believe that. I think it was you.”

“Prove it.”

He looked like Jack Palance, Wilson the gunslinger pulling on his black gloves and saying “Prove it” to Elisha Cook Jr., just before he whipped out his Colt and shot him in the chest, then threw him face down into the mud furrowed by wagon wheels.

“There are a lot of Rodolfos in the world. I can prove I never saw the girl in my life. Do you know where I was at the time the crime was committed? Having dinner with the Governor. He can confirm it. You’re a man consumed by envy, aren’t you? You hate people who made it in life, who didn’t end up as jailhouse lawyers, don’t you?”

“I don’t hate anyone. I merely feel contempt for scum like you.”

“Then what are you doing here? After money?”

“No, after your daughter.”

Cavalcante Meier raised his hand to hit me. I stopped his hand in midair. His arm had no strength to it. I released his hand. He was a piece of filth, a courtly exploiter of people, sybarite, parasite.

Raul was waiting for me at the office.

"Guedes has been taken off the Marly Moreira case by order of the Commissioner, as of today. He gave interviews against regulations. They think he's bucking for promotion. He's been transferred to a precinct in the sticks. He can't open his trap."

Guedes wasn't out for promotion. He believed Cavalcante Meier was guilty and wanted to go public before they could cover it up. He believed in the media and in public opinion. Naive, but that kind of person often achieves incredible things.

"So how's it going?" Wexler asked.

"Ah, Leon, I'm in love!"

"Aren't you always? Berta is a nice girl."

"It's a different one. Senator Cavalcante Meier's daughter."

"You want to screw every woman in the world," Wexler said in recrimination.

"That's true."

It was true. I had the soul of a sultan out of the thousand and one nights; when I was a boy, at least once a month I would fall in love and cry myself to sleep. As an adolescent, I began dedicating my life to screwing. The daughters of friends, the wives of friends, women I knew, and women I didn't know—I screwed everybody. The only one I didn't screw was my mother.

"There's a girl in the outer office who wants to speak to you," Dona Gertrudes, the secretary, told me. Dona Gertrudes was becoming uglier by the day. She was starting to get a humpback and mustache, and I had the impression that she looked cross-eyed at me, one eye in each direction. A saintly woman. On second thought, was she really?

Eve, in the outer office. We stood there reading each other's expression.

"Do you play chess?" I asked.

"No. Bridge."

"Will you teach me?" I asked.

"Yes."

I held myself in check so I wouldn't fly around the room like a June bug.

"It wasn't my father, I know it wasn't."

"I love you," I said. "From the first day I met you." Her look was like a blowtorch.

"I was pretty shaken myself that day."

We were holding hands when Wexler came into the room.

"Raul is here. I told him you were busy. You want to talk to him?"

"It must be something to do with the Marly case. Yes, I'll talk to him. Wait here," I told Eve.

I was at the door when Eve said, "Save my father."

I turned. "You have to help me do that."

"How?"

"You can begin by not lying to me any more."

"I won't lie again."

"What did you say to Márcio the Suzuki at your house? Where did you know him from?"

"Márcio supplied cocaine for my cousin Lilly. But she kicked the habit about six months ago. That day I asked Márcio if Lilly had gone back to snorting, and he said no. I was afraid he was there to bring drugs for her."

"Where did Lilly get the money to buy the stuff?"

"Daddy gives Lilly anything she asks for. She's the daughter of his brother who died when Lilly was a child. Her mother remarried and wanted nothing to do with her, so Lilly came to live with us when she was eight."

"Why did you say you know your father didn't kill Marly and Márcio?"

"My father couldn't kill anyone."

"So it's just a feeling, a simple assumption?"

"Yes," she said, refusing to meet my eyes.

Raul was pacing back and forth in Wexler's office.

"Guedes says he's going to publicly name the senator as the murderer and that he doesn't care what happens."

"Guedes is crazy," I said. "We can't let him make that blunder."

Raul and I went looking for Guedes. Eve went home. I promised to call her later.

Guedes was at the morgue, talking to a technician friend of his. He was working on his statement to the press.

"Cavalcante Meier didn't do it," I said.

"Two days ago you didn't know the first thing about the case, now you show up with total insight."

I told him part of what I knew.

"If it wasn't Cavalcante Meier, who was it?"

"I don't know. Maybe a drug dealer."

"I went through Marly Moreira's life with a fine-tooth comb. There's not the slightest chance she was involved in dealing drugs. And both were killed by the same person. Your reasoning is full of holes."

I attempted to defend my point of view. I mentioned Cavalcante Meier's alibi. After all, the testimony of the Governor couldn't be ignored.

"They're all corrupt. Just wait, when the Governor leaves office he'll become a partner in one of Cavalcante Meier's businesses."

"Guedes, you're going to come out of this looking real bad."

"It doesn't matter. What've I got to lose—my job? I'm sick of being a cop."

"Accusing an innocent man is slander; it's a crime."

"He isn't innocent. I have my proof." Guedes's eyes blazed with rectitude, justice, integrity, and probity. "Did you know that Senator Cavalcante Meier is the registered owner of a .38 Taurus revolver, the same caliber as the bullets that caused the deaths of Marly and Márcio?"

"Lots of people keep a .38 in their house. When's the press conference?"

"Tomorrow at ten a.m."

I arrived at the house in Gávea just as night was falling.

"What happened?" Eve asked. "The look on your face—"

"Where's your father?"

"In his bedroom. He's not feeling well."

"I have to speak to him. It's important."

I got a surprise when I saw Cavalcante Meier. His hair was uncombed, he hadn't shaved, and his eyes were red, as if he'd been drinking too much, or crying. The look of Jannings, Professor Rath, in *The Blue Angel,* struggling to hide his shame, surprised by the world's incomprehension. Lilly was at his side, her face paler than ever, her skin looking as if it had been whitewashed. She held a purse in her hand. Her black dress heightened her phantasmagoric beauty.

"I did it," Cavalcante Meier said.

"Daddy!" Eve exclaimed.

Cavalcante Meier didn't ring true. I've been to enough movies to know a bad actor when I see one.

"I did it, I already said I did. Tell your policeman friend to come pick me up. Get out of my house!"

He came toward me as if to attack. Eve held him back.

"Go away, please go away," Eve begged.

As I left, Lilly went with me. She stopped next to my car.

"Okay if I come along?"

"Sure."

Lilly sat beside me. I drove slowly through the dark tree-lined gardens and toward the entrance.

"He's lying," I said. "It must be to protect someone. Maybe Eve."

Lilly's body began to tremble, but no sound came from her throat. As we passed a lamppost I saw that her face was wet with tears.

"It wasn't him. Or Eve," Lilly said, so low I could barely make out the words.

So that was it. I already knew the truth, and what the hell good did it do me? Is there really any such thing as guilty and innocent?

"I'm listening, you can begin," I said.

"I discovered I loved Uncle Rodolfo two years ago, not as an uncle, or father, which is what he'd been to me till then, but as one loves a lover."

I said nothing. I know when a person is about to bare their soul.

"We've been lovers for six months. He's everything in my life, and I'm everything in his."

"Is that why you killed Marly?"

"Yes."

"Did he know?"

"No. I told him today. He tried to protect me. He loves me as much as I love him."

In the half-darkness of the car she looked like a fluorescent statue bathed in black light.

"I can tell you how it happened."

"Tell me."

"My uncle told me he was having problems with a girl he'd had an affair with and who worked for one of his firms. She was threatening to cause a scandal, to tell my aunt everything. My aunt is a very sick woman, and I love her as if she were my mother."

I had never seen her. Rich families have inviolable secrets, private faces, dark complicities.

"She never leaves her room. There's always a nurse at her side; she could die at any time."

"Go on."

"My uncle received the letter, on a Monday I think. Every night, around eleven, I would go to his room, then leave early the next morning before the maids came to straighten up."

"Did Eve know about this?"

"Yes."

"Go on," I said.

"That day Uncle Rodolfo was very nervous. He showed me the letter, said that Marly was crazy, that the scandal could kill Aunt Nora and ruin him politically. Uncle Rodolfo is a very good man, he doesn't deserve anything like that."

"Go on," I said.

"Uncle Rodolfo showed me the letter from that Marly woman and then left it on the night table. The next day I took the letter, found that woman's phone number, and called her. I said who I was and that I had a message from Uncle Rodolfo. We arranged a meeting for after office hours. I chose a deserted beach where I swim sometimes. She was arrogant and said to tell Uncle Rodolfo not to treat her like dirt. When the old lady dies, she threatened, that bastard will have to marry me. I had Uncle Rodolfo's revolver in my bag. It only took one shot. She fell forward, moaning. I ran and got my car, found Márcio, and asked him to sell me some coke. I did a few lines at his place, the first time in six months. I was desperate. I dozed off, and Márcio must have gone through my bag and taken the letter while I was asleep. When Uncle Rodolfo told me you were meeting Márcio at Gordon's, I got there first so you wouldn't find him. I made up a story that Uncle Rodolfo had sent the police after him."

"Please stop calling him uncle."

"That's what I always called him, and I'm not going to change now. Márcio was furious and went to Uncle Rodolfo's house the next day. You know that part, you saw it all."

"Not everything."

"I met Márcio in the garden, when he was leaving. He told me Uncle Rodolfo was going to pay him off, but that he wasn't going to return the letter. I set up a time with him to buy some cocaine; I'd already made up my mind to get him out of the way. Márcio was in an easy chair watching television, already spaced out on coke and whiskey. I went up to him and shot him in the head. I felt nothing, except disgust, as if he were a cockroach."

"You didn't find the letter. It was in Márcio's pocket."

"I searched everywhere, but I'd never look in his pocket. Touching him would make me sick," Lilly said.

"What happened to the money?"

"It was in a suitcase. I took it home. It's in my bedroom closet."

I stopped the car. She was holding her purse tightly between trembling hands.

"Give that to me," I said.

"No!" she answered, clutching the bag to her chest.

I tore the bag from her grasp. The Taurus was inside: two-inch barrel, mother-of-pearl handle. Her eyes were a bottomless abyss.

"Leave the gun with me," Lilly asked.

I shook my head.

"Then take me back, so I can be with Uncle Rodolfo."

"I have to find Guedes. Take a cab. And I'd hire a lawyer right away."

"Everything's ruined, isn't it?"

"Unfortunately it is. For all of us," I replied.

I put her in a taxi and went looking for Guedes. I thought about Eve. Farewell, my lovely. The long good-bye. The big sleep. There was no one inside my body. The hands on the steering wheel seemed to belong to someone else.

guardian angel

THE HOUSE HAD SEVERAL BEDROOMS. I asked which of them I was supposed to sleep in. She took me to a bedroom that was close to hers.

I sat on the bed, tested the mattress.

"No good, it's too soft. It'll kill my back."

I tested the mattresses in all the bedrooms until I found a firm one.

"This one's good. You got a shirt I can use? I forgot to bring anything to sleep in."

The woman came back right away with a white shirt.

"This is the largest I have. I just wore it once, does it matter?"

I thanked the woman and said good night. I put on the shirt, smelled the scent in the fabric, a mixture of clean skin and perfume.

I looked for a position for sleep. My back hurt. I had a lot of broken and badly healed bones scattered around my body.

The woman knocked on the door so softly that I nearly didn't hear her.

"Yes?"

"It's me. I'd like to speak to you."

"One moment."

I put on my pants and opened the door.

She was wearing a robe, and a woman in a robe always reminds me of my mother. In fact, the only thing I remember about my mother is the robe.

"You're too far away; I don't feel protected. I can't sleep. Can't you go to the room next to mine? We can take the firm mattress from this bed and exchange it for the other one."

I took my firm mattress to the bedroom next to hers.

I sat on the bed.

"I think everything's all right now. I can sleep on this. Good night."

"Good night."

I couldn't take more than ten minutes lying down. The pain in my spine increased. I got out of bed and sat in an armchair that was in the room.

Another knock on the door.

"What is it?"

"I heard a noise in the garden," she whispered through the door. "I think there's someone in the garden."

I put on my pants. Opened the door. She was still in her robe.

"It must be your imagination. You're very nervous. Where in the garden?"

"In the magnolia grove. There aren't any lights there, and I had the impression that I saw a light going on and off."

"You have a flashlight?"

"Yes."

The woman gave me the flashlight.

"Be careful. I've told you the horrible things that have been happening with me, haven't I?"

"You ought to go to your apartment in the city."

"It's worse there. I had to disconnect the telephone because of the calls in the middle of the night, threatening me. And there are people following me in the street. Here, at least, there are bars on all the windows, and the doors are metal. Take the revolver."

"It's better if you keep the revolver. Lock the door. And don't go looking out through the window."

It was a large country estate. A lawn with flowerbeds ringed the house. In the middle of the grass, a swimming pool. In the rear, the caretaker's house and the garden. The rest of the estate was woods and large trees, which made the night even darker. Stone benches were scattered among the trees. I sat down on one of them, in the magnolia grove. I waited, with the lit flashlight on the bench.

Sonya emerged silently from the darkness and sat down beside me on the stone bench.

"Did you leave the revolver where she could see it?"

"I left it in her hand. I'm following your plan."

"Listen to this noise," Sonya said, taking a recorder from her purse and turning it on. It sounded like the moan of someone dying. "Doesn't it sound like a ghost?"

"You two are lucky there's no dog here."

"There was. We poisoned it. Jorge poisoned it. When's she going to use the revolver?"

"She's scared to death, let's wait a bit. Who's Jorge?"

"If you don't know, I'm not going to tell you."

"Why do you want the woman dead?"

"That's none of your concern."

"I'm going back to the house. Turn off the moans. That's enough for now."

"Don't forget our agreement," Sonya said. "This has to be taken care of within three days. If she's still undecided, you put the bullet in her head yourself."

I went back to the house. The woman opened the door, holding my revolver. She was trembling, her eyes wide.

"What was that noise?"

"Nothing."

"Nothing? I heard it. Do you think I'm crazy?"

"No."

"I know, I know you think I'm crazy."

The woman pointed the revolver at me.

"Tell me the truth. You think I'm crazy. The caretakers thought I was crazy and ran off one night without saying a word. I've just heard a loud moan, the sound of a soul in agony, like mine, and you tell me it was nothing? And this revolver with no bullets? Is that how you were going to defend me? With an unloaded gun?"

"How do you know it's not loaded?"

"I put it up to my head and pulled the trigger six times. Nothing happened."

"I forgot to load it. I don't know how that happened; I'm very careful."

"You removed the bullets because you thought I was crazy and would shoot myself."

"I'm here to protect you. Go to sleep. Tomorrow we'll talk."

"Don't speak to me that way. I'm very nervous. Come sleep in my room."

"All right."

The woman lay down without taking off her robe, covering herself with a sheet. I sat down in the armchair in the room. All the bedrooms had armchairs and their own bathroom.

She looked at me from the bed, sighing like someone about to cry.

"Come over here, hold my hand."

I held her hand.

"You have large hands. Did you used to be a manual laborer?"

"No."

"Have you always been a companion for sick people?"

"When I was young, I spent two years pushing an old man's wheelchair. It was the best time of my life. I liked to read, he had thousands of books, and I spent all day reading."

"I've never seen you reading here."

"I haven't had time yet, and your books don't appeal to me."

"I'm sorry. And after you worked in the house with all those books that appealed to you?"

"Then I took care of the old man."

"Was he mentally ill?"

"No. It was a sickness of old age." The guy killed himself, with my help, but I wouldn't tell her that. "Now try to get a little sleep."

"Am I crazy?"

"No. You're just very nervous."

The woman fell asleep. I let go of her hand. I went to the armchair and spent the entire night awake, thinking, smelling the scent of her shirt on my body and looking at the woman as she slept. Primitive man would devour, like a hyena, the remains of dead animals that had been hunted down by other animals. He didn't become a hunter himself until he invented pointed weapons. I loaded the bullets into the chamber of the revolver.

The woman in the bed looked like a dead dog that would be easy to kick. I don't ask questions when I'm hired for a job. But in this case I'd like to know who wanted her to put a bullet in her head. Some scumbag husband terrifying his hysterical wife to make her kill herself so the bastard could keep the money? I'd been through a situation more or less like that once, during Carnival week.

Dawn broke, birds started to chirp, and the woman woke up. She smiled at me.

"I feel better today. I think the nightmare is coming to an end. I'm going to do some work in the garden, will you stay close to me?"

I left her bedroom. In my bathroom, I washed my face and brushed my teeth. I went to the garden.

The woman was wearing a hat to protect her from the sun. She asked me to accompany her to the tool shed next to the garage. There were pickaxes, shovels, an electric lawnmower, a pump for cleaning the pool. She picked up a pair of shears, the kind used in gardens.

"My garden is pretty, isn't it? I planted those flowers myself; aren't they pretty?"

I don't care much about flowers, but I listened patiently as she mentioned the names of the ones growing in the flowerbeds.

"I have to make a phone call."

"The telephone is disconnected."

"I'll go to the village."

"Please, don't leave me by myself."

"Then come with me. You can work in the garden later."

We took her car.

"Do you like music?"

"If you want to listen to music, it doesn't bother me."

She popped a violin concerto into the car's player.

"Doesn't it give you a peaceful feeling?"

Violin music makes me restless, but I put up with it without saying anything. We arrived at the small square in the village. I stopped at the door of the little market, full of sacks of cat and dog food.

She got out of the car with me. "I'm going to buy some things. I'm tired of eating frozen food."

The man in the market greeted her amicably; the woman had owned the estate for many years. The man asked if I was the new caretaker, and the woman replied that I was a friend.

Nearby there was a bakery. I called Sonya from there.

"I'm going to do the job. But first I want to talk to you and Jorge. I want the rest of the money. Tonight, the same place where we met last night."

"Jorge won't go.

"That's his problem. If he doesn't come talk to me, the deal's off. Nine o'clock."

I hung up the phone and went back to the market. I picked up the bag of groceries, and we went back to the car.

The woman worked in the garden, then made something for us to eat. But she just sat at the table, without eating a thing. Then she went back to work in the garden, while listening to music, with me at her side the whole time, suffering from the music, wanting everything to be over and done with.

At fifteen till nine I told the woman that I was going to take a look around the grounds and might be gone for a while.

"Don't leave me alone."

I got the flashlight.

"I won't be far away, nothing to worry about. Lock everything and only open the door to me. And stay away from the window."

"Please . . ."

"Don't worry."

I left, taking the revolver. At the tool shed I grabbed two shovels and a pickax and went to the magnolia grove. I sat down on the stone bench, with the flashlight on. I placed the shovels and pickax beside the bench.

Sonya and Jorge were slow to show up. The man was wearing a hat that covered half his face.

"Turn off that flashlight. What did you want with me?"

I recognized him at once. If you want to stay alive in this shitty world, you can't forget anyone's face or voice. It was the son of old man Baglioni, who I had helped make it to the other world. I pretended not to recognize him.

"Just one question. Is the woman your wife?"

"That old bag? She's my partner. She's off her rocker and has been screwing up the business. What did you want from me?"

"To get what you owe me."

"Before you do the job? Impossible. A deal's a deal."

"I'm going to kill the woman today and disappear. How am I supposed to get the rest?"

"You know where to find Sonya. She'll pay you later."

I turned on the flashlight. I pointed to the shovels and pickax.

"I want you two to help me dig a grave. If I do it by myself it'll take a really long time. The body has to vanish. I went shopping with her in the village today, and they saw my face."

"That's all we needed," said Jorge.

"No grave, no body."

"All right, all right," Jorge said, grabbing one of the shovels. I picked up the other one and the pickax.

"Not here. We have to go outside the estate, in the forest."

"I can't walk very far in these high heels," Sonya said.

"That's your problem."

We went into the forest, with Sonya complaining that her shoes were getting ruined.

"This is good," I said.

Sonya refused to dig. Jorge and I worked in silence, the way gravediggers do. It's not easy to open up a large grave, especially in that type of hard earth. Our shirts were soaked in sweat. Jorge was sweating more than me but didn't take off the hat that concealed his face.

Jorge laid down the shovel. "That's deep enough," he said.

I still had the pickax in my hand.

"There's still one thing missing," I said.

I struck Jorge in the head with all my strength, using the point of the pickax. He fell. Sonya began to run but only managed a few steps and a shout of fear, not really a shout, more a kind of howl.

I checked to see they were really dead; I didn't want to bury them alive. I deepened the cavity a little more. I threw them into the hole and covered it with dirt. I patted down the earth with the shovel and covered the grave with rocks and tree branches. In the forest there was nothing but birds, toads, snakes, insects, and other harmless animals. They weren't going to dig up that grave, but I didn't want to take any chances.

I washed the shovels and the pickax and returned them to the tool shed. I knocked on the iron door of the house.

"It's me, you can open the door."

The woman opened the door, as frightened as ever. "Did you see anything?"

"No. And I didn't hear any strange noises. Did you?"

"No," she answered. "Would you like some tea? I'll make us some tea."

I stayed at the estate for another week with the woman, despite the music. There's nothing more irritating than violin music. Every day I would go to the grave where those two were rotting, to see if there was any bad smell in the air. Nothing. In the market in the village they recommended an elderly couple as caretakers for the woman. The old man was a robust type who worked all day in the garden, him and my mother. I'm joking, but I wish she could have been my mother. I liked her. If I'd had a mother like her, I'd be a different man, my fate would be different, and I'd take care of her. I'd have someone to love.

She was in the garden with the caretaker, puttering in the soil. "I have to leave," I said.

"I don't know how to repay you for what you've done for me. I'm well. I'm no longer afraid."

"You're not well. But no one is going to phone you in the middle of the night anymore or follow you in the streets to frighten you."

"How can I pay you? You must be needing some money."

"I've already been paid. But you can give me a ride to the bus station in the city."

The woman drove me to the bus station.

"When you need anything, look for me. Give me your telephone number," she said.

"I don't have a phone."

"Sonya must know how to find you if I need you, doesn't she? She was very kind, recommending you as my guardian angel."

I didn't answer. The woman waited with me until the bus arrived, the two of us in the car listening to the music she liked, and the violin didn't seem so irritating.

I got on the bus. She waved at me as the bus pulled away.

the ship *catrineta*

I AWOKE TO THE SOUND OF AUNT OLYMPIA declaiming "The Ship *Catrineta*" in her grave and powerful contralto voice.

> My soul I deny thee, O demon,
> Thou serpent of land and of sea.
> To God and His hosts it looks upward,
> From body and torment to flee.
> An angel descended from Heaven,
> Delivered him safe to the lee.
> The demon was rent by his fury
> And peace again ruled o'er the sea.
> Come ev'ning the ship *Catrineta*
> Had landed, from Satan set free.

Then I remembered that today was my twenty-first birthday. All my aunts must be in the hall, waiting for me to wake up. "I'm awake," I shouted. They came into my room. Aunt Helena was carrying an old, dusty book with a leather cover and gilded clasps. Aunt Regina was bringing a tray with my breakfast, and Aunt Julieta a basket with fresh fruit gathered from our orchard. Aunt Olympia had on the dress she wore in Molière's *École des Femmes.*

"It's all a lie," Aunt Helena said. "The demon didn't explode, and no angel saved the captain; the truth is all in the old 'Ship's Log', written by our ancestor Manuel de Matos, which thou hast already read, and in this other book, 'The Secret Decalogue of Uncle Jacinto', which thou art to read for the first time today."

In "The Secret Decalogue" my mission was defined. I was the only male in a family reduced, besides myself, to four unmarried and implacable women. The sun was coming through the window, and I could hear the birds singing in the garden. It was a beautiful morning. My aunts asked anxiously if I had chosen the girl. I answered yes.

"We'll have a birthday party tonight. Bring her here, so we can meet her," said Aunt Regina. My aunts have taken care of me since I was born. My mother died in childbirth and my father, my mother's first cousin, committed suicide a month later.

I told my aunts that they would meet sweet Ermelinda Balsemão that night. Their faces beamed with satisfaction. Aunt Regina handed me "The Secret Decalogue of Uncle Jacinto" and they all solemnly left the room. Before beginning to read the Decalogue, I telephoned Ermê, as I called her, and asked if she'd like to have dinner with my aunts and me. She was happy to accept. Then I opened "The Secret Decalogue" and began to read the commandments of my mission: *It is the inescapable obligation of every first-born male of our Family, above the laws of society, religion, and ethics . . .*

My aunts dug their most extravagant formal dresses out of trunks and closets. Aunt Olympia was wearing her favorite clothing, which she saved for very special occasions, the dress she had worn the last time she played Phaedra. Dona Maria Nunes, our housekeeper, constructed enormous and elaborate hairdos for each of them; as was the custom in our family, none of the women had ever cut her hair. I stayed in my room, after reading the Decalogue, getting up from the bed now and then to look at the garden and the woods. It was a hard mission, one which my father had carried out, and my grandfather and great-grandfather and all the rest. I got my father out of my head right away. This wasn't the right moment to think about him. I thought about my grandmother, who had been an anarchist and manufactured bombs in her basement without anyone suspecting. Aunt Regina liked to say that every bomb that exploded in the city between 1920 and 1960 had been made and thrown by Grandma. "Mom," Aunt Julieta would say, "could not tolerate injustice, and that was her way of showing her disapproval; the ones who died were for the most part guilty, and the few innocents sacrificed were martyrs in a good cause."

From my window, by the light of the full moon, I could see Ermê's car, its top down, as it came slowly through the stone gate, climbed the hydrangea-lined road, and stopped in front of the beefwood tree that stood in the middle of the lawn. The cool evening breeze of May tossed her fine blonde hair. For an instant, Ermê seemed to hear the sound of the wind in the tree; then she looked toward the house, as if she knew I was observing her, and drew her scarf around her throat, pierced by a coldness that didn't exist, except within herself. With an abrupt gesture she accelerated the car and, now resolute, drove toward the house. I went down to receive her.

"I'm afraid," Ermê said. "I don't know why, but I am. I think it's this house, it's very pretty but so gloomy!"

"What you're afraid of is my aunts," I said.

I took Ermê to the Small Parlor, where my aunts were waiting. They were most impressed with Ermê's beauty and breeding and treated her with great affection. I saw at once that Ermê had won the approval of all. "It will be tonight," I told Aunt Helena, "let the others know." I wanted to finish my mission as soon as possible.

Aunt Helena told lively adventures of our relatives, who went back to the sixteenth century. "By obligation, all the first-born were, and are, artists and carnivores, and whenever possible they hunt, kill, and eat their prey. Vasco de Matos, one of our ancestors, even ate the foxes he hunted. Later, when he began to keep domestic animals, we ourselves would slaughter the lambs, rabbits, ducks, chickens, pigs, and even the calves and cows. We're not like others," said Aunt Helena, "who lack the courage to kill an animal or even see one killed, and want to savor it in innocence. In our family we're conscious and responsible carnivores. Both in Portugal and in Brazil."

"And we have eaten people," said Aunt Julieta. "Our ancestor Manuel de Matos, was first mate on the *Catrineta* and ate one of the crewmen who was sacrificed to save the others from starving to death."

"'Hear now, ladies and gentlemen, an astonishing tale, of the ship *Catrineta,* which has much to tell . . . ,'" I recited, imitating Aunt Olympia's grandiloquent tone. All my aunts, with the exception of Olympia, burst out laughing. Ermê appeared to be taking it all in with curiosity.

Pointing at me with her long, white, bony finger, where the ring with our family coat of arms shone, Aunt Julieta said, "José has been trained since he was a little boy to be an artist and a carnivore."

"An artist?" Ermê asked, as if the idea amused her.

"He is a Poet," said Aunt Regina.

Ermê, who was majoring in literature, said she loved poetry—"later I'd like you to show me your poems"—and that the world truly needed poets. Aunt Julieta asked if she was familiar with the Portuguese "Book of Songs." Ermê said she had read a few things in school, and that she took the poem to be an allegory of the struggle between Good and Evil, with the eventual triumph of the former, as is common in so many medieval homilies.

"Then thou believest that the angel saved the captain?" asked Aunt Julieta.

"That's what is written, isn't it? In any case, they're just verses from the fanciful popular imagination," said Ermê.

"Then thou dost not believe that an actual incident, similar to the poem, took place on the ship carrying Jorge de Albuquerque Coelho from here to Portugal in 1565?" asked Aunt Regina. Ermê smiled delicately without answering, as the young will do with old people whom they have no wish to displease.

Saying that they, she and her sisters, knew every novel of the sea that dealt with the *Catrineta,* Aunt Regina left the parlor, to return shortly with an armload of books. "This is *Salvation of the Shipwreck* by the Spanish poet Gonçalo Berceo; this is *Cantigas de Santa María,* by Alfonso el Sabio;

this is the book by that poor man Teófilo Braga; this is the Carolina de Michaelis; this is an unfinished novel of the cycle, found in Asturias, with verses reproduced from the Portuguese originals. And this one, and this one, and this"—and Aunt Regina kept piling the books on the antique table in the middle of the Small Parlor—"all of them full of speculation, unfounded reasoning, humbug, and ignorance. We have the historical truth here in this book, the 'Ship's Log' of our ancestor, Manuel de Matos, second in command on the ship that in 1565 took Jorge de Albuquerque Coelho from here to Portugal."

After that we went to the table. But the subject had not yet been closed. It was as if Ermê's silence encouraged my aunts to speak further about the subject. "In the poem, which balladeers took upon themselves to spread about, the captain is saved from death by an angel," said Aunt Julieta. "The true story, which is in the Log kept by our ancestor, was never told, in order to protect Albuquerque Coelho's name and reputation. Art thou enjoying the squid? It's an old family recipe, and the wine is from our country residence in Vila Real," said Aunt Regina. "The historian Narciso Azevedo, from Oporto, a relative of ours, though fortunately not by blood—he's only married to our cousin Maria da Ajuda Fonseca, from Sabrosa—claims that during the voyage some crewmen came to Albuquerque Coelho with a petition asking authorization to eat several of their companions who had starved to death, and that Albuquerque Coelho adamantly refused, saying that while he lived he would not allow such a brutish desire to be satisfied. Now that's all very well," said Aunt Olympia, "but in reality what happened was quite different; the seamen who starved to death had been thrown into the sea, and Manuel de Matos saw that the entire crew, including Jorge Albuquerque Coelho, would all starve to death simultaneously. Speaking of which, this kid we're eating we raised ourselves, dost thou like it?" Before Ermê could reply, Aunt Julieta went on: "The crew was called together by Manuel de Matos, our ancestor, and while Jorge Albuquerque Coelho absented himself, stretched out in the berth in his cabin, it was decided by majority vote—and I quote the very words of the Log, which I know by heart—to draw lots to see who would be killed. Lots were cast four times, and four crewmen were killed and eaten by the survivors. And when the *Santo Antônio* arrived in Lisbon, Albuquerque Coelho, who prided himself on his reputation as a Christian, a hero, and a disciplinarian, forbade any crewmen to speak of the affair. From what eventually came to light, the romantic *Ship Catrineta* was created. But the cruel and bloody truth is here in Manuel de Matos's Log."

The parlor seemed to darken, and an unexpected gust of cold air came in the window and ruffled the curtains. Dona Maria Nunes, who was serving, shrugged her shoulders, and for several instants a powerful, almost unbearable silence could be heard.

"This house is so large," Ermê said. "Does anyone else live here?"

"Just us," said Aunt Olympia. "We do everything ourselves, with Dona Maria Nunes's help. We take care of the garden and orchard, clean and cook, wash and iron our clothes. That's what keeps us busy and healthy."

"Doesn't José do anything?"

"He's a Poet; he has a mission," said Aunt Julieta, the Keeper of the Ring.

"And because he's a poet he doesn't eat? You didn't touch your food," Ermê said.

"I'm saving my hunger for later."

When dinner was over, Aunt Helena asked Ermê if she was a religious person. My aunts, accompanied by Dona Maria Nunes, always prayed a novena after dinner in the small chapel in the house. Before they retired to the chapel—Ermê declined the invitation, which pleased me, for we could be alone—I kissed them aunt by aunt, as I always did. First Aunt Julieta—a thin, bony face with a long hooked nose, delicate lips like the drawing of the sorceress in my childhood fairy tale books, small and brilliant eyes, contrasting with the pallor of her face—till then I had not found out why she was Keeper of the Ring and I wanted to ask her, Why it is thou who wearest the Ring? but I felt I would know very soon. Aunt Olympia was dark with yellowed eyes, she kissed me with her heavy lips and wide mouth and her large nose and her well-pitched voice; for every feeling she had a corresponding mimicry, almost always expressed facially with glances, scowls, and grimaces. Aunt Regina looked at me with the small, clever, mistrusting eyes of a Pekingese puppy—she was perhaps the most intelligent of the four. Aunt Helena stood up when I went to her. She was the tallest of all, as well as the oldest and prettiest; she had a strong and noble face, like that of my grandmother Maria Clara, the bomb-throwing anarchist, and her sisters called her the archetype of the family; they said all the men of the family were good-looking like her, but the photo of Uncle Alberto, their other brother, younger than my father, who died of the plague in Africa while fighting beside the blacks, showed a figure of singular ugliness. Aunt Helena asked to have a word with me in private. We left the dining room and spoke for a few moments behind closed doors.

When I returned, my other aunts had already retired.

"It's funny the way all of you talk. It's 'thou' this, 'thou' that," Ermê said.

"We use 'you' with the servants and unimportant people we don't know," I said. "It was that way in Portugal and continued in Brazil when the family came here."

"But you don't use 'you' with the housekeeper."

"Dona Maria Nunes? But she's like one of the family; she's been in this house since the time of Grandmother Maria Clara, even before my father and my aunts were born. Dost thou know how old she is? Eighty-four."

"She looks like a sailor, with her face all wrinkled and sunburned," Ermê said. "She's different from you, you're so pale!"

"It's so I can keep my poet's face," I said. "Let's go to my favorite place in the house."

Ermê looked at the shelves full of books. "I spend most of my time here," I said. "Sometimes I sleep here on the sofa; it's a kind of bedroom-library. It has a small bathroom off to the side."

We were standing, so close our bodies were almost touching. Ermê wore no makeup on her face, her neck, her arms, but her skin shone with health. I kissed her. Her mouth was fresh and warm like mature wine.

"What about your aunts?" Ermê asked as I placed her on the sofa.

"They never come here. Don't worry." Her body had the firmness and scent of a tree of many fruits and flowers, the strength of an animal wild and free. I shall never be able to forget her.

"Why don't you find a job and marry me?" Ermê asked. I laughed, for the only thing I knew how to do was write poems. And why work? I was quite rich and when my aunts died would be richer still. "I'm rich too but I plan to work," Ermê said. "All right, let's get married," I said. I got dressed, left the library, and went to the pantry.

Without a word, Dona Maria Nunes handed me the bottle of champagne and two glasses. I took Ermê to the Small Parlor, pushed aside the books that still occupied the antique table, and placed the champagne and glasses on it. Ermê and I sat down, side by side.

I took from my pocket the black crystal flask that Aunt Helena had given me that night, and I recalled our conversation behind the door: I myself must choose and sacrifice the person I am to eat on my twenty-first year of life, isn't that it? I asked. Yes, thou must kill her thyself; use no foolish euphemisms; thou wilt first kill her and then eat her, today, the day thou thyself hast chosen, and that is all, Aunt Helena replied. And when I said I did not want Ermê to suffer, Aunt Helena said: Do we ever make people suffer? And she gave me the black crystal flask decorated with wrought silver, explaining that it contained an extremely powerful poison, the smallest drop of which was enough to kill; as colorless, tasteless, and odorless as pure water, it would cause instant death—we have had this poison for centuries and it grows even stronger, like the pepper our ancestors brought from India.

"What a lovely bottle!" Ermê exclaimed.

"It's a love potion," I said, laughing.

"Really? Do you swear?" Ermê was laughing too.

"One small drop for you, one small drop for me," I said, letting a drop fall into each glass. "We're going to fall madly in love with each other." I filled the glasses with champagne.

"I'm already madly in love with you," Ermê said. With an elegant gesture she raised the glass to her lips and took a small sip. The glass fell from her hand onto the table and broke, and Ermê's face fell against the fragments of crystal. Her eyes were still open as though she were lost in thought. She never even knew what happened to her.

My aunts came into the room, along with Dona Maria Nunes.

"We are proud of thee," said Aunt Helena.

"Nothing will be wasted," said Aunt Regina. "The bones will be ground up and given to the pigs, along with corn meal and cobs. We'll make sausage from the intestines. The brains and the choice cuts thou shalt eat. Where dost thou wish to begin?"

"With the tenderest part," I said.

From the window of my room I could see the beginning of daybreak. As commanded in the Decalogue, I donned my dress coat and awaited my summons.

At the great table in the Banquet Hall, which I had never in my life seen in use, my mission was fulfilled amid great pomp and circumstance. Every light of the immense chandelier was burning, making the black formal attire of my aunts and Dona Maria Nunes glow.

"We seasoned it very lightly in order not to spoil the taste. It's almost raw. It's a piece of rump, very tender," said Aunt Helena. Ermê was slightly sweet like veal, but tastier.

As I swallowed the first mouthful, Aunt Julieta, who had been watching me attentively, seated like the others around the table, removed the Ring from her forefinger and placed it on mine.

"It was I who took it from thy father's finger on the day he died, and kept it for today," said Aunt Julieta. "Now art thou head of the family."

In a word, the state of immorality
was general. Clergy, nobility and the
common people were all perverted.

JOAQUIM MANUEL DE MACEDO, *A Walk Through the Streets of Rio de Janeiro* (1862–63)

the art of walking in the streets of rio de janeiro

AUGUSTO, THE WALKER, WHOSE REAL NAME IS EPIFÂNIO, lives in a space above a women's hat shop on Sete de Setembro, downtown, and he walks the streets all day and part of the night. He believes that by walking he thinks better, finds solutions to his problems; *solvitur ambulando,* he tells himself.

In the days when he worked for the water and sewerage department, he thought of giving up everything to live off writing. But João, a friend who had published a book of poetry and another of short stories and was writing a six-hundred-page novel, told him that a true writer shouldn't live off what he wrote, it was obscene, you couldn't serve art and Mammon at the same time, therefore it was better for Epifânio to earn his daily bread at the water and sewerage department and write at night. His friend was married to a woman who suffered from bad kidneys, was the father of an asthmatic child, his mentally defective mother-in-law lived with them, and even so he met his obligations to literature. Augusto would go home and find he was unable to rid himself of the problems of the water and sewerage department; a large city uses a lot of water and produces a lot of excrement. João said there was a price to pay for the artistic ideal—poverty, drunkenness, insanity, the scorn of fools, affronts from the envious, lack of understanding from friends, loneliness, failure. And he proved he was right by dying from a sickness caused by fatigue and sadness, before completing his six-hundred-page novel. Which his widow threw in the trash along with other old papers. João's failure did not dishearten Epifânio. When he won a prize in one of the city's many lotteries, he resigned from the water and sewerage department to dedicate himself to the task of writing, and adopted the name Augusto.

Now he is a writer and a walker. Thus, when he isn't writing—or teaching whores to read—he walks the streets. Day and night he walks the streets of Rio de Janeiro.

At exactly three a.m., when Haydn's *Mit dem Paukenschlag* sounds on his Casio Melody, Augusto returns from his walks to the empty upstairs apartment where he lives, and sits down, after feeding the rats, in front of the small table occupied almost entirely by the enormous notebook with lined pages where he writes his book, under the large skylight through which a ray of light enters from the street, mixed with moonlight on nights when there is a full moon.

In his walks through the city's downtown, since he began writing the book, Augusto looks attentively at all there is to be seen—facades, roofs, doors, windows, posters stuck on walls, commercial signs, whether luminous or not, holes in the sidewalk, garbage cans, sewer drains, the ground he steps on, birds drinking water from puddles, vehicles, and especially people.

Another day he went into the theater-temple of Pastor Raimundo. He found the theater-temple by chance; the doctor at the Institute had told him that a problem in the macula of his retina demanded treatment with vitamin E in combination with selenium and had sent him imprecisely to a pharmacy that prepared the substance, on Senador Dantas Street, somewhere near the intersection with Alcindo Guanabara. Upon leaving the pharmacy, and after walking a little, he passed the door of the movie theater, read the small poster that said CHURCH OF JESUS SAVIOR OF SOULS FROM 8 TO 11 DAILY and went in without knowing why.

Every morning, from eight to eleven, every day of the week, the theater is occupied by the Church of Jesus Savior of Souls. Starting at two in the afternoon it shows pornographic films. At night, after the last show, the manager puts the posters with naked women and indecorous publicity slogans away in a storage area next to the bathroom. To the church's pastor, Raimundo, as well as the faithful—some forty people, most of them elderly women and young people with health problems—the theater's usual program is unimportant; all films are in some way sinful, and none of the church's believers ever go to the movies, because of an express prohibition from the bishop, not even to see the life of Christ at Eastertide.

From the moment that Pastor Raimundo places a candle, actually an electric light bulb, on a pedestal that imitates a lily, in front of the screen, the locale becomes a temple consecrated to Jesus. The pastor hopes the bishop will buy the theater, as he has done in certain districts in the city, and install a permanent church there, twenty-four hours a day, but he knows that the bishop's decision depends on the results of his, Raimundo's, work with the faithful.

Augusto is going to the theater-temple that morning, for the third time in a week, with the idea of learning the songs the women sing, *Flee from me, flee from me, O Satan, my body is not thine, my soul is not thine, Jesus has defeated thee,* a mixture of rock and samba. Satan is a word that attracts him. It has been a long time since he went into a place where people pray or do anything like it. He remembers as a child having gone for years on end to a large church full of images and sad people, on Good Friday, taken by his mother, who forced him to kiss the feet of Our Lord Jesus Christ lying with a crown of thorns on his head. His mother died. A diffuse memory of the color purple has never left him. Jesus is purple, religion is linked to purple, his mother is purple, or was it the purple satin lining her coffin? But there is nothing purple in that theater-temple with bouncers who watch him from a distance, two young men, one white and one mulatto, thin, small, short-sleeved dress shirt and dark tie, circulating among the faithful and never coming near the chair in the rear where he is sitting, motionless, wearing dark glasses.

When they sing *Flee from me, O Satan, Jesus has defeated thee,* the women raise their arms, throwing their hands backwards above their heads, as if they were rebuffing the demon; the bouncers in short sleeves do the same; Pastor Raimundo, however, holding the microphone, directs the chorus by raising only one arm.

Today, the pastor focuses his attention on the man in dark glasses, missing an ear, in the back of the theater as he says, "Brethren, everyone who is with Jesus raise your hands." All the faithful raise their hands, except Augusto. The pastor, very disturbed, sees that Augusto remains immobile, like a statue, his eyes hidden by the dark lenses. "Raise your hands," he repeats with emotion, and some of the faithful respond by standing on tiptoe and extending their arms even higher. But the man without an ear does not move.

Pastor Raimundo came from the state of Ceará to Rio de Janeiro when he was seven years old, along with his family, who were fleeing drought and hunger. At twenty he was a street vendor on Geremário Dantas Street, in the Madureira district; at twenty-six, pastor of the Church of Jesus Savior of Souls. Every night, he gave thanks to Jesus for this immense gift. He had been a good vendor, he didn't cheat his customers, and one day a pastor, hearing him selling his merchandise in a persuasive way, as he knew how to speak one word after another at the correct speed, invited him to enter the Church. In a short time Raimundo became a pastor; he was now thirty, had almost lost his Northeastern accent and acquired the neutral speech of certain Rio natives, for it was like that, impartial and universal, that the word of Jesus must be. He is a good pastor, just as he was a good vendor and a good son, since he took care of his mother when she became paralyzed and dirtied her bed, until the day of her death. He cannot forget the senile, failing, and moribund body of his mother, especially the genital and excretory areas that he was obliged to clean every day; sometimes he has disgusting dreams about his mother and regrets that she didn't die of a heart attack at fifty, not that he remembers what she was like at fifty; he only remembers his mother as old and repellent. Because he knew how to say words rapidly one after the other, and with correct meanings, he was transferred from the outlying Baixada district to downtown, as the Church of Jesus Savior of Souls wanted to bring the word of God to the most impenetrable districts, like the center of the city. The center of the city is a mystery. The South Zone is also difficult; the wealthy disdain the evangelical churches, the religion of the poor, and in the South Zone the church is frequented during weekdays by old women and sickly young people, who are the most faithful of the faithful, and on Sundays by maids, doormen, cleaning workers, dark-skinned and poorly dressed folk. But the rich are worse sinners and need salvation even more than the poor. One of Raimundo's dreams is to be transferred from downtown to the South Zone and find a way into the heart of the rich.

But the number of faithful going to the theater-temple hasn't increased, and Raimundo may have to go to preach in another temple; perhaps he will be forced to return to the Baixada, for he has failed, he has not been able to take the word of Jesus convincingly where the Church of Jesus Savior of Souls most needs to be heard, especially these days, when the Catholics, with their churches nearly empty, have abandoned their intellectual posture and are counterattacking with the so-called charismatic movement, reinventing the miracle, resorting to faith healing and exorcism. They, the Catholics, had already gone back to admitting that the miracle exists only if the devil exists, good dominating evil; but it was still necessary for them to perceive that the devil is not metaphysical. You can touch the devil—on certain occasions he appears as flesh and blood, but he always has a small difference in his body, some unusual characteristic—and you can smell the devil, who stinks when he is distracted.

But his, Raimundo's, problem is not with the lofty politics of the relations of his Church with the Catholic Church; that's a problem for the bishop. Raimundo's problem is the faithful of his parish, the dwindling collection of tithes. And he is also disturbed by that man in dark glasses, missing one ear, who didn't raise his hand in support of Jesus. Since that man appeared, Raimundo has begun suffering from insomnia, having headaches, and emitting gases with a fetid odor from his intestines that burn his ass as they are expelled.

Tonight, while Raimundo doesn't sleep, Augusto, sitting in front of his enormous notebook with lined pages, jots down what he has seen as he walked through the city and writes his book *The Art of Walking in the Streets of Rio de Janeiro.*

He moved upstairs over the hat shop to facilitate writing the first chapter, which comprises only the art of walking in the downtown area of the city. He doesn't know which chapter will be the most important, when it is done. Rio is a very large city, protected by hills from whose top you can take in the whole of it, in stages, with a look, but the downtown is more diversified and dark and old, the downtown has no true hill; as occurs with the centers of things in general, which are flat or shallow, the downtown has only a single hillock, unduly called Saúde Hill, and to see the city from above, and even then only poorly and incompletely, you must go to Santa Teresa Hill, but that hill isn't above the city, it's somewhat to the side, and from it you don't get the slightest idea of what the downtown is like. You don't see the streets' sidewalks; at best, on certain days you see the polluted air hovering over the city.

In his wanderings Augusto still has yet to leave the downtown, nor will he do so any time soon. The rest of the city, the immense remainder that only the Satan of the Church of Jesus Savior of Souls knows in its entirety, will be traversed in due time.

The first owner of the hat shop lived there with his family many years before. His descendants were some of the merchants who continued to live downtown after the great flight to the districts, especially to the South Zone. Since the 1940s, almost no one lived in the two-story houses on the major streets of the downtown area, in the city's commercial core, which could be contained in a kind of quadrilateral with one of its sides Avenida Rio Branco, another a meandering line beginning at Visconde de Inhaúma and continuing along Marechal Floriano to Tomé de Souza Street, which would be the third side, and finally, the fourth side, a rather twisted course born at Visconde do Rio Branco, passing through Tiradentes Square and Carioca Street to Rio Branco, enclosing the space. The two-story houses in this area have become warehouses. As the hat shop's business dwindled year by year, for women had stopped wearing hats, even at weddings, and there was no further need for a storage space, as the small stock of merchandise could all fit in the store, the upstairs, which was of interest to no one, became empty. One day Augusto passed by the door of the hat shop and stopped to look at the wrought iron balconies on its facade, and the owner, an old man who had sold just one hat in the last six months, came out of the store to talk with him. The old man said that the house of the Count of Estrela had been located there, in the time when the street was called Cano Street because the water pipes for the fountain of Palace Square ran through it, a square that later would be called Dom Pedro II Square and then Quinze Square. "The habit people have of changing the names of streets. Come see something." The old man climbed to the second floor with Augusto and showed him a skylight whose glass was from the time the house was built, over ninety years old. Augusto was enchanted by the skylight, the enormous empty room, the bedrooms, the bathroom with English porcelain, and by the rats that hid when they walked past. He liked rats; as a child he had raised a rat that he had become attached to, but the friendship between the two had ended the day the rat bit him on the finger. But he continued to like rats. They say that the waste, the ticks, and the fleas from rats transmit horrible diseases, but he had always gotten along well with them, with the exception of that small problem of the bite. Cats also transmit horrible diseases, they say, and dogs transmit horrible diseases, they say, and human beings transmit horrible diseases, that much he knew. "Rats never vomit," Augusto told the old man. The old man asked what they did when they ate food that was bad for them, and Augusto replied that rats never ate food that was bad for them, for they were very cautious and selective. The old man, who had a sharp mind, then asked why lots of rats died of poisoning, and Augusto explained that to kill a rat it was necessary to use a very potent poison that killed with a small, single bite from the rodent, and, in any case, not many rats died from poisoning, considering their total population. The old man, who also liked rats and for the first time had met someone who had the same affection for the rodents and liked old skylights, invited him to live in the space, despite having inferred from the conversation that Augusto was a "nihilist."

Augusto is in the enormous room, under the large skylight, writing his book, the part referring to the center of the immense city. From time to time he stops and contemplates, with a small loupe used to examine weaves, the bulb hanging from the ceiling.

When he was eight years old, he got hold of a loupe used to examine textile fibers in his father's shop, the same loupe he is using at this moment. Lying down, in the distant year, he looked through the loupe at the bulb in the ceiling of the house where he lived, which was also a two-story dwelling in the center of the city and whose facade was destroyed to make room for the immense glowing acrylic sign of a small-appliances store; on the ground floor his father had a shop and talked with the women as he smoked his thin cigarette, and laughed, and the women laughed. His father was a different man in the shop, more interesting, laughing with those women. Augusto remembers the night when he was looking through the loupe at the bulb in the ceiling and saw beings full of claws, paws, menacing horns, and imagined in his fright what could happen if one of those things came down from the ceiling; the beasts appeared and disappeared, leaving him terrified and fascinated. He finally discovered, at daybreak, that the beasts were his eyelashes; when he blinked, the monster would appear in the loupe, and when he opened his eyes, it would vanish.

After observing, in the skylight, the bulb monsters of the large room—he now has long eyelashes and still has the loupe for looking at textiles—Augusto returns to writing about the art of walking in the streets of Rio de Janeiro. Because he is on foot, he sees things differently from those who travel in cars, buses, trains, launches, helicopters, or any other vehicle. He plans to avoid making his book into some kind of tourist guide for travelers in search of the exotic, of pleasure, the mystical, horror, crime, and poverty, such as interests many people of means, especially foreigners; nor will his book be one of those ridiculous manuals that associate walking with health, physical well-being, or notions of hygiene. He also takes precautions so that his book does not become a pretext, à la Macedo, for listing historical descriptions about potentates and institutions, although, like that creator of novels for damsels, he sometimes yields to prolix digressions. Neither will it be an architectural guide to old Rio or a compendium of urban architecture; Augusto hopes to find a peripatetic art and philosophy that will help him establish a greater communion with the city. Solvitur ambulando.

It is eleven p.m. and he is on Treze de Maio Street. Besides walking, he teaches prostitutes to read and to speak correctly. Television and pop music had corrupted people's vocabulary, especially the prostitutes'. It is a problem that has to be solved. He is aware that teaching prostitutes to read and to speak correctly in his rooms over the hat shop can be a form of torture for them. So he offers them money to listen to his lessons, little money, much less than the usual amount a customer pays. From Treze de Maio he goes to Avenida Rio Branco, which is deserted. The Municipal Theater advertises an opera recital for the following day; opera has gone in and out of fashion in the city since the beginning of the century. With spray paint, two youths are writing on the theater walls, which have just been painted and show few signs of the work of graffiti artists, WE THE SADISTS OF CACHAMBI GOT THE MUNI'S CHERRIE GRAFITTI ARTISTS UNITE; under the phrase, the logo-signature of the Sadists, a penis, which had at first caused some consternation among the students of graffitology but is now known to be that of a pig with a human glans. "Hey," Augusto tells one of the youths, "cherry is with a *y*, not *ie*, graffiti is with two *f*'s and one *t*, and you need punctuation between the two sentences." The youth replies, "Old man, you understood what we mean, didn't you? So fuck you and your shitass rules."

Augusto sees a figure trying to hide on Manoel de Carvalho, the street behind the theater, and recognizes a guy named Hermenegildo who does nothing in life but hand out an ecological manifesto against the automobile. Hermenegildo is carrying a can of glue, a brush, and eighteen rolled-up manifestoes. The manifesto is pasted with a special high-adhesive glue onto the windshields of cars parked on the street. Hermenegildo motions Augusto toward the place where he's hiding. It's common for them to bump into each other late at night, on the street. "I need your help," Hermenegildo says.

The two walk to Almirante Barroso Street, turn to the right and continue to Avenida Presidente Antônio Carlos. Augusto opens the can of glue. Hermenegildo's objective tonight is to get inside the Menezes

Cortes public parking garage without being seen by the guards. He has already made the attempt twice, unsuccessfully. But he thinks he'll have better luck tonight. They walk up the ramp to the first level, closed to traffic, where the cars with long-term parking contracts are, many of them parked overnight. Usually one or two guards are there, but tonight there's no one. The guards are probably all upstairs, talking to pass the time. In a little more than twenty minutes, Hermenegildo and Augusto paste the seventeen manifestoes on the windshields of the newest cars. Then they leave by the same route, turn onto Assembléia Street and go their separate ways at the corner of Quitanda. Augusto goes back to Avenida Rio Branco. At the avenue he turns to the right, again passes by the Municipal Theater, where he stops for a time to look at the drawing of the eclectic penis. He goes to the Cinelândia area, to urinate in McDonald's. The McDonald's bathrooms are clean places to urinate, even more so when compared to the bathrooms in luncheonettes, whose access is complicated; in luncheonettes or bars it's necessary to ask for the key to the bathroom, which comes attached to a huge piece of wood so it won't get lost, and the bathroom is always in some airless place, smelly and filthy, but in McDonald's they're always odorless, even if they have no windows, and they are well situated for someone walking downtown. This one is on Senador Dantas almost across from the theater, has an exit onto Álvaro Alvim Street, and the bathroom is close to that exit. There's another McDonald's on São José, near Quitanda Street, another on Avenida Rio Branco near Alfândega. Augusto opens the bathroom door with his elbow, a trick he invented; the doorknobs of bathrooms are full of germs of sexually transmitted diseases. In one of the closed stalls some guy has just defecated and is whistling with satisfaction. Augusto urinates in one of the stainless steel urinals, washes his hands using the soap he takes by pressing the metal tab on the transparent glass holder on the wall next to the mirror—a green, odorless liquid that makes no suds no matter how much he rubs his hands, then he dries his hand on a paper towel and leaves, again opening the door with his elbow, onto Álvaro Alvim.

Near the Odeon Cinema a woman smiles at him. Augusto approaches her. “Are you a female impersonator?” he asks. “Why don't you find out for yourself?” says the woman. Further on, he goes into the Casa Angrense, next to the Cinema Palácio, and orders mineral water. He opens the plastic cup slowly and, as he drinks in small sips, like a rat, he observes the women around him. A woman drinking coffee is the one he chooses, because she's missing a front tooth. Augusto goes up to her. “Do you know how to read?” The woman looks at him with the seduction and lack of respect that whores know how to show men. “Of course I do,” she says. “I don't, and I wanted you to tell me what's written there,” says Augusto. Businessman's lunch. “No credit,” she says. “Are you free?” She tells him the price and mentions a hotel on Marrecas Street, which used to be called Boas Noites Street, and where the Foundlings House of the Santa Casa stood more than a hundred years ago; and the street was also called Barão de Ladário and was called André Rebouças before it was Marrecas; and later its name was changed to Juan Pablo Duarte Street, but the name didn't catch on and it went back to being Marrecas Street. Augusto says he lives nearby and suggests they go to his place.

They walk together, awkwardly. He buys a newspaper at the newsstand across from Álvaro Alvim Street. They head toward the upstairs room above the hat shop by following Senador Dantas Street to Carioca Square, empty and sinister at that hour. The woman stops in front of the bronze lamppost with a clock at its top, decorated with four women, also bronze, with their breasts exposed. She says she wants to see if the clock is working, but as always the clock is stopped. Augusto tells the woman to keep walking so they won't get mugged; on deserted streets it's necessary to walk very fast. No mugger runs after his victim; he has to come close, ask for a cigarette, ask the time. He has to announce the robbery so the robbery can take place. The short stretch of Uruguaiana Street to Sete de Setembro is silent and motionless. The homeless sleeping under marquees have to wake up early and are sleeping peacefully in the doors of shops, wrapped in blankets or newspapers, their heads covered.

Augusto enters the building, stamps his feet, walks with a different step; he always does that when he brings a woman, so the rats will know a stranger is arriving and hide. He doesn't want her to be frightened;

women, for some reason, don't like rats. He knows that, and rats, for some even more mysterious reason, hate women.

Augusto takes the notebook where he writes *The Art of Walking in the Streets of Rio de Janeiro* from the table under the skylight, replacing it with the newspaper he bought. He always uses a just-published newspaper for the first lessons.

"Sit here," he tells the woman.

"Where's the bed?" she says.

"Go on, sit down," he says, sitting in the other chair. "I know how to read; forgive me for lying to you. Do you know what was written on that sign in the bar? Businessman's lunch. They don't sell on credit, that's true, but that wasn't written on the wall. I want to teach you how to read. I'll pay the sum we agreed on."

"Can't you get it up?"

"That's of no concern. What you're going to do here is learn to read."

"It won't work. I've tried already and couldn't do it."

"But I have an infallible method. All you need is a newspaper."

"I can't even spell."

"You're not going to spell. That's the secret of my method. Spot doesn't run. My method is based on a simple premise: no spelling."

"What's that thing up there?"

"A skylight. Let me show you something."

Augusto turns out the light. Gradually a bluish glow penetrates the skylight.

"What's that light?"

"The moon. There's a full moon tonight."

"Damn! I haven't seen the moon for years. Where's the bed?"

"We're going to work." Augusto turns on the lamp.

The girl's name is Kelly, and she will be the twenty-eighth whore whom Augusto has taught to read and write in two weeks by his infallible method.

In the morning, leaving Kelly to sleep in his bed—she asked to spend the night in his room and he slept on a mat on the floor—Augusto goes to Ramalho Ortigão Street, passes beside the Church of São Francisco, and enters Teatro Street, where there is now a new post for the illegal lottery, a guy sitting in a school desk writing on a pad the bets of the poor who never lose hope, and there must be many, the poverty-stricken who don't lose faith, for there is an ever-growing number of such posts throughout the city. Augusto has a destination today, as he does every day when he leaves his place; though he appears to wander, he never walks totally aimlessly. He stops on Teatro Street and looks at the two-story house where his grandmother lived, the upstairs of which is now occupied by a store selling incense, candles, necklaces, cigars, and other macumba materials but which just the other day was a store that sold remnants of cheap fabric. Whenever he passes by there he remembers a relative—his grandmother, his grandfather, three aunts, the husband of an aunt, a cousin. He dedicates this day to the memory of his grandfather, a gray man with a large nose from which he used to pick snot, and who used to make small mechanical toys, birds that sang on perches in cages, a small monkey that opened its mouth and roared like a lion. He tries to remember his grandfather's death and can't, which makes him very nervous. Not that he loved his grandfather; the old man always gave to understand that the toys he built were more important than his grandchildren, but he understood that, thought it reasonable that the old man would prefer the toys and admired his grandfather for tending to his mechanisms day and night. Maybe he didn't even sleep in order to dedicate himself to the task, which was why he was so gray. His grandfather was the person who came closest to the notion of a flesh-and-blood sorcerer and both frightened and attracted him; how could he have forgotten the circumstances of his death? Had he died suddenly? Had he been killed by his grandmother? Had he been buried? Cremated? Or had he simply disappeared?

Augusto looks at the top floor of the building where his grandfather lived, and a bunch of idiots gather around him and look upward too—voodoo followers, buyers of fabric remnants, idlers, messenger boys, beggars, street peddlers, pedestrians in general, some asking "What happened?" and "Did he already jump?"; lately lots of people in downtown have been jumping out of windows from high-rise offices and splattering themselves on the sidewalk.

Augusto, after thinking about his grandfather, continues in the direction of his objective for today, but not in a straight line; in a straight line he should go to Tiradentes Square and along Constitution, which leads almost to the large gate of the place he's going, or along Visconde do Rio Branco, which he usually chooses because of the Fire Department. But he is in no hurry to arrive where he wants to go, and from Teatro Street he goes to Luiz de Camões to make a quick stop at the Portuguese Royal Academy reading room; he insists that this library have his book once it is finished and published. He feels the cozy presence of that vast quantity of books. He leaves immediately for Avenida Passos, not to be confused with Senhor dos Passos Street, arrives at the Tesouro alleyway and heads toward Visconde do Rio Branco by way of Gonçalves Ledo, in the midst of Jewish and Arab merchants, bumping into their poorly dressed customers, and when he gets to Visconde do Rio Branco trades the commerce of clothing for that of second-hand items, but what interests him on Visconde do Rio Branco is the barracks of the Fire Department; not that this was his destination, but he likes to look at the Fire Department building. Augusto stops in front of it; the courtyard inside is full of large red vehicles. The sentry at the door watches him suspiciously. It would be nice if one of those enormous red trucks with its Magirus ladder came out with its siren on. But the large red vehicles don't come out, and Augusto walks a bit further to Vinte de Abril Street and arrives at the gate of the Campo de Santana, across from Caco Square and the Souza Aguiar Hospital.

The Campo de Santana has in its vicinity places that Augusto is in the habit of visiting: the mint where the government used to print money, the archives, the new library, the old college, the former army general headquarters, the railroad. But today he just wants to see the trees, and he enters through one of the gates, passing the one-armed man sitting on a stool behind a tray and selling cigarettes by the unit, the pack sliced in half by a razor, which the one-armed man keeps hidden in a sock held by a rubber band.

As soon as he enters, Augusto goes to the lake; the French sculptures are nearby. The Campo has a long history: Dom Pedro was acclaimed emperor in the Campo de Santana, rebellious troops camped there while they awaited orders to attack, but Augusto thinks only of the trees, the same ones from that far-off time, and strolls among the baobabs, the fig trees, the jackfruit trees displaying their enormous fruit; as always, he feels the urge to kneel before the oldest trees, but getting down on his knees reminds him of the Catholic religion, and he now hates all religions that make people get down on their knees, and he also hates Jesus Christ, from so often hearing priests, pastors, ecclesiastics, businessmen talk about him; the ecumenical movement in the church is the cartelization of the business of superstition, a political non-aggression pact among mafiosi: let's not fight among ourselves because the pie is big enough for everybody.

Augusto is sitting on a bench, beside a man who is wearing a Japanese digital watch on one wrist and a therapeutic metal bracelet on the other. At the man's feet lies a large dog, to which the man directs his words, with measured gestures, looking like a philosophy professor talking to his students in a classroom, or a tutor giving explanations to an inattentive disciple, for the dog appears not to pay great attention to what the man says and merely growls, looking around him with his tongue hanging out. If he were crazy, the man wouldn't be wearing a wristwatch, but a guy who hears answers from a dog that growls with its tongue hanging out, and replies to them, has to be crazy, yet a crazy man doesn't wear a watch; the first thing he, Augusto, would do if he went crazy would be to get rid of his Casio Melody, and he's sure that he's not crazy yet because, besides the watch he carries around on his wrist, he also has a fountain pen in his pocket, and crazy people hate fountain pens. That man sitting beside Augusto, thin, hair combed, clean-shaven, but with groups of pointed hairs showing under his ear and others coming out of his nose, wearing sandals, jeans too big for his legs, with the cuffs rolled up to different lengths, that crazy man is perhaps only half crazy because he appears to have discovered that a dog can be a good psychoanalyst, besides being cheaper and prettier. The dog is tall, with strong jaws, a muscular chest, a melancholy gaze. It is evident that, besides the dog—the conversations are, cumulatively, a sign of madness and of intelligence—sanity, or the man's mental eclecticism, can also be proved by the watch.

"What time is it?" Augusto asks.

"Look at your watch," says the man with the dog, the two of them, man and dog, observing Augusto with curiosity.

"My watch isn't working very well," claims Augusto.

"Ten hours thirty-five minutes and two, three, four, five—"

"Thank you."

"—seconds," the man concludes, consulting the Seiko on his wrist.

"I have to go," Augusto says.

"Don't go yet," says the dog. It wasn't the dog; the man is a ventriloquist, he wants to make me look like a fool, thinks Augusto; it's better for the man to be a ventriloquist, dogs don't talk, and if that one talks, or if he heard the dog talk, it could become a cause for concern, like seeing a flying saucer, for example, and Augusto doesn't want to waste time on matters of that sort.

Augusto pats the dog's head. "I have to go."

He doesn't have to go anywhere. His plan that day is to remain among the trees until closing time, and when the guard starts blowing his whistle he'll hide in the grotto; it irritates him to be able to stay with the trees only from seven in the morning till six in the afternoon. What are the guards afraid will happen at night at the Campo de Santana? Some nocturnal banquet of agoutis, or the use of the grotto as a brothel, or cutting down the trees for lumber, or some such thing? Maybe the guards were right and starving criminals go around eating agoutis, and fucking among the bats and rats in the grotto, and cutting down trees to build shacks.

When he hears the beep of his Casio Melody alerting him, Augusto goes into the farthest point of the grotto, where he remains as motionless as a stone, or rather, a subterranean tree. The grotto is artificial; it was built by another Frenchman, but it has been there so long that it appears real. A loud whistle echoes through the stone walls, making the bats flap their wings and squeal; the guards are ordering people to leave, but no guard comes into the grotto. He remains immobile in the total darkness, and now that the bats have quieted down he hears the delicate little sound of the rats, already used to his harmless presence. His watch plays a rapid jingle, which means an hour has passed. Outside, it is surely nighttime and the guards must have gone, to watch television, to eat; some of them may even have families.

He leaves the grotto along with the bats and rats. He turns off the sound on his Casio Melody. He has never spent an entire night inside the Campo de Santana; he has walked around the Campo at night, looking at the trees longingly through the bars, now painted gray with gold at the top. In the darkness the trees are even more disturbing than in the light, and they allow Augusto, walking slowly under their nocturnal shadows, to commune with them as if he were a bat. He embraces and kisses the trees, something he is embarrassed to do in the light of day in front of other people; some are so large that he can't get his arms around them. Among the trees Augusto feels no irritation, nor hunger, nor headache. Unmoving, stuck in the earth, living in silence, indulging the wind and the birds, indifferent even to their enemies, there they are, the trees, around Augusto, and they fill his head with a perfumed, invisible gas that he senses and that transmits such lightness to his body that if he had the aspiration, and the arrogance of will, he could even try to fly.

When day breaks, Augusto presses one of the buttons on his watch, bringing back the drawing of a small bell on the dial. He hears a beep. Hidden behind a tree, he sees guards opening one of the gates. He looks with affection at the trees one last time, running his hand along the trunks of some of them in farewell.

At the exit is the one-armed man selling one or two cigarettes to guys who don't have the money to buy an entire pack.

He walks down Presidente Vargas cursing the urban planners who took decades to understand that a street as wide as this needed shade and only in recent years planted trees, the same insensitivity that made them plant royal palms along the Mangue canal when it was built, as if the palm were a tree worthy of the name, with a long trunk that neither gives shade nor houses birds and looks like a column of cement. He goes along Andradas as far as Teatro Street and stands once more in front of his grandfather's house. He hopes that someday his grandfather will appear in the doorway, absent-mindedly picking his nose.

When he enters his walk-up on Sete de Setembro, he finds Kelly pacing back and forth under the skylight.

"I looked for coffee and couldn't find any. Don't you have coffee?"

"Why don't you leave and come back tonight, for the lesson?"

"There was a rat, and I threw a book at it but didn't hit it."

"Why did you do that?"

"To kill the rat."

"We start out by killing a rat, then we kill a thief, then a Jew, then a neighborhood child with a large head, then a child in our family with a large head."

"A rat? What's the harm in killing a rat?"

"What about a child with a large head?"

"The world is full of disgusting people. And the more people, the more disgusting ones. Like it was a world of snakes. Are you gonna tell me that snakes aren't disgusting?" Kelly says.

"Snakes aren't disgusting. Why don't you go home and come back tonight for the lesson?"

"Let me stay here till I learn how to read."

"Just for two weeks."

"All right. Will you help me bring my clothes from home?"

"You have all that many clothes?"

"Know what it is? I'm afraid of Rezende. He said he'd slash my face with a razor. I stopped working for him."

"Who's this Rezende?"

"He's the guy who—He's my protector. He's gonna get me the money to put in a tooth and work in the South Zone."

"I didn't think there were any pimps these days."

"A girl can't live by herself."

"Where's your place?"

"Gomes Freire near the corner of Mem de Sá. Know where the supermarket is?"

"Show me."

They walk along Evaristo da Veiga, go underneath the Arches, turn onto Mem de Sá, and immediately find themselves at the building where Kelly lives with Rezende.

Kelly tries to open the door to the apartment, but it's locked from inside. She rings the bell.

A guy in a green T-shirt opens the door saying "Where've you been, you whore?" but draws back when he sees Augusto, gestures with his hand, and says politely, "Please come in."

"Is this Rezende?" Augusto asks.

"I came to get my clothes," says Kelly shyly.

"Go get your clothes while I chat with Rezende," Augusto says.

Kelly steps inside.

"Do I know you?" Rezende asks uncertainly.

"What do you think?" Augusto says.

"I've got a rotten memory," Rezende says.

"That's dangerous," Augusto says.

Neither says anything further. Rezende takes a pack of Continentals from his pocket and offers Augusto a cigarette. Augusto says he doesn't smoke. Rezende lights the cigarette, sees Augusto's mutilated ear and quickly averts his gaze to the interior of the apartment.

Kelly returns with her suitcase.

"Do you have a sharpened razor?" Augusto asks.

"What do I need with a sharpened razor?" Rezende says, laughing like an idiot, avoiding looking at the remains of Augusto's ear.

Augusto and Kelly wait for the elevator to arrive while Rezende smokes, leaning against the apartment door, looking at the floor.

They are in the street. Kelly, seeing the bookie sitting in his school desk, says she's going to place a small bet. "Should I bet on the lamb or the stag?" she asks, laughing. "He didn't do anything because you were with me. He pulled in his horns because he was afraid of you."

"I thought you women were organized and there weren't any more pimps," Augusto says.

"My friend Cleuza invited me to join the Association, but—Five on the stag," she tells the bookie.

"The Whores' Association?"

"The Prostitutes' Association. But then I found out there are three different prostitutes' associations, and I don't know which one to join. My friend Slackmouth told me that organizing criminals is the most complicated thing there is; even crooks who live together in jail have that problem."

They take the same route back, passing under the Arches again, over which a trolley is crossing at that moment.

"Poor man, I was the only thing he had in the world," Kelly says. She's already feeling sorry for the pimp. "He'll have to go back to selling coke and marijuana in the red light district."

On Carioca Street, Kelly repeats that in Augusto's place there's no coffee and that she wants coffee.

"We'll have some coffee in the street," he says.

They stop at a juice bar. They don't have coffee. Kelly wants a coffee with cream and bread and butter. "I know it's hard to find a place that serves coffee with cream and bread and butter, especially toasted," Kelly says.

"There used to be luncheonettes all over the city, where you'd sit down and order: 'Waiter, please bring me right away a nice cup of coffee that hasn't been reheated, some bread straight from the oven and butter by the ton'—do you know the song by Noel?"

"Noel? Before my time. Sorry," says Kelly.

"I just meant that there were an endless number of luncheonettes all over downtown. And you used to sit down, not eat standing up like us here, and there was a marble-top table where you could doodle while you waited for someone, and when the person arrived you could look at her face while you talked."

"Aren't we talking? Aren't you looking at me? Doodle on this napkin."

"I'm looking at you. But I have to turn my head. We aren't sitting in chairs. This paper napkin blots when you write on it. You don't understand."

They have a hamburger with orange juice.

"I'm going to take you to Avenida Rio Branco."

"I'm already familiar with Avenida Rio Branco."

"I'm going to show you three buildings that haven't been demolished. Did I show you the photo of how the avenue used to be?"

"I'm not interested in old stuff. Cut it out."

Kelly refuses to go see the old buildings, but since she likes children she agrees to visit little Marcela, eight months old, daughter of Marcelo and Ana Paula.

They're on Sete de Setembro, and so they walk to the corner of Carmo, where, on the sidewalk under the marquee, in cardboard shacks, the Gonçalves family lives. Ana Paula is white, as Marcelo is white, and they are just satellites of the family of blacks who control that corner. Ana Paula is nursing little Marcela. As it is Saturday, Ana Paula was able to set up the small cardboard shack in which she lives with her husband and their daughter under the marquee of the Banco Mercantil do Brasil. The board that serves as wall, some five feet in height, the highest side of the shack, was taken from an abandoned subway construction site. On weekdays the shack is dismantled, the large sheets of cardboard and the board from the subway excavation are leaned against the wall during work hours, and only at night is Marcelo's shack, and the Gonçalves family's cardboard shacks, reassembled so that Marcelo, Ana Paula, and little Marcela and the twelve members of the family can go inside them to sleep. But today is Saturday; on Saturdays and Sundays the Banco Mercantil do Brasil doesn't open, and Marcelo and Ana Paula's shack, a cardboard box used to house a large refrigerator, has not been disassembled, and Ana Paula luxuriates in that comfort.

It is ten in the morning and the sun casts luminous rays between the black, opaque monolith of the Cândido Mendes skyscraper and the turret of the church with the image of Our Lady of Carmona, she standing up as Our Ladies usually do, a circle of iron, or copper, over her head pretending to be a halo. Ana Paula is giving the naked girl a sunbath; she has already changed her diaper, washed the dirty one in a bucket of water she got from a chicken restaurant, hung it on a wire clothesline that she puts up only on weekends by attaching one end to an iron post with a metal sign that reads *TurisRio—9 parking places* and another to an iron post with an advertising sign. Besides the diapers, Augusto sees Bermudas, T-shirts, jeans, and pieces of clothing that he can't identify, out of consideration, so as not to appear nosey.

Kelly remains on the corner, unwilling to approach the small shack where Ana Paula is taking care of Marcela. Ana Paula has gentle eyes, has a narrow, calm face, delicate gestures, slim arms, a very pretty mouth, despite the cavities in her front teeth.

"Kelly, come see what a pretty baby Marcelinha is," Augusto says.

At that instant, Benevides, the head of the clan, a black man who's always drunk, comes out from one of the cardboard boxes, followed by the two adolescents Zé Ricardo and Alexandre, the latter the most likable of them all, and also Dona Tina, the matriarch, accompanied by some eight children. There used to be twelve minors in the family, but four had left and no one knew of their whereabouts; they were known to be part of a juvenile gang that operated in the city's South Zone, acting in large bands to rob the elegant stores, well-dressed people, tourists, and on Sundays the patsies tanning on the beach.

One of the children asks Augusto for money and gets a cuff from Benevides.

"We're not beggars, you brat."

"It wasn't charity," says Augusto.

"The other day some guy came by saying he was organizing beggars in a group called Beggars United. I told him to shove it. We're no beggars."

"Who is the guy? Where does he hang out?"

"On Jogo da Bola Street."

"How do you get to that street?"

"From here? You go in a straight line to Candelária Church, once you're there you take Rio Branco, from there you go to Visconde de Inhaúma Street, picking it up on the left side, go to Santa Rita Square where it ends and Marechal Floriano starts, that's Larga Street, and you go down Larga until you come to Andradas, on the right-hand side, cross Leandro Martins, get onto Júlia Lopes de Almeida, go left to Conceição Street, follow it till Senador Pompeu, take a right onto Colonel something-or-other, and stay to the right till you get to Jogo da Bola Street. Ask for him, his name's Chicken Zé. A black guy with green eyes, all the time surrounded by suck-ups. He's gonna end up on the city council."

"Thanks, Benevides. How's business?"

"We've hauled in twenty tons of paper this month," says Alexandre.

"Shut up," says Benevides.

A truck comes by periodically to pick up the paper that's been collected. Today it came early and took away everything.

Dona Tina says something that Augusto doesn't understand.

"Shit, ma, keep your mouth shut. Shit," shouts Benevides, furious.

His mother moves away and goes to put some pans over a dismountable stove made of bricks, in the Banco Mercantil's doorway. Ricardo combs his thick hair using a comb with long steel teeth.

"Who's the babe?" Benevides points to Kelly, in the distance, at the street corner. Kelly looks like a princess of Monaco, in the midst of the Gonçalves family.

"A friend of mine."

"Why doesn't she come any closer?"

"She must be afraid of you, of your shouts."

"I have to shout. I'm the only one here with a head on his shoulders . . . Sometimes I'm even suspicious of you . . ."

"That's silly."

"At first I thought you were from the police. Then from the Leo XIII, then somebody from the bank, but the manager's a good guy and knows we're workers and wouldn't send some spy to rat on us. We've been here for two years, and I plan to die here, which may not be that long, 'cause I've got this pain in the side of my belly . . . You know this bank's never been robbed? Only one in the whole area."

"Your presence keeps robbers away."

"I'm suspicious of you."

"Don't waste your time on that."

"What do you want here? Last Saturday you didn't want to have some soup with us."

"I told you. I want to talk. And you only have to tell me what you want to. And I only like green-colored soups, and your soups are yellow."

"It's the squash," says Dona Tina, who is listening to the conversation.

"Shut up, ma. Look here, man, the city's not the same anymore. There's too many people, too many beggars in the city, picking up paper, fighting with us over territory, a whole lot of people living under overhangs; we're all the time throwing out bums from outside, and there's even fake beggars fighting us for our paper. All the paper thrown away on this part of Cândido Mendes is mine, but there's guys trying to grab it."

Benevides says that the man on the truck pays more for white paper than for newsprint or scrap paper, dirty paper, colored paper, torn paper. The paper he collects on Cândido Mendes is white. "There's a lot of continuous computer forms, reports, things like that."

"What about glass? It can also be recycled. Have you thought about selling bottles?"

"Bottle men have to be Portuguese. We're black. And bottles are giving out, everything's plastic. The only bottle man who works these parts is Mané da Boina, and he came by the other day to have some soup with us. He eats yellow soup. He's in deep shit."

Kelly spreads her arms, displays an impatient expression, at the corner across the street. Augusto says good-bye, embracing everyone. Benevides pulls Augusto to his naked torso, bringing his alcoholic mouth close to the other man's, and looks at him closely, curiously, shrewdly. "They're saying there's going to be a big convention of foreigners and that they're going to try to hide us from the gringos. I don't want to leave here," he murmurs menacingly. "I live beside a bank, there's safety, no crazy man's going try to set us on fire like they did with Maílson, behind the museum. And I've been here for two years, which means nobody's going to try and mess with our home; it's part of the atmosphere, you understand?" Augusto, who was born and raised in the downtown area, although in a more lustrous era when the stores' facades sported their names in glowing twisted glass tubes filled with red, blue, and green gases, understands completely what Benevides is telling him with his endless embrace; he too wouldn't leave downtown for anything, and he nods, involuntarily brushing his face against the face of the black man. When they finally separate, Augusto manages to slip the clever little black boy a bill, without Benevides seeing it. He goes to Ana Paula and says good-bye to her, to Marcelo and to little Marcela, who is now wearing a pair of floral-patterned overalls.

"Let's go," says Augusto, taking Kelly by the arm. Kelly pulls her arm away. "Don't touch me; those beggars probably have the mange. You'll have to take a bath before going to bed with me."

They walk to the used-book store behind the Carmo church, while Kelly spins her theory that beggars, in hot places like Rio, where they walk around half-naked, are even poorer; a shirtless beggar, wearing old, dirty, torn pants that show a piece of his butt is more of a beggar than a beggar in a cold place dressed in rags. She saw beggars when she went to São Paulo one winter, and they were wearing wool overcoats and caps; they had a decent look to them.

"In cold places beggars freeze to death on the streets," Augusto says.

"Too bad that heat doesn't kill them too," Kelly says.

Whores don't like beggars, Augusto knows.

"The difference between a beggar and others," Kelly continues, "is that when he's naked a beggar doesn't stop looking like a beggar, and when others are naked they stop looking like what they are."

They arrive at the used-book shop. Kelly looks at it from the street, suspicious. The shelves inside are crammed with books. "Are there enough people in the world to read so many books?"

Augusto wants to buy a book for Kelly, but she refuses to go into the bookstore. They go to São José Street, from there to Graça Aranha Street, Avenida Beira Mar, the Obelisk, the Public Promenade.

"I used to work the streets here, and I've never been inside this place," Kelly says.

Augusto points out the trees to Kelly, says that they're over two hundred years old, speaks of Master Valentim, but she's not interested and only comes out of her boredom when Augusto, from the small bridge over the pond, at the opposite side from the entrance on Passeio Street, at the other end where the terrace with the statue of the boy, now made of bronze, when Augusto, from the small bridge spits in the water for the small fishes to eat his spittle. Kelly finds it funny and spits too, but she quickly gets bored because the fish seem to prefer Augusto's spit.

"I'm hungry," Kelly says.

"I promised to have lunch with the old man," Augusto says.

"Then let's go get him."

They go up Senador Dantas, where Kelly also worked the streets, and come to Carioca Square. There the portable tables of the street vendors are in greater number. The main commercial streets are clogged with tables filled with merchandise, some of it contraband and some of it pseudo-contraband, famous brands crudely counterfeited in small clandestine factories. Kelly stops before one of the tables, examines everything, asks the price of the transistor radios, the battery-driven toys, the pocket calculators, the cosmetics, a set of plastic dominoes that imitate ivory, the colored pencils, the pens, the blank videotapes and cassettes, the coffee strainer, the penknives, the decks of cards, the watches and other trinkets.

"Let's go, the old man is waiting," Augusto says.

"Cheap crap," Kelly says.

At his walk-up, Augusto convinces the old man to comb his hair and to replace his slippers with one-piece high-lace boots with elastic on the sides and straps at the back for pulling them on, an old model but still in good condition. The old man is going out with them because Augusto promised they'd have lunch at the Timpanas, on São José, and the old man once courted an unforgettable girl who lived in a building next to the restaurant, built in the early nineteen hundreds, and which still has, intact, wrought-iron balconies, tympanums, and cymas decorated with stucco.

The old man takes the lead with a firm step.

"I don't want to walk too fast. They say it causes varicose veins," protests Kelly, who in reality wants to walk slowly to examine the street vendors' tables.

When they arrive in front of the Timpanas, the old man contemplates the ancient buildings lined up to the corner of Rodrigo Silva Street. "It's all going to be torn down," he says. "You two go on in, I'll be along shortly; order rice and peas for me."

Kelly and Augusto sit at a table covered with a white tablecloth. They order a fish stew for two and rice with peas for the old man. The Timpanas is a restaurant that prepares dishes to the customer's specifications.

"Why don't you hug me the way you did that dirty black guy?" Kelly asks.

Augusto doesn't want to argue. He gets up to look for the old man.

The old man is looking at the buildings, quite absorbed, leaning against an iron fence that surrounds the old Buraco do Lume, which after it was closed off became a patch of grass with a few trees, where a few beggars live.

"Your rice is ready," Augusto says.

"You see that balcony there, in that blue two-story building? The three windows on the second floor? It was in that window to our right that I saw her for the first time, leaning on the balcony, her elbows resting on a pillow with red embroidery."

"Your rice is on the table. It has to be eaten as soon as it comes from the stove."

Augusto takes the old man by the arm, and they go into the restaurant.

"She was very pretty. I never again saw such a pretty girl."

"Eat your rice, it's getting cold," Augusto says.

"She limped on one leg. That wasn't important to me. But it was important to her."

"It's always like that," Kelly says.

"You're right," the old man says.

"Eat your rice, it's getting cold."

"The women of the oldest profession possess a sinuous wisdom. You gave me momentary comfort by mentioning the inexorability of things," the old man says.

"Thanks," Kelly says.

"Eat your rice, it's getting cold."

"It's all going to be torn down," the old man says.

"Did it used to be better?" Augusto asks.

"Yes."

"Why?"

"In the old days there were fewer people and almost no automobiles."

"The horses, filling the streets with manure, must have been considered a curse equal to today's cars," Augusto says.

"And people in the old days were less stupid," the old man continues with a melancholy gaze, "and not in such a hurry."

"People in those days were more innocent," Kelly says.

"And more hopeful. Hope is a kind of liberation," the old man says.

Meanwhile, Raimundo, the pastor, called by his bishop to the world headquarters of the Church of Jesus Savior of Souls, on Avenida Suburbana, listens contritely to the words of the supreme head of his Church.

"Each pastor is responsible for the temple in which he works. Your collection has been very small. Do you know how much Pastor Marcos, in Nova Iguaçu, collected last month? Over ten thousand dollars. Our Church needs money. Jesus needs money; he always has. Did you know that Jesus had a treasurer, Judas Iscariot?"

Pastor Marcos, of Nova Iguaçu, was the inventor of the Offerings Envelope. The envelopes have the name of the Church of Jesus Savior of Souls printed on them, the phrase *I request prayers for these people,* followed by five lines for the petitioner to write the people's names, a square with $ in large type, and the category of the offering. The SPECIAL prayers, with larger quantities, are light green; the REGULAR are brown, and in them only two prayers can be requested. Other churches copied the Envelope, which greatly annoyed the bishop.

"The devil has been coming to my church," Raimundo says, "and since he starting going to my church the faithful aren't making their offerings, or even paying the tithe."

"Lucifer?" The bishop looks at him, a look that Raimundo would like to be one of admiration; probably the bishop has never seen the devil personally. But the bishop is inscrutable. "What disguise is he using?"

"He wears dark glasses, he's missing one ear, and he sits in the pews at the back, and one day, the second time he appeared at the temple, there was a yellow aura around him." The bishop must know that the devil can take any appearance he wants, like a black dog or a man in dark glasses and missing one ear.

"Did anyone else see this yellow light?"

"No, sir."

"Any special smell?"

"No, sir."

The bishop meditates for some time.

"And after he appeared, the faithful stopped tithing? You're sure it was—"

"Yes, it was after he showed up. The faithful say they don't have any money, that they lost their job, or they're sick, or they were robbed."

"And you believe they're telling the truth. What about jewels? Don't any of them have jewels? A gold wedding ring?"

"They're telling the truth. Can we ask for jewels?"

"Why not? They're for Jesus."

The bishop's face is unreadable.

"The devil hasn't been there lately. I've been looking for him. I'm not afraid; he's walking around the city and I'm going to find him," Raimundo says.

"And when you find him, what do you plan to do?"

"If the bishop could enlighten me with his counsel . . ."

"You have to discover for yourself, in the sacred books, what you must do. Sylvester II made a pact with the devil, to achieve the Papacy and wisdom. Whenever the devil appears, it's always to make a pact. Lucifer appeared to you, not to me. But remember, if the devil outsmarts you, it means you're not a good pastor."

"All good comes from God and all evil from the Devil," Raimundo says.

"Yes, yes," the bishop says with a bored sigh.

"But good can overcome evil."

"Yes," another sigh.

The lunch at the Timpanas continues. The old man speaks of the Ideal Cinema, on Carioca Street.

"The Ideal was on one side on the street, the Iris Cinema on the other. The Iris is still there. Now it shows pornographic films."

"It may become a church," Augusto says.

"At the night showings the Iris's ceiling would open and let in the evening cool. You could see the stars in the sky," the old man says.

"Only crazy people go to the movies to see stars," Kelly says.

"How did the ceiling open?" Augusto asks.

"A very advanced engineering system for the time. Pulleys, pulleys . . . Rui Barbosa always used to go there, and sometimes I sat near him."

"You sat near him?"

The old man notes a certain incredulity in Augusto's voice. "What do you think? Rui Barbosa died just the other day, in 1923."

"My mother was born in 1950," Kelly says. "She's an old woman who's falling apart."

"For a long time, after Rui died, and until the theater became a shoe store, his seat was separated by a velvet rope and there was a plaque saying *This seat was occupied by Senator Rui Barbosa.* I voted for him for president, twice, but Brazilians always elect the wrong presidents."

"The theater became a shoe store?"

"If Rui were alive, he wouldn't let them do that. The two facades, one of stone and the other of marble, and the glass marquee, a glass just like that in my skylight, are still there, but inside there's nothing but piles of cheap shoes; it's enough to break your heart," says the old man.

"Shall we go there?" Augusto suggests to Kelly.

"I'm not going anywhere with you to see fountains, buildings falling to pieces and disgusting trees until you stop and listen to my life story. He doesn't want to listen to the story of my life. But he listens to the story of everybody else's life."

"Why don't you want to hear the story of her life?" the old man asks.

"Because I've already heard the life stories of twenty-seven whores, and they're all the same."

"That's not the way to treat a girlfriend," the old man says.

"She's not my girlfriend. She's someone I'm teaching to read and speak."

"If she'd put in a front tooth, she might even be pretty," says the old man.

"Why put in a tooth? I'm not going to be a whore anymore. I've given it up."

"What are you going to do?"

"I'm still thinking about it."

On Monday, regretting having treated Kelly badly, even more so in light of the fact that she is learning to read with great rapidity, Augusto leaves his lodgings to go to Tiradentes Square to buy a semiprecious stone in the rough to give her as a gift. He has a friend, who goes by the false name Mojica, who buys and sells these stones and lives in the Hotel Rio on Silva Jardim and can give him a good price. Mojica, before establishing himself as a seller of stones, earned his living as a bagger of fat women, a specialty of lazy gigolos.

On Uruguaiana, hundreds of street vendors, prohibited by City Hall from setting up their stalls and assisted by unemployed youths and other passersby, plunder and sack the stores. Some security guards hired by the stores shoot into the air. The noise of broken store windows and of steel doors being battered down mixes with the screams of women running through the street. Augusto turns onto Ramalho Ortigão and takes Carioca in the direction of Tiradentes Square. The weather is overcast and it's threatening to rain. He is almost at Silva Jardim when Pastor Raimundo appears unexpectedly in front of him.

"You disappeared," says Pastor Raimundo, his voice tremulous.

"I've been very busy. Writing a book," Augusto says.

"Writing a book . . . You're writing a book . . . Can I ask about the subject?"

"No. Sorry," says Augusto.

"I don't know your name. May I ask your name?"

"Augusto. Epifânio."

At that moment it starts to thunder and a heavy rain begins to fall.

"What do you want from me? A pact?"

"I went into your theater by chance, because of some selenium capsules."

"Selenium capsules," says the pastor, paling even more. Wasn't selenium one of the elements used by the devil? He can't remember.

"Good-bye," says Augusto. Standing in the rain doesn't bother him, but the ex-bagger of fat women is waiting for him.

The pastor grabs Augusto by the arm, in a flight of courage. "Is it a pact? Is it a pact?" He staggers as if about to faint, opens his arms, and doesn't fall to the ground only because Augusto holds him up. Recovering his strength, the pastor frees himself from Augusto's arms, yelling "Let me go, let me go, this is too much."

Augusto disappears, entering the Hotel Rio. Raimundo shakes convulsively and falls in a faint. He lies for some time with his face in the gutter, wetted by the heavy rain, white foam coming out of the corner of his mouth, without attracting the attention of charitable souls, the police, or passersby in general. Finally, the water running in the gutter rises over his face and brings him back to consciousness; Raimundo gathers the strength to stand and walk unsteadily in search of the devil; he crosses the square, then Visconde do Rio Branco, proceeds staggeringly between the jobless musicians who meet at the corner of Avenida Passos under the marquee of the Café Capital, across from the João Caetano Theater; he passes the door of the church of Our Lady of Lampadosa, smells the odor of candles being burned inside there and crosses the street to the side where the theater is, running to avoid the automobiles; all over the city automobiles hit one another in the search for space to move in, and they run over slower or careless pedestrians. Dizzy, Raimundo leans against the base of a bronze statue of a short, fat man covered with pigeon crap, wearing a Greek skirt and Greek sandals and holding a sword, in front of the theater; beside it, a vendor selling undershorts and rulers pretends not to see his suffering. Raimundo turns left onto Alexandre Herculano, a small street with only one door, the back door of the School of Philosophy that appears never to be used, and finally enters a luncheonette on Conceição where he has a glass of guava juice and mulls over his unspeakable encounter. He has discovered the name behind which Satan is hiding, Augusto Epifânio. Augusto: magnificent, majestic; Epifânio: originating in a divine manifestation. Ha! He could expect nothing from Beelzebub less than pride and mockery. And if the one who calls himself Augusto Epifânio is not the Evil One himself, he is at least a partner in his iniquity. He remembers Exodus 22:18: "Thou shalt not suffer a witch to live."

The thunder and lightning begins again.

Mojica, the ex-bagger of fat women, tells Augusto that business isn't very good; the crisis has hit him too, and he's even thinking of going back to his old business; for reasons he can't explain, there's been an increase in the city in the number of middle-aged women with money wanting to marry a thin, muscular man with a big prick like him. Fat women are gullible, have good temperaments, are almost always cast aside, and they're easy to deceive. "One a year is enough for yours truly to lead a comfortable life; and it's a big city."

From Tiradentes Square, ignoring part of Benevides's instructions, Augusto goes to Jogo da Bola Street, taking Avenida Passos to Presidente Vargas. Crossing Presidente Vargas, even at the traffic light, is always dangerous; people are constantly getting killed crossing that street, and Augusto waits for the right moment and crosses it by running between the automobiles speeding past in both directions and makes it to the other side panting but with the euphoric sensation of one who has achieved a feat; he rests for a few minutes before proceeding to his right to Andradas and from there to Júlia Lopes de Almeida Street, from which he sees Conceição Hill and quickly comes to Tenente Coronel Julião, then walks a few yards and finally finds Jogo da Bola.

"Where can I find Chicken Zé?" he asks a man in Bermudas, Hawaiian sandals and a T-shirt with a three-strand gold chain wrapped around his neck, but the man looks at Augusto with an ugly expression, doesn't answer, and walks away. Further ahead, Augusto sees a boy. "Where can I find the boss of the beggars?" he asks, and the boy replies, "You got any change for me?" Augusto gives the boy some money. "I don't know who you mean. Go to the corner of Major Valô Square, there's people there who can tell you."

At the corner of Major Valô Square are a few men, and Augusto heads toward them. As he approaches, he notices that the man in Bermudas with the three-strand gold chain is in the group. "Hello," Augusto says, and no one answers. A large black man without a shirt asks, "Who was it said my name is Chicken Zé?"

Augusto senses that he is unwelcome. One of the men has a club in his hand.

"It was Benevides, who lives on Carmo, corner of Sete de Setembro."

"That lush is a sell-out, happy to be living in a cardboard box, grateful to be picking up paper in the street and sell it to the sharks. People like that don't support our movement."

"Somebody needs to teach the fucker a lesson," says the man with the club, and Augusto is uncertain whether he or Benevides is the fucker.

"He said you're president of the Beggars Union."

"And who're you?"

"I'm writing a book called *The Art of Walking in the Streets of Rio de Janeiro.*"

"Show me the book," says the guy with the gold chain.

"It's not with me; it's not ready."

"What's your name?"

"Aug—Epifânio."

"What the shit kind of name is that?"

"Search him," says Chicken Zé.

Augusto allows himself to be searched by the man with the club. The latter gives Chicken Zé Augusto's pen, his ID card, his money, the small pad of paper, and the semiprecious stone in a small cloth sack that Augusto received from the bagger of fat women.

"This guy's nuts," says an old black man observing the goings on.

Chicken Zé takes Augusto by the arm. He says: "I'm going to have a talk with him."

The two walk to the Escada da Conceição alleyway.

"Look here, Mr. Fancy, first of all, my name isn't Chicken Zé, it's Zumbi from Jogo da Bola, you understand? And second, I'm not president of any fucking Beggars Union; that's crap put out by the opposition. Our name is the Union of the Homeless and Shirtless, the UHS. We don't ask for handouts, we don't want handouts, we demand what they took from us. We don't hide under bridges or inside cardboard boxes like that fucker Benevides, and we don't sell gum and lemons at intersections."

"Correct," says Augusto.

"We want to be seen, we want them to look at our ugliness, our dirtiness, want them to smell our bodies everywhere; want them to watch us making our food, sleeping, fucking, shitting in the pretty places where the well-off stroll and live. I gave orders for the men not to shave, for the men and women and children not to bathe in the fountains; the fountains are for pissing and shitting in. We have to stink and turn people's stomachs like a pile of garbage in the middle of the street. And nobody asks for money. It's better to rob than to panhandle."

"Aren't you afraid of the police?"

"The police don't have any place to put us; the jails are full and there are lots of us. They arrest us and have to let us go. And we stink too bad for them to want to beat up on us. They take us off the streets, and we come back. And if they kill one of us, and I think that's going to happen any time now, and it's even a good thing if it does happen, we'll get the body and parade the carcass through the streets like Lampião's head."

"Do you know how to read?"

"If I didn't know how to read, I'd be living happily in a cardboard box picking up other people's leavings."

"Where do you get the resources for that association of yours?"

"The talk's over, Epifânio. Remember my name, Zumbi from Jogo da Bola; sooner or later you're going to hear about me, and it won't be from that shitass Benevides. Take your things and get out of here."

Augusto returns to his walkup on Sete de Setembro by going down Escada da Conceição to Major Valô Square. He takes João Homem to Liceu, where there's a place called the Tourist House, from there to Acre Street, then to Uruguaiana. Uruguaiana is occupied by police shock troops carrying shields, helmets with visors, batons, machine guns, tear gas. The stores are closed.

Kelly is reading the part of the newspaper marked by Augusto as homework.

"This is for you," Augusto says.

"No, thank you. You think I'm some kind of performing dog? I'm learning to read because I want to. I don't need little presents."

"Take it, it's an amethyst."

Kelly takes the stone and throws it with all her strength. The stone hits against the skylight and falls to the floor. Kelly kicks the chair, wads the newspaper into a ball, which she throws at Augusto. Other whores had done things even worse; they have attacks of nerves when they spend a lot of time alone with a guy and he doesn't want to go to bed with them. One of them tried to take Augusto by force and bit off his entire ear, which she spat into the toilet and flushed.

"Are you crazy? You could break the skylight. It's over a hundred years old. The old man would die of a broken heart."

"You think I've got the clap, or AIDS, is that it?"

"No."

"You want to go to the doctor with me for him to examine me? You'll see I don't have any kind of disease."

Kelly is almost crying, and her grimace reveals her missing tooth, which gives her an unprotected, suffering air, which reminds him of the teeth he, Augusto, doesn't have and awakens in him a fraternal and uncomfortable pity, for her and for himself.

"You don't want to go to bed with me, you don't want to hear the story of my life, I do everything for you, I've learned to read, I treat your rats well, I even hugged a tree in the Public Promenade, and you don't even have one ear, and I never mentioned that you don't have one ear so as not to annoy you."

"I was the one who hugged the tree."

"Don't you feel like doing it?" she yells.

"I don't have desire, or hope, or faith, or fear. That's why no one can harm me. To the contrary of what the old man said, the lack of hope has liberated me."

"I hate you!"

"Don't yell, you're going to wake the old man."

The old man lives in the rear of the store, downstairs.

"How am I going to wake him up if he doesn't sleep?"

"I don't like to see you yelling."

"I'm yelling! I'm yelling!"

Augusto embraces Kelly and she sobs, her face against his chest. Kelly's tears wet Augusto's shirt.

"Why don't you take me to the Santo Antônio Convent? Please, take me to the Santo Antônio Convent."

Saint Anthony is considered a saint for those seeking marriage. On Tuesdays the convent is filled with single women of all ages making vows to the saint. It's a very good day for beggars, as the women, after praying to the saint, always give alms to the poor petitioners, and the saint may notice that act of charity and decide in favor of their petition.

Augusto doesn't know what to do with Kelly. He says he's going to the store to talk with the old man.

The old man is lying in bed in the small room at the rear of the store. The bed is so narrow that he doesn't fall out of it only because he never sleeps.

"May I speak with you a bit?"

The old man sits up in bed. He motions for Augusto to sit beside him.

"Why do people want to go on living?"

"You want to know why I want to go on living, as old as I am?"

"No, all people."

"Why do *you* want to go on living?" the old man asks.

"I like trees. I want to finish writing my book. But sometimes I think about killing myself. Tonight Kelly hugged me, crying, and I felt the urge to die."

"You want to die so as to put an end to other people's suffering? Not even Christ managed that."

"Don't talk to me of Christ," Augusto says.

"I stay alive because I don't have a lot of pains in my body and I enjoy eating. And I have good memories. I'd also stay alive if I didn't have any memories at all," says the old man.

"What about hope?"

"In reality hope only liberates the young."

"But at the Timpanas you said—"

"That hope is a kind of liberation . . . But you have to be young to take advantage of it."

Augusto climbs the stairs back to his walkup.

"I gave the rats some cheese," Kelly says.

"Do you have some good memory of your life?" Augusto asks.

"No, my memories are all horrible."

"I'm going out," Augusto says.

"Will you be back?" Kelly asks.

Augusto says he's going to walk in the streets. Solvitur ambulando.

On Rosário Street, empty, since it's nighttime, near the flower market, he sees a guy destroying a public telephone; it's not the first time he's run into that individual. Augusto doesn't like to interfere in other people's lives, which is the only way to walk in the streets in the late hours, but Augusto doesn't like the destroyer of public phones. Not because he cares about the phones—since he left the water and sewerage department he has never once spoken on a telephone—but because he doesn't like the guy's face; he shouts "Cut that shit out," and the vandal runs off in the direction of Monte Castelo Square.

Now Augusto is on Ouvidor, heading toward Mercado Street, where there's no more market at all; there used to be one, a monumental iron structure painted green, but it was torn down, and they left only a tower. Ouvidor, which by day is so crammed with people that one can't walk without bumping into others, is deserted. Augusto walks along the odd-numbered side of the street, and two guys come toward him from the opposite direction, on the same side of the street, some two hundred yards away. Augusto quickens his pace. At night it's not enough to walk fast in the street, it's also necessary to avoid having the path blocked, and so he crosses over to the even-numbered side. The two guys cross to the even-numbered side, and Augusto returns to the odd-numbered side. Some of the stores have security guards, but the guards aren't stupid enough to get involved in someone else's mugging. Now the guys separate, and one comes down the even-numbered side and the other down the odd-numbered side. Augusto continues walking, faster, toward the guy on the even side, who hasn't increased the speed of his steps and seems even to have slowed his pace a little, a thin guy, unshaven, designer shirt and dirty sneakers, who exchanges a look with his partner on the other side, somewhat surprised at the speed of Augusto's steps. When Augusto is about five yards from the man on the even-numbered side, the guy on the odd-numbered side crosses the street and joins his accomplice. They both stop. Augusto comes closer and, when he is slightly more than a yard from the men, crosses to the even-numbered side and continues ahead at the same speed. "Hey!" one of the guys says. But Augusto keeps on going without turning his head, his good ear attuned to the sound of footsteps behind him; by the sound he can tell if his pursuers are walking or running after him. When he gets to the Pharoux pier, he looks back and sees no one.

His Casio Melody plays Haydn's three a.m. music; it's time to write his book, but he doesn't want to go home and face Kelly. Solvitur ambulando. He goes to the Mineiros pier, walks to the boat moorings at Quinze Square, listening to the sea beat against the stone wall.

He waits for day to break, standing at dockside. The ocean waters reek. The tide rises and falls as it meets the sea wall, causing a sound that seems like a sigh, or a moan. It's Sunday; the day comes forth gray. On Sunday the majority of restaurants downtown don't open; like all Sundays, today will be a bad day for the poor who live on the remains of discarded food.

belle

"THE WALTHER'S HOT, IF THEY CATCH YOU WITH IT, it'll spill over to us. After you do the job, throw it away, in the ocean or the lake."

"Leave it to me," I said.

The Dispatcher went on. "Remember the Glock and the shit storm it caused?" As if I could forget the black guy who pretended he was living in the rocks with the cockroaches but wasn't one of us, and smelled of scented soap and wore a fancy watch and when he stuck his hand in his waistband to pull out the piece, I shot him in the head and took his weapon, a Glock 18, automatic, a beauty, the best thing to ever come out of Austria. But it was hot, and when they caught me with it, they worked me over and broke two teeth here in front, crippled my right hand. They wanted me to confess to killing the black guy and said they'd go easy on me if I told them who'd hired me, but I didn't open my trap and didn't confess to a goddamn thing.

"You didn't know who ordered it."

"By the victim, you suspect who's behind it. It's simple. Want me to say his name? Don't fuck with me, old pal, look at my false teeth, my gimpy hand. I knew, I was tortured, and I didn't rat anyone out."

"They broke the wrong hand," said the Dispatcher. "If they knew you were a lefty . . ."

I walked away with the fool still talking to himself. I went to the hotel where the customer was staying—that was the name, *customer,* we used for the guy who was going to be hit. I called my girlfriend to be beside me at the door.

I don't enjoy popping anybody, but it's my job. The Dispatcher told me one day he read in a book that a man just needs two things, fucking and working, but all I needed was fucking; work is for shit. But I use a disguise: to everyone I'm a vendor of computer products, and I always carry around a small leather briefcase full of brochures.

Before we went to the hotel, my girlfriend arrived at my apartment and took off her clothes and her white body filled the darkened room with light and I looked at her ass to see if it had any marks from her bikini or the sun. She knew if she showed the least hint of suntan I'd beat the hell out of her, but her ass was whiter than an ambulance.

Her name was Belinha, she was eighteen, she liked me because I was an outlaw, and because she knew my hard-on was for real. She despised those guys who take pills to get it up, said she couldn't love a man who faked it like that. And she sucked my cock and I made her get on her knees on the bed and I sucked her pussy; she got off on being sucked like that. I would stick my tongue in there, and sometimes she'd ask me to put my nose in. Her pussy was fragrant and I would stick my nose in. I forgot to say that besides a large cock, I also have a large nose. Then I'd ram my cock in and she would come; that was the beginning.

She didn't know the kind of work I did, she thought it was something to do with smuggling or drugs and asked to see my tools and said she liked being an outlaw's girl, but I couldn't explain my job to her; I myself didn't really know what was behind it all. The Dispatcher would call me and say he had a job and give me the file on the customer, sometimes it was some important guy whose name was in the newspapers. I've even done foreigners. I was well paid, trustworthy, proof of which were the false teeth in my mouth, the scar on my face, and my busted right hand with fingers bent like thick pieces of wire.

My girlfriend came from an important family rolling in dough, was educated in the finest schools, and spoke French. She called herself Belinha or Isabel or Isabella or Belle. I preferred Belle because she was the most beautiful girl in the world. We were in my apartment waiting for the time to go to the hotel where I was going to meet the customer. Lying in bed after fucking, she said, "Explain that stuff about pistols and revolvers, the difference." I said that in a revolver the bullets are in a cylinder we call a drum, each cartridge has its own ignition chamber, and after each shot the cylinder rotates, bringing a new cartridge into alignment with the barrel. There are six-cartridge drums, the most common, and nine-cartridge, depending on the size of the revolver. A pistol, like the Walther semiautomatic P99, has a clip with cartridges that slides into the handle, and after each shot the empty cartridge is ejected and a new cartridge is loaded from the clip and placed in position for firing.

She also wanted to know why I used a pistol and not a revolver, so I explained, while she held the Walther as if it were a dead rat, that pistols were smaller, lighter, and more reliable, and besides, a pistol allowed the use of a silencer. "This fucker screwed into the barrel of the pistol is the silencer. There's no such thing as silencers for revolvers—I mean, there is, but they're bulky mothers that enclose the drum and make the weapon too heavy. Nobody uses them, they're a museum piece."

She also asked what I felt when I snuffed a guy, and I answered I didn't think about anything, just like a soldier in war. The difference is that I didn't win a medal when I killed the enemy.

I put on a coat, and she dressed in some high-class women's clothes, and we went to the customer's hotel and waited in the lobby for the guy to arrive. Belle was an elegant girl when it came to dressing, sitting, speaking. Anyone who looked at her would say: This is a well-born girl from a good family. That's why I told her I'd beat the hell out of her if she got a tattoo like she'd been talking about doing.

My appearance is nondescript: I'm a thin guy with a big nose, an inoffensive look, hair starting to go gray. Wearing that dark suit I looked like an insurance salesman. The Dispatcher had told me the customer was going to a meeting away from the hotel and should be back around nine that night. I had two pictures of his face in my pocket.

Then the customer showed up. I was a bit surprised to see him, not much, I'm an old whore and don't really get surprised. But the guy was in a wheelchair, being pushed by a young woman who looked like a nurse. That fucker the Dispatcher hadn't told me the customer was a cripple.

"Wait here for me," I told Belle, and got into the elevator with the nurse and the crippled guy.

I got out on the same floor. The corridor was empty, I could snuff the two of them right there, but my jobs are always done intelligently. I took a paper from my pocket and pretended I was trying to read something on it, while looking nearsightedly at the numbers on the doors and following the wheelchair. I waited for the nurse to open the door of the apartment, and when she went in, pushing the wheelchair, I went in too. Her eyes widened, but before she could make a peep, I shot her in the head. I always go for the head.

"Take it easy," said the customer, facing me with both hands palms outward. He was in the business, he looked me in the eye. "We can make a deal, I'll pay you more," he said.

I fired two shots into his head. Then I unscrewed the silencer, stuck the Walther in my belt, the silencer in my pocket, and left, shutting the door. I got in the elevator and went downstairs. If I was lucky, it'd be some time before they found the pair of stiffs.

When I got to the lobby, I took Belle by the arm and we left. No one looked at me, anyone looking in our direction would see only Belle.

I got in the car and said, "Let's go to the lake." But when we arrived at the lake, I didn't have the heart to toss the pistol in the water. Shit, a Walther P99, the best thing to ever come out of Germany.

"Let's go to the movies," Belle said. We went to see a detective film; she was crazy about detective films. If someday she ever cuckolded me, it'd be with a cop.

We got out of the theater at midnight and Belle said she wanted to go dancing at the discotheque. But first we stopped at my place, and I put away the Walther, after patting it like it was a puppy.

At the discotheque Belle led me to the floor right away to dance. Watching her dance was mind-blowing, but I danced shaking like a dead tree branch in a high wind. Then we had a drink, and she asked what I thought when I saw I was about to kill a cripple. "Nothing," I answered, "and you, what did you think?" She said she thought it better to kill a cripple than a healthy guy who could dance and do aerobics on a treadmill.

When we got back to the apartment, Belle, in bed, said she wanted to talk to me about something serious. Her father was threatening to cut off her allowance.

"Fuck your father's allowance, I'll give you the money," I said.

"But that's not all, he's so pissed at me that he says he's going to leave everything to charity, so that when he dies I won't inherit a penny."

"Fuck your father's money, I'll support you."

"Man, it's a lot of money," she said. "I think it's very cruel. I'm only eighteen, I'm going to last at least another sixty. Can you imagine sixty years in poverty?"

"I've already said I'll take care of you," I insisted.

She looked at me pensively and said, "Sweetheart, I love you, but who can guarantee that you—in the business you're in, that you're, you're . . ."

She stopped, and I finished the thought for her: "Who can say if I'm going to stay alive for long, isn't that it?"

She answered, "That's it, I'm very sorry, but that *is* it." Then she gave me lots of little kisses and told me she loved me, and added that she had a proposition for me.

"Leave it till tomorrow," I said. "Let's go to sleep. It's almost dawn, and if day breaks I can't get to sleep." I took off my clothes, stripping down to my undershorts, and got into bed. She remained seated in the armchair.

When I woke up, Belle was still sitting in the chair.

"I couldn't sleep," she said, "can we talk now?"

"Talk about what?"

"My proposition," she replied.

"Talk," I said.

She got up from the chair and sat down beside me on the bed. "I want you to kill my father."

I remained silent. Shit, I thought, you can kill everybody, except your own father and mother.

"Give it some thought," I said.

And she answered, "I spent all night thinking about it, and all week, there's nothing left to think about. What's the problem? Since I've known you you've killed five people. Yesterday you killed a cripple, and now you've got scruples about killing my son of a bitch father who wants to leave me without a penny? If you tell me to jump off a bridge I'll do it, and I ask you for one little thing and you hesitate, is that how much you love me?"

She bent over me, took off my shorts, and started sucking my cock. "Is that good?"

Some five hundred women have sucked my cock, but none of them had such a magical mouth as hers. "Is that good?" After repeating that, she stopped, sat down on the bed and said, "If you don't kill my father I'm leaving you. You'll have to find some other girl to fuck."

There wasn't another girl like her in the whole world. But Belle wanting to kill her father made her ugly, and my cock wilted.

"I'll think about it," I said.

"I'll give you a week," she said.

I shadowed her father during that week. He was a tall man with white hair, nice looking, who left the house every day and got into the chauffeured car waiting in front. One day, before he got into the car, I went up to him and said, "Excuse me, I'm not from here. How do I get to downtown?"

He answered, "I'm heading there, I'll give you a lift. Please, get in."

We talked in the car. I told him I was from Minas Gerais and was looking for work. It could be as a servant, anything, I just needed work, and he handed me a card and wrote a name on the back.

"This is Dona Estela, my secretary. I'm going to tell her to look for a position for you. Come to this address tomorrow morning and speak to her."

I thought it was time to leave and said, "I'll get out here. Thank you very much. I'll be there tomorrow."

I got out of the car and walked down the street, thinking. When I got to my apartment there was a message from Belle on the answering machine asking me to call her.

"How's it coming?" she asked.

"I'm setting things up," I said, "it won't be long. I'll do the job in a few days."

"I'll come by there later," Belle said, "and I'm giving you my sweet little ass."

Normally that would have aroused me, but that day, I don't know why, it was disagreeable. "I can't today, I've got a meeting with the Dispatcher."

The next day I went to look for Dona Estela. She was very pleasant and said she'd found me a position as a driver and that I should bring my documents to her as soon as possible.

At that moment Belle's father came into the waiting room and clapped me on the back, saying, "Everything all right? Is there anything you need, an advance?"

"No, sir. Thank you very much."

When I got to the apartment, I called Belle and said that doing her father at the office would be hard; it had to be on the street or at his home.

"I'll arrange a key for you," Belle said. "I'm coming over there so we can fool around a bit; I want to suck you."

"It's not possible today either," I said.

"Hey," said Belle, "I miss that big dick."

"There's been a screw-up," I said. "I've got another meeting with the Dispatcher to straighten it out."

She gave me a key.

"What about the servants?" I asked.

"Not to worry, they stay in an apartment over the garage."

I called Belle and asked, "Is tonight okay?"

"Yes," she replied, "he always takes a sleeping pill around eleven. Get here at midnight, but when you arrive, first let's go to my room to fool around a little."

I got there at exactly midnight, the Walther with its silencer in my pocket. When I entered, Belle was standing in the living room waiting for me. We went upstairs. "His room is that one over there, and mine is here. Come on." We went into her room, and Belle immediately got naked and asked, "What do you want, my ass? Want me to suck you? Want to suck me? Whatever you want, that's what I want."

That talk didn't appeal to me anymore. It used to get me excited, now it kind of disgusted me. She lay down on her stomach, arching her ass. In the world, the entire world, there wasn't a prettier ass than hers, and she knew it. I approached Belle, took the Walther out of my pocket and shot her in the head, right in the back of the neck, for her to die instantaneously and painlessly. Then I covered her body with a sheet and left, closing the door to the street. How could anyone want to kill their father or mother?

Now the Walther was really hot. I drove to the lake and sat down, thinking, without the heart to throw that jewel in the water. Day was starting to break, and I could feel something happening to me. I felt like crying, but crying is for fags, and I didn't cry. I took the Walther and threw it as far as I could. It hit the water without making much noise. The sun was so white it hurt my eyes.

xania

I PHONED THE DISPATCHER.

"You sent a girl to do the job? You sent a virgin to face off against an old whore?"

"I was counting on your weakness for women."

"It didn't work."

"She's very pretty."

"Was. I had to sacrifice the girl, you sonofabitch."

"I made a mistake. It happens. Zé, Zé, don't take it the wrong way, but you've become a problem."

"Shit, what kind of problem?"

"You can't give up the business, you know too much."

"You clown, they knocked my teeth out in the Glock case, but did I do the job? They tortured me, I'm crippled in one hand, but did I do the job?"

"They got the wrong hand. They didn't know you're a lefty. But look, Zé, we gotta do what we gotta do. Rules of the game. You know who gives the orders."

"I don't fucking know about anybody ordering anything."

"You said it yourself, not too long ago, that by knowing the victim you know who ordered it. Remember?"

I did say that. Fuck.

I hung up the phone.

This was my situation: The Dispatcher had put out a contract on me and thought that a pretty girl could get to me, but he screwed up and now he was sending The Man after me. I'd always thought I was The Man, and I'm sure I'm right, but there must be others. The problem was that I didn't know where to find the Dispatcher; he was the one who set up the meetings. He'd call and say, "We're going to meet at such-and-such restaurant," a different one each time, and he paid in cash. Every week he got a new prepaid cell phone and threw the old one away.

I rented a place at another apartment hotel using fake ID and passport. They knew my real name. I was thinking of the Dispatcher and the ones who were after me as *they,* a sign my paranoia was increasing. Fuck.

I started wearing loose-fitting shirts and carrying two pistols, one under my right armpit and the other in my belt. I let my beard grow and dyed the hairs that were gray a light brown. In my family we go gray early. I bought a pair of glasses with clear lenses from a street vendor. I inspected myself in the mirror. It didn't look like a disguise; my face is so common that it goes with everything.

I went on paying for the old apartment hotel and left my car in the garage. I wanted them to think I still lived there. Under my false name, Manoel de Oliveira, I rented an apartment on the same floor. The doormen didn't recognize me with my brown hair, beard, glasses, and Portuguese accent. Besides that, my apartment hotel was constantly changing its personnel. And doormen at apartment hotels by the water only look at the women, preferably at their asses in bathing suits as they head for the beach.

I was in luck. The peephole in my new apartment allowed me to see the door of the old one where I used to live and which to all intents and purposes was still my address.

I spent all day looking through the peephole. My neck ached, but I knew that one day someone would show up, and this time it wouldn't be some beginner of a girl.

The woman was wearing the uniform of the restaurant on the ground floor and had a tray in her hand. She rang the doorbell of my old apartment.

The Dispatcher must've thought, Zé will never suspect I've sent another woman.

I came out from where I was, calmly. The woman with the tray gave me a perfunctory glance—she must know me only from an old photograph—and rang the bell again. I went up to her, stuck the pistol in her ribs, and put the key to the apartment in her free hand.

"Open the door," I said.

She opened the door and we went inside.

"Put the tray on the table," I said, "and lie down on the floor with your hands behind you."

She lay down and I handcuffed her. I removed the napkin covering the tray; on it was a cheese sandwich, a Coca-Cola, and a Luger Parabellum, 9mm, with silencer.

I like cheese sandwiches. While I ate the sandwich I asked, "Where'd you get this piece? It's a collector's item. I'm honored you chose such a tool to do me."

"Are you Zé?" she asked.

"I am. What's your arrangement with the Dispatcher?"

"A shot in the head."

"Nine millimeter . . . Gray matter all over the wall. What's your name?"

"Xania."

"Xania? You're The Man? A woman?"

The Man is what the Dispatcher's best operator was called.

"If you're asking if I'm the best, if I handled the most complicated cases, yeah, I'm The Man."

"Xania."

"You think my name is odd? There's a TV character named Xania, but my parents chose the name of a city on the island of Crete. I think in Portuguese it's spelled with *Ch*, but they thought it was more interesting with *X*."

"Xania, I have a proposition for you. Here it is. By the rules, I ought to eliminate you. But I want the Dispatcher, understand? I want peace and quiet, to go somewhere and raise chickens. The Dispatcher won't let me."

"You want to raise chickens?"

"It's a metaphor. I'm tired of this work. I kill you, and the Dispatcher will send somebody else, I think he'll send a man next time, and I'll go on killing people, something I don't want to do anymore, especially when it doesn't pay me a cent. I want you to tell me where I can find the Dispatcher, the address where he lives."

"I don't know. I meet him in a restaurant, never the same one twice, every time he sets it up in a different one."

"Did he already pay you for the job? How much?"

"He gave me half."

Xania mentioned the amount.

"You make more than I do."

"I'm The Man," she said, laughing.

"What about the other half?"

"He's going to give it to me when I—I mean, was going to give it to me—"

"Let's agree on something. You call him and say the job's done. Ask him to set a time and place to pay you the rest."

"I'm running the risk of death if he learns I'm ratting him out."

"You're already at risk of death, immediate death right here. Besides which, I'm going to eliminate the sonofabitch, don't worry about that. Go on, Xania, make the call."

I stuck the pistol against the back of her neck.

"I'll count to three. One, two—"

"Wait, wait," said Xania, taking the cell phone from her purse.

It took a while, at least that was my impression, for the Dispatcher to answer. With my pistol in Xania's neck I leaned my body so close to hers that I could feel her ass against my groin.

"The job's done," Xania said.

I heard the Dispatcher's voice asking if I'd given her a hard time.

"Not at all. He thought I was the waitress. What now?"

"Put another bullet in his head," I heard the Dispatcher say.

I took the Parabellum from the tray and fired. I gestured for Xania to continue the conversation.

"Done. There's brains splattered all over the floor."

"In an hour, come to Niraki, the Japanese restaurant," I heard the Dispatcher say. "Know where it is?"

Goddamn, the Japanese restaurant where Olive Oyl tried to teach me how to use chopsticks. What was the Japanese name for them? For chopsticks?

Xania and I got a taxi.

"You go in first. Sit down with the Dispatcher if he's already there. If not, wait for him. I'm only going to shoot the sonofabitch after he pays you the other half."

The restaurant was surrounded by glass, and from the street I could see what was going on inside. It was six p.m. and beginning to get dark. The Niraki was empty. The Dispatcher hadn't arrived yet. Xania sat down at a table.

It crossed my mind that the Dispatcher might not show up. After I'd waited for fifteen minutes that seemed like fifteen hours, he finally showed up. He arrived in a large chauffeur-driven car and went into the Niraki.

The Dispatcher sat down at Xania's table, and after they exchanged a few words he handed her an envelope. I entered quickly and shot him twice in the head. I've already said that I always shoot for the head. The fucker had his back to me and never even saw me.

I looked at Xania, who looked back at me and saw what was going to happen. I felt bad and hesitated a little, but I did what had to be done. The two collapsed on top of each other.

The Dispatcher had made me kill two women, and I hate killing women. I pressed the pistol against his face and opened a large hole where his nose had been. The fucker would need to have a closed-coffin funeral.

The waiters looked at me in horror.

I left, went to the Dispatcher's car, and knocked on the window. The driver opened the glass, and I put two bullets in him, in the head like always.

Afterward, I went to the apartment I'd just rented, shaved off my beard, threw the glasses into the trash. The Portuguese tenant was no more.

I put on a beret and went back to my old place. The Luger and the tray were still on the table. I needed to make plans for a trip, but I was tired and it could wait till the next day. I lay down and slept badly.

It was a relief when day began to dawn.

be my valentine

IF THERE'S ONE THING I CAN'T STOMACH, it's a blackmailer. If it weren't for that, I wouldn't have left home that Saturday for all the money in the world.

Medeiros, the lawyer, called me and said, "It's blackmail and my client will pay." His client was J.J. Santos, the banker.

"Mandrake," Medeiros continued, "the matter has to be settled without leaving a trace, understand?"

"I understand, but it's going to cost a bundle," I said, looking at the blonde princess who was with me.

"I know, I know," Medeiros said. And he did know; he'd been a politician, he'd been in the government, he was a retired cabinet minister, he was on top of things.

I got off to a bad start that Saturday. I woke up out of sorts, with a headache, hung over from a night of drinking. I walked around the house, listened to some Nelson Gonçalves, opened the fridge, and had a piece of cheese.

I got my car and headed for Itanhangá, where the upper crust play polo. I like to see rich people sweat. That's where I met the blonde. She looked like a dew-covered flower, her skin healthy and clean, her eyes shining with health.

"Polo players are going to hell," I said.

"What?" she asked.

"On the Day of Judgment the rich will get screwed," I answered.

"A romantic socialist!" she laughed disdainfully.

That was the blonde who was in my apartment when Medeiros, the lawyer, called.

J.J. Santos, the banker from Minas Gerais, was arguing with his wife that same Saturday about whether they should go to the wedding of the daughter of one of his partners.

"I'm not going," J.J. Santos's wife said. "You go." She preferred to stay home and watch television and eat cookies. Married for ten years, they were at that point where you either resign yourself and die imprisoned or send your wife packing and live free.

J.J. Santos put on a dark suit, white shirt, silver tie.

I grabbed the blonde princess and said, "Come with me." It was Valentine's Day.

"Did you ever read a book of poetry?" she asked me.

"Look," I replied, "I've never read any kind of book, except law books."

She laughed.

"Do you have all your teeth?" I asked.

She did have all her teeth. She opened her mouth, and I saw the two rows, upper and lower. That's the rich for you.

We got to my apartment. I said, "What's going to happen here, between the two of us, will be different from anything that ever happened to you before, princess."

"Roll the preview," she said.

When I was born they called me Paulo, my father's name, but I became Mandrake, a person who doesn't pray and speaks little but makes the necessary gestures. "Prepare yourself, princess, for something never before seen."

Then the phone rang. It was Medeiros, the lawyer.

The altar was covered with flowers. The bride, escorted by her father, came slowly down the aisle of the church, to the sound of choir voices singing in harmony. The groom, as always, wore a foolish expression as he waited for the bride at the altar.

At eight o'clock J.J. Santos left the church, got into his Mercedes, and went to the home of the bride's parents in Ipanema. The apartment was packed. J.J. Santos exchanged greetings with people, joked with the bride and groom, and left unnoticed half an hour later. He didn't know for sure what he wanted to do. He certainly had no desire to go home and watch old dubbed movies on the color TV. He got his car and drove along Ipanema beach, in the direction of the Barra da Tijuca. He had only been living in Rio for half a year and found the city fascinating. About five hundred yards ahead, J.J. Santos saw the girl, standing on the sidewalk. Stereo music poured from his car's speakers, and J.J. Santos was emotionally predisposed. He had never seen such a pretty girl. He had the impression that she had looked at him, but he must be mistaken; she wasn't the type for a street hooker, like those who pick up customers in passing cars. He was to the end of Leblon when he decided to go back. Maybe the girl was still there; he wanted to see her again. The girl was there, leaning over the door of a Volkswagen—haggling over price? J.J. Santos stopped some twenty yards behind, blinking his high beams. The girl looked, saw the big Mercedes, and left the guy in the Volks talking to himself. She approached slowly, with perfect balance, knowing how to put one foot on the ground and distribute her weight along the muscles of her body as she moved.

She stuck her head in the door and said, "Hello." Her face was very young, but there was greater maturity in her voice.

"Hello," J.J. Santos replied, looking around in fear someone had seen him stopping there. "Get in."

The girl got in and J.J. Santos put the car in motion.

"How old are you?" asked J.J. Santos.

"Sixteen," replied the girl.

"Sixteen!" said J.J. Santos.

"What of it, you fool? If I don't go with you, I'll go with somebody else."

"What's your name?" asked J.J. Santos, his conscience relieved.

"Viveca."

In another part of the city, where I was:

"My name is Maria Amelia. Don't call me princess. How ridiculous!" the blonde complained.

"Bullshit," I answered.

"You're vulgar, gross, and ignorant."

"Right. Want out?"

"What does that mean?"

"You want to beat it? Beat it."

"Can't you even talk?"

"Right again."

"You're an idiot!" the blonde laughed noisily, amused, all her teeth shining.

I laughed too. We were both interested in each other. I go crazy over rich women.

"Just what is your name anyway? Paulo, Mandrake, Picasso?"

"That's not the question," I replied. "You have to ask me, just who are you anyway?"

"Just who are you anyway?"

"I don't know," I answered.

"Paranoia has filtered down to Class C," the blonde said.

J.J. Santos knew the Barra was full of hotels. He had never been to any of them but had heard the stories. He headed for the most famous one.

He chose the Presidential Suite.

The Presidential Suite had its own pool, color television, radio, and dining room, and the bedroom abounded with chandeliers and was lined with mirrors.

J.J. Santos was excited.

"Do you want anything?" he asked the girl.

"A soft drink," she answered modestly.

The waiter brought a soft drink and Chivas Regal.

J.J. Santos took a sip, removed his coat, and said, "I'm going to the bathroom, make yourself comfortable."

When he came out of the bathroom, the girl was naked, lying on the bed, on her stomach. J.J. Santos took off his clothes and lay down beside her, caressing her as he watched himself in the mirrors. Then the girl rolled over on her back, a smile on her lips.

It wasn't a girl. It was a man, his penis reflected, menacingly rigid, in the countless mirrors.

J.J. Santos leaped from the bed.

Viveca returned to her prone position. Turning her head, she stared at J.J. and asked sweetly, "Don't you want me?"

"You goddam pe—pervert," said J.J. He grabbed his clothes and ran to the bathroom, where he quickly dressed.

"You don't want me?" said Viveca, still in the same position, when J.J. Santos returned to the room. Distressed, J.J. Santos put on his coat and took out his wallet. He always carried a lot of money in his wallet. That day he had two thousand in bills of five hundred. People from Minas are like that. His papers were in the wallet. The money was gone.

"On top of everything else you stole my money!"

"What? What? Are you calling me a thief? I'm no thief!" Viveca screamed, getting up from the bed. Suddenly a razor blade appeared in her hand. "Calling me a thief!" With a rapid gesture Viveca made the first cut in her arm and a thread of blood welled on her skin.

J.J., dismayed, made a gesture of disgust and fear.

"Yes, I'm a faggot, I'm a FAAAAG-GOT!" Viveca's scream seemed capable of shattering every chandelier and mirror.

"Don't do that," J.J. begged, terrified.

"You knew what I was, you brought me here knowing everything, and now you scorn me as if I were trash," Viveca sobbed, as she gave her arm another cut with the razor.

"I didn't know anything; you look like a girl, with that makeup and wearing that wig."

"This isn't a wig, it's my own hair. See how you treat me?" Another slash on the arm, by now covered with blood.

"Stop that!" J.J. requested.

"I won't stop! I won't stop! I won't stop! You called me a thief, thief, thief! I may be poor but I'm honest. You have money and think everybody else is trash! I always wanted to die and destroy a big shot, like in the film *Black Widow*. Did you see *Black Widow?*" Viveca asked, resting the razor blade against her throat, over the carotid, which was standing out from the force of her screams.

"Forgive me," J.J. asked.

"It's too late now," said Viveca.

In the meantime I was arriving at my apartment with the high-toned blonde. She sat in the easy chair; that aura was building between us, two responsible people calmly exchanging significant glances.

"Roll the preview," she said.

"Prepare yourself, princess, for something never before seen."

At that instant Medeiros, the lawyer, called.

"My client, J.J. Santos, picked up a woman in the street, took her to a hotel, and when they got there he discovered it was a transvestite. The transvestite stole two thousand from my client. They had an argument, and the transvestite, armed with a razor blade, threatened to commit suicide unless he got ten thousand in cash. My client asked me for the money, which I have here with me now. We want to pay the money and put an end to the whole affair. You're experienced in police matters, and we'd like you to take charge of the thing. No police; we'll pay the money and want everything buried. The matter has to be covered up without a trace, understand?"

"I understand, but it's going to cost a bundle," I said, looking at the blonde princess beside me.

"I know, I know," said Medeiros, "money's no problem."

J.J. and Viveca were inside the Mercedes, parked at the beach.

J.J. was at the wheel, as pale as a corpse. Beside him, Viveca was holding the razor blade next to her throat. She really did look like a young woman. I pulled my old wreck up beside the huge Mercedes.

"I work with Mr. Medeiros," I said.

"Did you bring the money?" Viveca asked, brusquely.

"It was hard to arrange, today's Saturday," I alibied, humbly. "We're going to get it now."

I opened the door and pulled J.J. out.

I got in and tore off, with the door still open, leaving the dumbfounded J.J. on the sidewalk.

"Is it far? Where's the money?" asked Viveca.

"It's nearby," I said, driving at high speed.

"I want my money right now, otherwise I'll do something crazy!" Viveca screamed, cutting herself on the arm. The gesture was abrupt and violent, but the blade touched lightly on her skin, just enough to draw blood and scare the suckers.

"For God's sake don't do that!"

"I'll do something crazy!" Viveca threatened.

He must not have known Rio very well, or else he didn't know where the police stations were located. At the door of the Leblon precinct two cops were talking. I braked the car, almost on top of them, and jumped out, yelling, "Look out! The transvestite's got a razor blade!"

Viveca leaped from the car. The situation was truly confusing for him. One of the cops approached and Viveca lashed out, cutting his hand. The cop retreated a step, pulled a .45 from his belt, and said, "Drop that piece of shit unless you wanna die right now." Viveca hesitated. The other cop, who had approached him, gave Viveca a kick in the stomach. Viveca fell to the ground.

We all went into the precinct headquarters. There were four or five cops around us.

Viveca was crying.

"I beg the forgiveness of all the law enforcement officers here, especially the man that I injured and I'm very sorry about that. I am a man, yes, but since I was a child my mother dressed me as a girl and I always liked to play with dolls. I'm a man because my name is Jorge, but that's the only reason. I have the soul of a woman, and I suffer because I'm not a woman and can't have children like other women. I'm wretched. Then that man in the Mercedes picked me up at the beach and said, Come with me, boy; and I answered, I'm not a boy, I'm a woman; and he said, Woman my foot, get in, tonight I feel like something different. He said he'd pay me five hundred, and I have my mother and grandmother to support, and so I went. When we got there, besides doing all sorts of immoral things to me, he beat me and cut me with the razor blade. Then I grabbed the blade and said I'd kill myself if he didn't give me five hundred. He said he didn't have it and telephoned a friend of his and that man there showed up and brought me here and I lost my head, please forgive me. I'm a delicate person; I went crazy over the unfairness and the bad things they did to me."

"What's your client's name?" said a suspicious cop.

"I'm not at liberty to say. He's committed no crime. This guy's lying," I said.

In reality I wasn't sure of a damned thing, but a client is a client.

"Lying! Me?!" Tears ran down Viveca's makeup. "Just because I'm weak and poor and the other one's rich and powerful, I'm going to be crucified?" Viveca screamed, between sobs.

"Rich people don't run things here," one of the cops said.

"What about that car?" said the injured cop, in the middle of the confusion. Luckily nobody else heard him.

"It's mine, I bought it yesterday, I haven't had time to transfer the title yet," I said, as the cop took notes on a piece of paper.

"We're going to wait for the commissioner," the cop said.

"This guy stole two thousand from my client. It must be hidden somewhere on his person," I said.

"You can frisk me. Go ahead, frisk me!" Viveca challenged, spreading his arms.

None of the policemen showed any interest in frisking Viveca. That's when I had the flash. I grabbed Viveca's hair and yanked it. The hair came off in my hand and four bills of five hundred flew into the air and fell to the floor.

"That's the money he stole from my client," I said, relieved.

"He gave it to me, he gave it to me, I swear it," said Viveca, without much conviction.

Before they put Viveca in the lockup, they noticed he had a number of old marks on both arms. He must have used that trick several times before.

"You'll have to wait for the commissioner," the injured cop said.

I gave him my card. "I'll stop by later, OK? One other thing, let's pretend we didn't find the money, all right? My client won't mind."

"We'll need to talk with you, if not tonight, one of these days." I looked at him and saw we'd just made a deal.

"No problem. Just give me a call," I said.

I took off like a jet in the Mercedes. I got to the hotel and looked up the manager. I took two of the twenty notes of five hundred that I had in my pocket, gave them to him and said, "I want to see the registration card for a guest who was here a couple of hours ago."

"I can't do that," he said.

I gave him two more bills. "The guy's my client," I said.

"I don't want any trouble!"

"Give me the card, you sonofabitch, or you'll have trouble you'll never see the end of. It was a minor he had with him, and you'll be royally screwed."

The manager brought me the cards. There was J.J.'s full name. Profession: bank employee. Irony or lack of imagination? The other card read Viveca Lindfords, resident of Nova Iguaçu. Where the shit had he gotten that name? I put both cards in my pocket.

I rushed home. What a car that was. I'd have to transfer the title to my name backdated to Friday, for the protection of my client. . . . I got home and went in shouting, "Princess! I'm back." But the blonde had vanished. My pockets full of money, a Mercedes at the curb, and what? I was a sad and unlucky man. I'd never see the rich blonde again, I knew.

kisses on the cheek

"YOUR BLADDER WILL HAVE TO BE removed entirely," Roberto said. "And in these cases a place is prepared for the urine to be stored before it's excreted. A part of your intestine will be converted into a small sac, connected to the ureters. The urine from that receptacle will be directed to a bag placed in an opening in your abdominal wall. I'm describing the procedure in layman's terms so you can understand. The bag will be hidden by your clothes and will have to be emptied periodically. Have I been clear?"

"Yes," I replied, lighting a cigarette.

"I'd like to schedule the surgery immediately following the tests I'm asking for. Did I tell you about the relationship between bladder cancer and smoking?"

"I don't remember."

"Three out of five cases of bladder cancer are linked to smoking. The link between smoking and bladder cancer is especially strong among men."

"I promise I'll stop smoking."

"This year, worldwide, there will be close to three hundred thousand cases of bladder cancer."

"Really?"

"It's the fourth most common type of cancer and the seventh leading cause of death from cancer."

I felt like telling Roberto to stop bugging me, but besides being my doctor he was also my friend.

"Bladder cancer," he continued, "can occur at any age, but it usually hits people over fifty. You'll be fifty next month. You're a month older than me."

"I'm late for an appointment. I have to go, Roberto."

"Don't forget to have the tests done."

I ran out. I didn't have any appointment. I wanted to smoke another cigarette in peace. And I also needed to meet with someone who could get me a gun. I remembered my brother.

I phoned him.

"Do you still have that weapon?"

"Yes. Why?"

"Want to sell it?"

"No."

"Aren't you afraid one of your children will find the gun and shoot the other one in the head? Something like that happened the other day. It was in the papers."

"My gun is locked inside a drawer."

"According to the paper, so was that poor guy's."

"I didn't read anything about it."

"You always say you only read the headlines. That didn't make the headlines because it happens every day."

"And just how did it happen?"

"The boy was playing cowboys and Indians with his brother and the tragedy occurred. Any day now I'm going to read in the newspaper that one nephew of mine killed the other playing a game."

"Enough with the foreboding."

"I'll stop by there tonight."

When I got to my brother's house he said, "Take a look at this drawer. You think a couple of kids could break that lock?"

"Yes."

"How?"

"Want to see me break into that piece of shit?"

"You're an adult."

"Where's Helena?"

"In the bedroom."

"Have her come out here."

I told his wife about the article in the newspaper, which I had made up.

"I'm constantly asking Carlos to get rid of that damned thing, but he won't listen," said Helena.

"I came here to buy the revolver, but this idiot doesn't want to sell."

"What are you going to do with the gun?" Carlos asked.

"Nothing. Own it, that's all. I've always wanted a revolver."

Helena and my brother argued for a time. She won the debate when she said that one of the boys could get hold of the key while my brother was sleeping, or when he forgot the key in a place where the kids could find it, or on some other occasion. Finally, Carlos opened the drawer and took out the gun.

"And to make things worse, you keep the thing loaded," I said, after examining the firearm.

"You irresponsible madman," said Helena, furious, "you always told me the revolver wasn't loaded. Listen, let your brother take that piece of crap with him, now. Otherwise I'm moving out and taking the children."

I got the revolver and went back to my apartment. I phoned my girlfriend. I felt like going to the bathroom but knew I'd see signs of blood in the urine, which always sent a shiver down my spine. That could spoil my time with her. I urinated with my eyes closed and, also with my eyes closed, flushed the toilet several times.

While I was waiting for my girlfriend, I thought about the future, smoking and drinking whiskey. I was going to spend the rest of my life filling with urine a bag stuck to my body, which would then have to be emptied somehow or other. How could I go to the beach? How could I make love to a woman? I imagined the horror she would feel upon seeing that thing.

My girlfriend arrived and we went to bed.

"You're worried about something," she said, after a time.

"I'm not feeling well."

"Don't worry, sweetheart, we can just talk; I love talking with you."

This is one of the worst phrases a man can hear when he's naked with a naked woman in bed.

We got up and got dressed without looking at each other. We went into the living room. We talked a little. My girlfriend looked at her watch, said, "I have to go, love," kissed me on the cheek, left, and I shot myself in the chest.

But the story doesn't end there. I should have shot myself in the head, but it was in the chest and I didn't die.

During my convalescence, Roberto came to see me several times to say we didn't have much time, but we could still do the bladder surgery, successfully.

It was done. Now I easily empty the urine bag. It's well hidden under my clothes; no one realizes it's there, over my abdomen. The cancer appears to have been entirely eliminated. I no longer have a girlfriend, and I'm addicted to crossword puzzles. I stopped going to the beach. I did go once, to throw the gun into the sea.

marta

I'm forty years old, a sensitive man who likes music, poetry, and cinema. I'm a lawyer, single, and live alone. I'm looking for a lasting relationship of love and respect. INCORRIGIBLE ROMANTIC.

I spent a week, me, Incorrigible Romantic, visiting chat rooms and was getting discouraged, when the woman I was looking for showed up:

DEAR INCORRIGIBLE ROMANTIC, *Like you, I am also looking for a lasting relationship with someone worthy and affectionate. I too love music and poetry and especially cinema. Tell me more about yourself.* LOUISE BROOKS.

DEAR LOUISE BROOKS, *I've never married, not because I lacked the financial conditions to do so, just the opposite, I'm a man of means, despite living a modest life. I've never married because I haven't met the ideal woman. They say there's no such thing, that it's a romantic illusion. But I refuse to accept such pessimism. That's why I used the pseudonym Incorrigible Romantic. What about you? Why Louise Brooks?*

DEAR INCORRIGIBLE ROMANTIC, *Louise Brooks was a beautiful actress in silent films. One day a boyfriend gave me a picture of her that looked so much like me that I still have it even now. A woman with an air of mystery, which I, to tell the truth, don't have. I'm an open book. I've never been married either and am looking for the ideal man. I know I'm going to find him. Who knows if he's you. Do you have a girlfriend?* LOUISE BROOKS.

DEAR LOUISE, *No, I don't have a girlfriend. I would like to meet you. You must be thinking, he doesn't know me, how can he want to meet me? But I'm sure we're going to get along very well. Give it some thought.* ROMANTIC.

DEAR ROMANTIC, *I'm a shy person, I live with my mother, I'm doing this crazy thing for the first time in my life, talking with a stranger on the Internet. I don't know if I should go any further with this. I'm afraid.* LOUISE.

I was anxious to get that woman.

DEAR LOUISE, *I'm a shy person like you, it's the first time I've done this. But I know, a type of premonition, that we're going to get along very well. May I visit your home? I know your mother will like me.* ROMANTIC.

DEAR ROMANTIC, *At my house it's impossible, it will have to be at yours. Give me your address. I'll be there tomorrow, at nightfall.* KISSES, LOUISE.

DEAR LOUISE, *My address is on Gomes Monteiro, third floor. It's a four-story building, one apartment per floor, one of those old buildings that real estate speculation hasn't managed to destroy. Call on the intercom and I'll buzz you in. Anxiously awaiting you.* ROMANTIC.

I was tense all day, and as the time approached I got worse. I had to get that woman.

Then the intercom rang.

"It's Louise."

I pushed the button. A short time later the bell to my apartment rang. I opened the door.

She was a very pale woman, with hair so dark it looked dyed. She was wearing a miniskirt that displayed her beautiful, long white legs.

"Come in, please."

There she stood, the woman I was looking for. She came in. I asked her to have a seat.

"A lovely apartment. Is it yours?"

"I have another one, in the Barra. I rent this one."

"My real name is Diana."

"Mine is Carlos."

"Take a look at this photo of Louise Brooks," she said.

I looked. A black and white photo. Her hair was of an unusual blackness and her skin was very white. A beautiful woman.

"Want something to drink?"

"A little whiskey."

I got from the pantry a bottle of whiskey, one of mineral water, and a bucket of ice.

"I like mine without ice, just whiskey and water, more whiskey than water," I said.

"Ice with mine, please, and lots of water."

I fixed our drinks and put the glasses on a tray.

"Do you have anything to munch on?" she asked.

"I'll check inside there, be right back," I replied.

I dawdled, sitting in the pantry holding the bag of cookies. I wanted to give her time.

After some minutes I returned. Louise lifted her glass.

"I'd like to make a toast, in hopes that our relationship is a lasting one, as you said in your e-mail."

I raised my glass to my lips.

"Before drinking I'd like to get something salty from the kitchen," I said. "I only brought cookies."

I went to the kitchen, carrying my glass. I returned with a plate of savory snacks.

I raised the glass. "To a lasting relationship," I said.

"Cheers," she answered, clinking her glass against mine.

We drank while we chatted.

She had lost her father, and the widowed mother she lived with was very controlling. She had no other relatives.

I told her I had four sisters, all older than me. I said I would like to travel with her, go to Paris or New York. I already had the money for the trip put aside. She said she'd like to see Katmandu.

"I'm going to get more water from the kitchen," I said, getting up.

But as soon as I stood up, I staggered, supporting myself on the back on the armchair.

"I feel a bit dizzy . . ."

She hugged me.

"Are you really dizzy or is that just a trick so I'll put my arms around you?" She grabbed my cock, which was soft. "In a little while I'll make it hard. Sit down on the sofa for a moment," she said.

I sat down and immediately my head fell forward.

"Carlos, Carlos, are you all right?"

No answer.

Soon afterwards, she shook my arm.

"Carlos, can you hear me?"

I remained silent.

I heard the sound of Diana trying to open the bedroom door. I felt her hands going through my pockets. Then I heard her voice, she must be talking on a cell phone.

"Igor, he collapsed. The things must be locked in another room. Yes, I'll wait. You know the address, don't you? Ring the buzzer."

I lay there in the armchair, not moving. I heard the buzzer.

"It's Igor," said the voice on the intercom.

"Come on up," said Diana.

Sound of the door being opened.

"Was it easy?" A man's voice.

"A piece of cake. I think there's jewels, cash, everything that counts in that locked bedroom. But I couldn't find the key."

"It must be in his pocket."

"I searched him. There's no key. Igor, let's do the guy, the whole bit."

"I don't like that, Marta."

"He saw my goddamn face. If you cut his throat, he won't feel a thing. The whole bit, Igor, and you walk away with half and get to screw me too."

"Let's break down that door," said Igor.

But the door opened before they could break it down.

The two cops working with me came out of the bedroom with guns pointed at them. They ordered the couple to get down on the floor with their hands behind them.

While the pair were being handcuffed, I got up from the sofa.

"Marta Castro and Igor da Silva, you're under arrest for the murder of Edgard Gouveia," I said.

They began a heated argument in which Igor said that it was Marta's idea, that she had forced him to kill the guy, and Marta said she had tried to stop him but Igor had killed him anyway.

"It was you who killed him," Marta repeated.

"You gave the order, you whore," Igor said.

The argument went on all the way to the precinct, where they were booked and held without bail. They would be sentenced to long prison terms.

Before being locked away, Marta spoke with me.

"You didn't black out, and I put a heavy dose of barbiturates in your drink. What happened?"

"When I went to the kitchen, I switched glasses. The one I drank out of was clean."

"How did you discover me?"

"By examining the computer belonging to your victim, Edgard Gouveia, whom you killed by cutting his throat. It was all there, the chat with Louise Brooks. You should have changed names."

"But I wanted to be her. Louise looks a lot like me, doesn't she?"

"Yes, a lot," I replied.

And she did, really. An unusual face. Marta could be a photographic model or an actress in film. Without even changing her name. But by the time she gets out of prison it'll be too late.

passion

ONCE, I WAS IN LOVE WITH A GIRL and to prove to her the magnitude of my feeling cut off the little finger of my right hand. They say passion is a pathological condition, a sickness that luckily is transitory.

Though I was never in love with Nelly, I married her. I'm a writer, and all writers (with notorious exceptions) are poor devils. Nelly had money, inherited from her father, in addition to making quite a lot in her profession as a lawyer specializing in indemnities.

I have to tell the truth. I was a failure as a writer. Not even that, I wasn't even a failure, which would be something, I was a writer who'd never managed to get published. I sent my originals to countless publishers and every one, without exception, was returned, with those routine hypocritical explanations. I spoke with Nelly to see if she could finance the publication of one of my books, just one, with those publishing houses that do that, but she asked me if I had no shame and said she'd have no part of something as unworthy as that.

Nelly is very jealous and has hired a team of private detectives who watch me day and night. You know how I met Michele, the passion of my life? At the office of Dr. Amancio, a surgeon friend of mine. He let me use one of the rooms and I made love to Michele on one of the hospital beds.

Actually, it was Amancio who found the solution to my problem, about which I'll have more to say later.

For Michele I'd cut off any finger, my whole hand, anything but my dick. I like making love to Michele. Making love with passion demands a rite, a protocol, pomp, solemnity. But for that, the body of the woman you're going to make love to needs to be very beautiful, perfect, like Michele's. Or that you find to be perfect, which amounts to the same thing. Pirandello is right: if it seems that way to you, it is. Here's the rite, which encompasses the five senses: the woman lies down in bed, completely nude, and you contemplate her body, from head to toe, front and back. You look at every detail, the neck, the shoulder blades, the navel, the knee, the toes, the mouth, the eyes, open so you can distinguish the color, and closed, so you can see the lash and the dark circles, every woman has them, some more pronounced, others more subtle. Next you lightly brush the belly and the breasts, and the inside of the thighs. The skin has nerve endings and corpuscles, the so-called tactile receptors, which make the body sensitive to the caress. Next you bring your nose close to her body and smell the aroma of each part, the hair, the underarms, the breasts, the feet, the vagina, the back, the buttocks. Then, following the ritual, you taste the woman by lightly biting and running your tongue over her entire body, lips, tongue, breasts, again the underarms, the belly, navel, legs, not forgetting the part behind the knees, and also the feet and finally the vagina—in the vulva, where the tongue must explore all the recesses, for the tastes of the vagina are countless and varied in each fragment, and at certain moments you should shape your tongue into a cone and stick it as far as possible into that voluptuously flavorful fissure. Afterward, the buttocks and anus. The tongue must roam and discover the pleasures contained in that magic orifice of extremely high sensitivity that can afford a sublime delight.

Only after these prolegomena should we introduce the penis into the dazzling rift, which will be balsamically aromatic, prepared to receive it.

How to do that with Nelly? She has an ugly body, drooping breasts, flaccid ass and belly. And when I suggested that she consult a plastic surgeon, she asked bitingly, "You think I'm some kind of Botoxed social butterfly? I'm a professional, a famous lawyer, respected, who makes a living by working." Implicit in the way she said this was that I was a bum, a make-believe writer, who didn't work.

I had a long talk with my friend Amancio. "I don't know what to do about my life," I told him. "I'm in love with Michele, and my wife is suffocating me, humiliating me, making me unhappy."

Amancio was silent for some time. Then he said he had the answer to my problem. "I know you want to give Michele an apartment, don't you?"

"Yes, I'd like to satisfy her fondest dream, which is to have a penthouse apartment in Leblon. But I don't even have the money to buy a shack in a shantytown."

"I've got the solution to your problem."

Amancio's solution horrified me.

"I can't do that, Amancio, I don't have the courage."

"Think, think about it."

"I would never do something like that."

But that night, Nelly told me she was tired of living with a parasite and was going to find me a job in the bureaucracy that I couldn't refuse.

"Go on, say yes. I'm ordering it, I've already decided."

"All right, all right, Nelly, I'll go by the office tomorrow."

But I wasn't about to obey Nelly's intolerable *ukase*. Instead, I went to Amancio's office.

"I'm in," I said.

"Everything's ready," Amancio said.

He gave me a hypodermic needle and told me to scrape it on Nelly's skin as she slept; one scratch would be enough. The needle was infected with tetanus. I remembered someone saying that a good way of getting rid of a person was by infecting them with tetanus, but I couldn't recall who had said it.

I remained awake, holding the needle, without the courage to act. Then Nelly started snoring, and I believe that was what led me to do what Amancio recommended.

The next morning Nelly said she had a scratch on her leg, and I suggested she put a Band-Aid on it. Band-Aids don't do a goddamn bit of good, Amancio had told me. "Shut off the water so Nelly doesn't take a bath; if she washes the wound with soap and water, everything's ruined; soap and water kill any type of infection."

Nelly went to her office without taking a bath, with the Band-Aid on her leg. I stayed at home, suffering, judging myself a damnable murderer, a reprobate of the worst kind. I called Amancio's office.

"Take it easy, take it easy. Stop by here and we'll talk," he said.

"You two got married under community property," Amancio said. "When Nelly dies you'll get everything, you'll be able to write in peace, and if necessary, pay for publishing your book. Several writers who later became famous and important paid for the first printing of their books. Everybody knows that."

Amancio explained that the incubation period of tetanus could vary from three to twenty-one days; the further away from the nervous system the wound, the longer the incubation period, and the longer that incubation period, the greater the probability of death, which is why he ordered me to make the scratch in the leg.

"God forgive me," I said.

"What's done is done," said Amancio.

When you want time to go by quickly, it goes by very slowly. After ten days, nothing happened. But on the thirteenth day, Nelly began to experience contractions in her jaw muscles. I called Amancio.

"Ah, that's good," he said, "it's the first sign of tetanus, what's called *trismus*. Nelly's going to be unable to open her mouth. Call me to examine her."

"Nelly, my love, I've called Dr. Amancio; he's coming here to examine you."

Amancio examined Nelly at length.

"It's nothing," Amancio said, "just nervous tension. You must be having some problem at work. I'm going to give you a tranquilizer, an injection."

He applied an injection in Nelly's vein.

"Wonderful," Amancio said. "Just look at her face."

I looked. Nelly was laughing.

"She's laughing," I said.

"Exactly. It's called *risus sardonicus*, a spasm of the muscles surrounding the mouth. Wonderful. Now we'll wait for diaphoresis. She's going to sweat, sweat, sweat, her temperature will rise, she's going to suffer tachycardia and die of asphyxia caused by spasms of the diaphragm." (I forgot to mention that Amancio abused the word *wonderful*—the food was wonderful, the film was wonderful, the shoes were wonderful, and so on.)

Amancio himself wrote the death certificate: general failure of multiple organs, which is what doctors put on the death certificate when they're unsure of the *causa mortis*. Nelly had no other relatives, and since visits were forbidden, no one saw the *risus sardonicus* stamped on her face while she lay dying in bed, but I confess that I always remembered her Joker's physiognomy and even had nightmares of Nelly sitting at the dinner table looking at me with a scornful or disdainful smile as I ate a plate of onions, the food I hate most.

Nelly owned countless properties and a variety of investments. I took part of the money I got and bought a two-story penthouse at the beach in Michele's name. That was her dream, a penthouse on the oceanfront in Leblon. (In reality, I also had to spend a reasonably large amount to remodel the penthouse. The apartment was highly livable, but women are crazy about remodeling, and it was done: a new kitchen, two new baths, some walls torn down, a new sauna, a different floor—all in all, a new apartment. Plus the furniture . . . I spent a lot of money.)

"Look," she told me when the work was finished, "you go on living in your house, and I'll live in mine. The thing that kills love is two people living together, rubbing against each other all day. I know over a thousand cases. Another thing, nobody can show up at the other's house without calling ahead."

She was right. Since there was no friction, our relationship continued as perfect as before. Maybe it got even better, because we fucked in more comfort.

Amancio was constantly demanding. "You owe me," he would say. Amancio might be a good tetanus contaminator, but it seems as a doctor he was nothing special. He had few patients and spent much of his time in nightclubs and houses of ill repute; as he himself confessed, he was fond of fucking whores.

"You don't need to use a rubber if you fuck a whore. You need to use a rubber if you fuck a married woman, 'cause they catch diseases from their husbands, who're bisexual," he said.

Knowing his proclivities, I wasn't concerned when he and Michele would go to art exhibitions together, which they did often.

I gave him a large amount of money and also a full power of attorney to buy, sell, subrogate, everything.

One day Amancio said he needed my help. He had a place in the mountains, a little past Teresopolis, and wanted to invite an acquaintance of his to spend a few days there, but in reality he wanted to imprison him in the cellar.

"What then?" I asked.

"After a few days I'll let him go. It's just to scare him. He's a nobody."

"What if he yells for help?"

"He can yell as much as he wants, no one's going to hear. I don't have a caretaker, and I lock the place up tighter than a drum. Take it easy."

"Shit, you're going to kill the guy?"

"I don't know," he said, "he's a son of a bitch. And he's screwing up my life. He doesn't let me be with the woman I'm in love with."

"I didn't know you were in love too. Is she a whore?"

"No, she's not a whore."

The place in the mountains was in an isolated location. The house was old, made of stone, very pretty.

"What about the guy?" I asked.

"He'll be here soon," Amancio answered. "Come on, I'll show you the cellar."

A trapdoor was opened in one of the rooms, and Amancio pointed to the opening.

"See? We go down that wooden ladder and then pull the ladder up, leaving the son of a bitch to rot in there. Go on down to see."

The ladder had countless steps. The cellar was very dark. When I got to the final step, I said, "Shit, this place is really deep."

"There's a lantern and kerosene there. Please light the lantern."

Using my lighter, I illuminated the cellar. I found the lantern on a small table beside a bed with a straw mattress.

"It's a cubicle," I shouted.

At that moment, I saw the ladder being raised.

"Our visitor has arrived, I'll be right back," said Amancio.

After a time, I heard a female voice.

"Hello, Pedro."

"Michele?"

"In the flesh," she replied, her face appearing at the trapdoor.

"What are you doing here?" I asked, already knowing the answer.

I was in a state of shock, for I suddenly understood everything. The nobody that Amancio wanted to starve to death was me. I was fucked. I knew neither he nor Michele was joking. Now I understood those art exhibitions the two of them went to together, several times a week. And once they went to Paris to see an exhibition, and I thought nothing of it, they were my best friend and the woman who claimed to be madly in love with me. I was a naïve fool. The woman Amancio was in love with was Michele.

"What are you doing here, Michele?" I repeated.

"I came to help Amancio bury you. Bye-bye, sweetheart."

Before the trapdoor could be closed, I shouted, "Michele, Michele, please, call Amancio, call Amancio."

Amancio appeared at the trapdoor opening.

"What do you want?"

"Amancio, you're my best friend. Get me a thick notebook, several pens, and a little more kerosene. Before I starve to death, I want to write a novel. I have the feeling it'll be my masterpiece."

"I'll get it for you," I heard him say.

It took him some time to return. I thought about my power of attorney with subrogation rights. Then I remember who it was that once told me that causing a tetanus infection was a good way to get rid of any enemy. Michele.

Later, the trapdoor opened and several pens and a thick notebook were dropped down. And also several cans of food and drinks. I saw Amancio's face in the trapdoor opening.

"Amancio, did you subrogate to Michele the power of attorney I gave you?"

"Yes, why—?"

He didn't finish the sentence. I heard a shot and the thud of a body falling to the floor. Michele was a genius, an evil genius. She slammed the trapdoor shut.

Was Amancio lucky enough to have a quick, maybe painless death, or was Michele going to leave him bleeding like a pig? But there's nothing worse than starving to death, I thought. Those cans of food wouldn't last long. I had to find a way less slow and painful to dispatch myself. Using the lantern, I looked around the cellar for something sharp to cut my wrists. I didn't find anything. Perhaps I could tear open my veins with my teeth. It wouldn't be easy to do. But it didn't have to be that day. Another hypothesis was to set fire to the straw mattress and die of asphyxiation. But it didn't have to be that day.

I could take advantage of the silence, the solitude, to write. That was it: leave a message for posterity, a masterpiece that would surely be found one day beside my skull, which would generate great publicity for my book.

I sat down on the bed, placed the table in front of me, picked up one of the pens, opened the notebook, and began to write furiously.

Publishers would fight like hyenas over the right to publish my book.

the brotherhood of swords

I WAS ONCE A MEMBER of the Brotherhood of Swords. I still remember when we met to choose the name of our Brotherhood. I argued, at the time, that for our survival it was important to have a respectable name and purpose and gave as example what had happened to the Brotherhood of São Martinho, an association of wine fanciers who, like the character in Eça de Queirós, would sell their soul to the devil for a bottle of Romanée-Conti 1858, but which came to be known as a fraternity of drunks and, discredited, closed its doors, while the Brotherhood of the Most Holy, whose declared objective is to promote the worship of God through invocation of the Holy Sacrament, remained in existence. In other words, we needed a worthy title and objective. My colleagues replied that the society was a secret one, that in a way it was born (this was said ironically) discredited, and that its name didn't matter in the least, as it would never be made public. They added that the Masons and the Rosicrucians originally had nice titles and respectable objectives and ended up suffering accusations of every kind, from political manipulation to kidnapping and assassination. I insisted, asking them to suggest names for the Brotherhood, which in the end was done. And we began to examine the various proposals on the table. After heated discussions, four names were left. Brotherhood of the Good Bed was discarded because it sounded like an association of layabouts. Brotherhood of Fanciers of Feminine Beauty, besides being too long, was considered reductionist and aesthetical. We didn't consider ourselves aesthetes in a strict sense; Picasso was right in hating what he termed the aesthetic game of eye and mind manipulated by connoisseurs who "appreciated" beauty and, after all, what was "beauty"? Our brotherhood was one of Fuckers and, as the poet Whitman said in a poem correctly entitled "A Woman Waits for Me," sex encompasses everything: bodies, souls, meanings, tests, purities, gentleness, results, promulgations, songs, commands, health, pride, maternal mystery, seminal fluid, all the hopes, benefits, donations and concessions, all the passions, beauties, and delights of the earth. Brotherhood of Roving Hands, suggested by one of the poets in our group (we had lots of poets among us, obviously), who illustrated his proposal with a poem by John Donne—"License my roving hands, and let them go before, behind, between, above, below"—although pertinent because of its simplicity in privileging knowledge through touch, was rejected for being an elementary symbol of our objectives.

Finally, after much discussion, the name Brotherhood of the Swords was adopted. The richest of the Brothers were its main defenders: aristocrats are attracted by things of the underworld, fascinated by lawbreakers, and the term Sword as a symbol of the Fucker came from the criminal world. A sword penetrates and wounds, and is thus the penis as, erroneously, outlaws and the ignorant in general see it. I suggested that if some symbolic name were used by us, it should be that of an ornamental tree grown for its flowers, for after all the penis is commonly known in our language as wood or club, and wood is the generic name of any tree in many places in Brazil (but, correctly, not of bushes, which have a fragile trunk), but my reasoning came a cropper when someone asked what name the Brotherhood would have—Brotherhood of the Woods? the Stalks?—and I had no answer. Sword, according to my opponents, had vernacular power, so once again the riffraff made their valuable contribution to the enrichment of the Portuguese language.

As a member of the Brotherhood of Swords I believed, and I still believe, that copulation is the only thing that matters to the human being. To fuck is to live, nothing else exists, as the poets know very well. But was a Brotherhood needed to defend this absolute axiom? Of course not. There were prejudices, but they didn't interest us; social and religious repressions didn't affect us. So what was the objective in founding the Brotherhood? Very simple: to discover how to obtain, fully, orgasm without ejaculation. The queen of Aragon, as Montaigne relates, well before that ancient realm united with Castile, in the 14th century, following mature deliberation by her private counselor, established the rule, keeping in mind the moderation demanded by modesty within marriages, that the number of six copulations per day was the legal limit, necessary and suitable. In other words, in those days a man and a woman copulated, in a suitable and modest manner, six times a day. Flaubert, for whom "*une once de sperme perdue fatigue plus que trois litres de sang*" (I spoke of that in one of my books), thought six copulations a day humanly impossible, but Flaubert was not, we know, a Sword. Even today it's believed that the only way to come is by ejaculation, despite the Chinese for over three thousand years affirming that a man can have several consecutive orgasms without ejaculating, thus avoiding the loss of the ounce of sperm that is more tiring than hemorrhaging three liters of blood. (The French call the exhaustion that follows ejaculation "small death," which is why one of their poets said that the flesh was sad, but Brazilians say that the flesh is weak, in all senses, which strikes me as more poignant; it's worse being weak than sad.) It is calculated that a man ejaculates on average five thousand times during his lifetime, expelling a total of a trillion spermatozoa. All that for what and why? Because in reality we are still a species of monkey, and all of us function like a rudimentary genetic bank, when it would be enough for only some to operate that way. We of the Brotherhood of Swords knew that man, by freeing himself of his simian atrophy, backed by the peculiar virtues of his mind (our brain is not, I repeat, that of an orangutan), could have consecutive orgasms without ejaculating, orgasms that would give even more pleasure than those of the seminal kind, which make the man merely a blind instrument of the instinct of preservation of the species. And that result filled us with joy and pride; we had succeeded, through elaborate and difficult physical and spiritual exercises, to achieve the Multiple Orgasm Sans Ejaculation, which became known by the acronym MOSE. I cannot reveal what these "exercises" were, for the vow to maintain secrecy prevents me. Strictly speaking, I shouldn't even mention the subject, even in this limited way.

The Brotherhood of Swords functioned very well during the six months following our extraordinary discovery. Until the day that one of the Brothers, like me a poet, called for the convening of a General Assembly of the Brotherhood to relate a matter he considered of the utmost importance. His wife, noticing the nonoccurrence of *emissio seminis* during copulation, had concluded that there could be various reasons for it, which in summary would be: either he was saving up the sperm for another woman, or else he was feigning pleasure when in reality he was acting mechanically like a soulless robot. The woman even suspected that our colleague had an implant in his penis to keep it always rigid, an allegation that he easily proved to be groundless. In short, the poet's wife had stopped feeling pleasure from copulating. In reality she wanted the viscosity of sperm inside her vagina or on her skin; to her that white, sticky secretion was a powerful symbol of life. Sex, as Whitman would put it, after all included seminal fluid. The woman didn't say so, but surely the exhausting of him, the male, represented the strengthening of her, the female. Without those ingredients she couldn't feel pleasure, and, this is the worst part, if she felt no pleasure neither did our Brother, for we of the Brotherhood of Swords want (need) our women to come too. That's our motto (I won't cite it in Latin in order not to appear pedantic; I've already used Latin once): Come by Making Come.

At the end of our Brother's explanation the assembly fell silent. The majority of the members of the Brotherhood were present. We had just heard disquieting words. I, for example, no longer ejaculated. Ever since I had succeeded in dominating the Great Secret of the Brotherhood, the MOSE, I no longer produced a single drop of semen, even though all my orgasms were much more pleasurable. And what if my wife, whom I loved so, asked me, as she could at any moment, to ejaculate on her alabaster breasts? I asked one of the doctors in the Brotherhood—there were several doctors among us—if I could go back to ejaculating. Medicine knows nothing about sex, that's the regrettable truth, and my colleague replied that it would be very difficult, in light of the fact that I, like all the others, had created a strong dependency on that physical and spiritual conditioning; he had already tried, using every scientific resource to which he had access, to counteract that process, without success. All of us, upon hearing that frightful reply, became extremely dismayed. Immediately, other Brothers said they had encountered the same problem, that their wives were beginning to see as unnatural, or even frightening, that inexhaustible ardor. I think I've turned into a monster, said the poet who had raised the problem for our collective consideration.

And that is how the Brotherhood of Swords came to an end. Before disbanding we all swore a blood oath never to reveal to the world the secret of the Multiple Orgasm Sans Ejaculation, which we would take to our graves. We go on having a woman waiting for us, but in constant rotation, before she can discover that we are different, strange, able to come with infinite energy without shedding semen. We cannot fall in love, for our relationships are ephemeral. Yes, I too have turned into a monster, and my sole desire in life is to go back to being a monkey.

winning the game

WHEN I'M NOT READING SOME BOOK I get from the public library I watch one of those TV programs that show the life of the rich, their mansions, the cars, the horses, the yachts, the jewels, the paintings, the rare furniture, the silverware, the wine cellar, the servants. It's impressive how well served the rich are. I don't miss a single one of those programs, even though they're not of much use to me; none of those rich people live in my country. But I enjoyed hearing a millionaire interviewed during dinner say that he acquired a yacht worth hundreds of millions because he wanted to have a yacht bigger than some other rich guy. "It was the only way to put an end to my envy of him," he confessed, smiling, taking a swallow of the drink in his glass. The dinner companions around him laughed a lot when he said that. The rich can have everything, even envy of each other, and in them it's humorous; for that matter, everything is amusing. I'm poor, and envy in the poor is looked upon badly, because envy causes repression in the poor. Along with envy comes hatred of the rich; the poor don't know how to retaliate without a spirit of vengeance. But I don't feel rage against any rich person; my envy is like the guy with the bigger yacht: like him, I just want to win the game.

I've discovered how to win the game between a poor guy, like me, and a rich one. Not by becoming rich myself, I'd never manage that. "Getting rich," one of them said on a program, "is a genetic proclivity that not everyone has." This millionaire had made his fortune starting out from zero. My father was poor, and I inherited nothing when he died, not even the gene that motivates you to make money.

The only possession I have is my life, and the only way of winning the game is by killing a rich man and coming away alive. It's something like buying the bigger yacht. I know this seems like odd reasoning, but one way to win the game is by making up at least part of the rules, something the rich do. The rich man I kill has to be an heir; an heir is a person like me, often without the predisposition to get rich, but who was born rich and blithely enjoys the fortune that fell from the sky into his lap. Actually, to relish life to the fullest, it's preferable that just the father, and not the heir, be born with the gene.

I would prefer killing one of those foreign rich guys that I see on television. A man. Their wives, or their daughters, are even more ostentatiously rich, but a woman, however many jewels she has on her fingers and around her wrist and neck, isn't the bigger yacht. Nor would I be interested in one of those women who obtained their fortune by working, certainly carriers of the gene, clones who appear on television in suits. No, it would have to be a man. But since the ideal rich men live in other countries, I have to look for a rich man right here, one who inherited the money and goods that he enjoys.

The difficulty in achieving this goal doesn't worry me in the least. I painstakingly draw up my plans and when I lie down I'm asleep within minutes and don't wake up during the night. Not only do I have peace of mind but a well-functioning prostate, unlike my father, who used to get up every three hours to urinate. I'm in no hurry; I must choose with great care, somebody at least at the level of the rich guy who bought the big yacht. The majority of the people who appear in the magazines published here in my country can be called rich and famous, but killing one of them would be easy and wouldn't make me win the game.

Every rich person likes to show off his wealth. The *nouveau riche* flaunt it more, but I don't want to kill one of them, I want a rich man who inherited his fortune. These, belonging to the later generations, are more discreet, normally displaying their wealth through travel. They love shopping in Paris, London, New York. They also like to go to distant and exotic places that have good hotels with genteel help, and the more sports-minded can't pass up an annual ski trip, which is understandable because after all they do live in a tropical country. They display their wealth among themselves (there's nothing to be gained from playing with the poor), at millionaires' dinners where the winner can confess it was because of envy that he bought what he bought, and the others merrily drink to his health.

A guy like me, white, poor, skinny, and starving, has neither brothers nor allies. It wasn't easy to get a job with the most expensive and exclusive catering service in town. It took deliberate planning and maneuvering; I spent two years at it. Perseverance is the only virtue I possess. The rich had the habit of hiring that catering service when they gave a dinner. The owner, the descendant of an illustrious family, I'm not going to mention her name, just as I'm not going to mention anyone's name, not even mine, was a domineering woman who kept her notes and time charts in a small computer that she carried in a bag over her shoulder. She imposed rigid standards on those who worked for her, cooks, decorators, buyers, waiters, and all the rest. She was so competent that the employees, besides obeying without batting an eye, even admired her. If some employee acted in a way not in keeping with the established model, he was fired. That was rare, because all, before being hired, were subjected to a rigorous selection and training process. We did as we were told, and I was one of the most obedient. And the service charged a small fortune to cook for and feed those rich people. The owner of the catering service had the gene.

Before the evaluation and training to which I submitted to become a waiter at the catering service, I did an apprenticeship of my own. First, I did something about my appearance. I found a good, cheap dentist, which is very rare, and bought some decent clothes. Then, even more important, I learned, as part of my solitary training, to be a happy servant, as good waiters are. But faking those feelings is very difficult. That subservience and happiness can't be obvious, they must be very subtle, perceived subconsciously by the recipient. The best way of playing that impalpable dissimulation was to create a state of mind that could make me truly happy to be a waiter to the rich, even temporarily. The owner of the catering service pointed me out as an example of the employee who did his job by taking pride in what he did, which is why I was so efficient.

The rich, like the poor, aren't all the same. There are those who like to ramble on with a cigar between their fingers or a glass of precious liquid in their hand, there are those who play the gallant, those who are reserved, the solemn, those who sport their erudition, those who flaunt richness with their designer attire, there are even the circumspect ones, but deep down they're all show-offs; it's part of the pantomime. Which ends up being a true sign language, for it allows seeing what each of them really is. I know that the poor also do their pantomime, but the poor don't interest me, it's not in my plans to play with any of them; my game is that of the bigger yacht.

I waited patiently for the ideal rich man to come along. I was ready for him. It wasn't easy to get the poison, tasteless and odorless, that I transferred from one pocket to the other in my pilgrimage. But I'm not going to relate the risks I took and the vile things I did to obtain it.

Finally, a rich man of the type I was looking for appeared at the reserved-seating dinner at one of the five tables in the mansion's dining room. I knew his story, but I'd never seen him, not even his photo. It was the owner of the catering service who told me, and for the first time I saw her excited because "he" had just arrived, and I was designated to serve him personally. Rich people like to be well attended. I would remain at a certain distance, without looking at him, but at any gesture of command of his, however subtle, I was to approach and say simply, "Sir?" I knew how to do that very well; I was a happy waiter.

He had arrived, like the other guests, in a bulletproof car, surrounded by bodyguards. He was a short, dark guy, balding, with discreet gestures. His wife, his fourth, was a tall, slim blonde who appeared even taller thanks to the high heels she was wearing.

There were eight guests at each table, four men and four women. Even though the service wasn't French style, each table was attended to by a pair of waiters; my colleague was a tall black man with perfect teeth.

There were drinks for every taste, even beer, but I don't remember anyone at my table asking for that vulgar and fattening beverage. As per the owner's instructions, the other waiter was my subordinate. Discreetly, I decided that my colleague would handle the requests of the other diners, who were so engrossed in their conversations that they didn't notice the special treatment I afforded one of them.

I waited on him with perfection. He ate little, drank in moderation. He didn't use, with me, the words "please" or "thanks." His orders were laconic, unaffected. The dinner was nearing its end.

"Sir?" I approached when he turned his head an inch to the side, without looking at anyone, but I knew it was for me.

"Half a cup of coffee."

It was the chance I'd been waiting for.

I went to the kitchen and made the coffee in the state-of-the-art Italian machine supplied by the caterer. I added the poison.

"Here you are, sir."

He sipped the coffee, chatting with the lady beside him. Unhurriedly, I picked up the empty cup, went back to the kitchen, and washed it carefully.

It took some time for them to discover that he was dead, as he had rested his head on his arms on the table and appeared to be sleeping. But since millionaires don't do those things, take a nap at a banquet table, those around him found it odd and realized that something serious had occurred. A heart attack, probably.

There was a commotion, confronted with relevant elegance by the majority of those present, especially his svelte wife. The bodyguards, however, were much more nervous. The dinner was brought to a close shortly after a private ambulance took the corpse away.

I think I'm going to continue serving the rich for a time. It'll have to be another catering service; the one I worked for suffered a reversal of fortune. At first the newspapers said only that the cause of the rich man's death was a sudden illness. But one of the weekly magazines published a long cover story talking about poisoning, with pictures of the guests at the banquet, especially those, men and women alike, about whom malicious insinuations could be made. The life of the dead millionaire, his businesses, his marriages and divorces, especially the scandalous circumstances of one of the latter, were given extensive coverage.

The police are investigating. I enjoyed going to the precinct to make a statement. I wasn't there long; the police thought I couldn't have much to say about poisoning. After all, I was a stupid and happy waiter, above any suspicion. When I was dismissed by the interrogator in charge of the case, I said casually, "My yacht's bigger than his."

Someone had to know.

"I told you, we're through here, you can go."

As I was leaving, I heard him tell the recording clerk, "One more shitty statement."

I won the game. I'm uncertain whether I should play again. With envy but without resentment, just to win, like the rich. It's good to be like the rich.

acknowledgments

"The Art of Walking in the Streets of Rio de Janeiro" originally appeared in Cristina Ferreira-Pinto, ed., *Urban Voices: Contemporary Short Stories from Brazil*; "Belle" originally appeared in Words Without Borders; "Be My Valentine" originally appeared in *The Literary Review*; "The Blotter" originally appeared in Maria Angélica Lopes, ed., *The Brazilian Short Story in the Late Twentieth Century*; "The Game of Dead Men" originally appeared in *Review*; "Guardian Angel" originally appeared in *World Literature Today*; "The Hunchback and Botticelli's Venus" originally appeared in Words Without Borders; "Kisses on the Cheek" originally appeared in *Ezra*; "Lonelyhearts" originally appeared in *Brasil/Brazil*; "Mandrake" originally appeared in Words Without Borders; "Marta" originally appeared in *Ellery Queen Mystery Magazine*; "Xania" originally appeared in *BOMB*; "The Ship *Catrineta*" originally appeared in *Latin American Literary Review*; "Winning the Game" originally appeared in *Ellery Queen Mystery Magazine*.